VENGEFUL VOWS

THE BURKES MAFIA

KIRA COLE

1

———

DECLAN

SOMETIMES, I GET TIRED OF THE VIOLENCE, BUT IT'S A means to an end. I'm ready for this war to start. Today. So, I did what I had to do. Crossed a line I never had before.

Usually, I enjoy the sight of a woman tied up and begging me for mercy. Especially when I'm balls deep inside her.

But I can't say I mind it now either as I stare into the heated eyes of the daughter of my family's sworn enemy.

I look down into the wide, beautiful eyes of Bree Murphy. She looks like her lowlife father, but in the best possible way. She won the genetic lottery with her small, upturned features, wide, bright eyes, and her pouty, heart-shaped mouth. But the thing that's confusing me is what's *in* those hazel eyes.

Fear, of course. She's terrified, and she should be. I've taken her from her home, kidnapped her, tied her to a chair in my father's panic room. But it's not *just* fear in her eyes. There's something more. Something... defiant.

I have to admit, it intrigues me.

I can't deny that Bree, squirming in her seat, the

leather restraints digging into her wrists and ankles marking her alabaster skin, turns me on. Her cheeks are flushed, a slight sheen to her skin as she tries to pull herself free. Add to the fact that she's wearing a silk cami and shorts that show off her long legs and full tits, I'm practically a goner.

Too bad she's a dirty Murphy.

And I can only blame myself for my growing erection and choosing to kidnap her in the middle of the night.

At least she doesn't sleep naked...

I clear my throat and look at my brother, trying to ignore the sensation of blood rushing to my cock.

"What now?" I demand, perching against the mahogany desk that takes up most of my father's office, crossing one ankle over the other.

My brother Gray simply rolls his eyes, lounging on the leather sofa in the corner of the room, sipping a glass of whiskey.

"Slice off a finger and send it to Niall?"

Gray chuckles, taking a swig of the amber liquid.

"This isn't some seventies gangsta movie shit," my father snaps from behind me where he sits at the desk, going through some documents.

"I thought you'd be a little more pleased with my efforts, Da." My eyes flick back to Bree, whose hazel eyes stay locked on mine—filled with loathing, and that something extra that is driving me crazy.

"What do you think, Bree?" I tilt my head to the side, letting a smirk tug at my lips.

Her eyes flash, but she stays silent.

"Maybe we cut out your tongue instead since you apparently don't use it much? Though maybe I keep that for myself." I chuckle.

She flushes a beautiful shade of pink, but if looks could kill, I'd be long buried by now.

"Simmer down, Declan. I've taught you better than that. She's the daughter of an enemy, not our enemy himself. We treat women with the utmost respect."

He is right. Even considering our line of "business," there are lines we don't cross, and mistreating women is one of them. Which is why she doesn't have a single mark on her.

But I'm so ready for this war to start already, and taking her was the only way to make that happen.

I'm looking down at Bree.

Damn. Her skin looks like silk. I bet it's soft too.

Doesn't matter.

"She has his blood. Works with him. That makes her an enemy too."

"Not for much longer." He rises from behind the desk and walks over to Bree, taking her chin in his hand and tilting her head up.

She bares her teeth like a cornered animal, and I smile.

She has bite. Many would be screaming, begging for their lives if they encountered the head of the Burke family and his two heirs. But not Bree Murphy.

"Wanting to claim the kill for yourself, Da?" Gray sets his empty glass down on the table beside him.

"The opposite."

I frown, watching as my father tilts Bree's face left, then right. "I don't understand."

"You need to clean up this mess," Da snaps, letting go of Bree and turning on me. "You had the brilliant idea of kidnapping Niall Murphy's daughter, putting us at the top of his hit list, so you're going to marry her to fix that little predicament."

I blink. Once. Twice.

"Oh fuck!" Gray howls with laughter, clutching his chest as he tries to catch his breath.

"No!" Bree snarls.

All this time, through when I clamped one hand over her mouth, threw her into my arms, and carried her out, she hadn't spoken a single word. She fought me, of course, and I have the claw marks along my forearms to prove it. She'd even gotten in a swift kick to my nether regions that is still aching, but she hadn't screamed. She had kept that pretty mouth closed, and I almost found it intriguing.

I guess this is her line.

But this is kind of my line too.

My eyes go to my dad. "You can't be serious."

"Oh, I'm deadly serious."

"Never pictured you as the settling down type," Gray teases, standing up and strolling over to the bar cart.

I clench my hands into fists and round on my father.

"Is this some kind of sick joke?" I spit. "Why not Gray? He's the oldest."

"Fuck off." Gray chuckles as he lifts the lid of the whiskey decanter and pours himself another large glass. "She's what, nineteen?"

"Twenty-one," I correct.

Gray cocks an eyebrow at me.

"Yeah no. I like mine with a little experience if you catch my drift. No offense, little girl." He winks in Bree's direction.

She bares her teeth, straining against the leather bindings once more, making her tits bounce.

Fuck.

I try to erase the image from my mind as I try to work through my racing thoughts.

"No, not happening." I shake my head.

"Too late. Gray is too old for her, and you need to suffer the consequences of your actions." My father jams his index finger into my chest.

Despite the fact that I'm a six-foot-two adult man, my stomach still twists at the look of disappointment in his gray eyes.

"I don't see how marrying the daughter of our enemy is going to solve our issues with Niall. If anything, you're adding fuel to the fire."

"Yeah. You don't scream son-in-law of the year," Gray chimes in.

"Fuck off, Gray."

"Don't get pissy at me, little brother, you poked the sleeping dragon. I was all for letting it rest."

"We should ransom her—"

Dad's eyes narrow as they snap to me.

When my father decides on something, it might as well be set in stone.

It's just that I never thought I would get married.

I'm no slouch, but I'm just not interested in romantic entanglements outside the bedroom. I'm the type of man with blood on my hands, and I can't imagine ever letting a woman get close enough to see it.

And I may not be what I would call a womanizer, but I don't discriminate. A beautiful woman is a beautiful woman, and they're all welcome to warm my bed for a night or two. Maybe three, if they're lucky.

Lately, I've been more focused on growing the Burke name.

And, of course, one day, I'll have to worry about having an heir, but right now? With a Murphy?

I want to help my father keep Niall Murphy out of our

territory. Niall's actions have nearly destroyed this family more than once. He is a monster. A snake. And I just want him gone. But at what cost?

My freedom? My sanity?

Sure, she looks good. And sometimes, I wish things were different. Sometimes, I wish I could have a wife, a family, a normal life. But at the same time, I'm terrified of it. If things go the way it went for my mother and father... I don't think I could handle it.

And now that choice has been taken away from me. It is no longer a matter of if I'll get married, but when.

No more women warming my bed. No more being married to the business.

This is happening.

Well, fuck.

My shoulders sag as my father places a hand on my shoulder.

"Father Harrington will be here in two hours. Send Paige in here to help Bree get ready."

Two hours?

"I won't marry him!" Bree cries. "I won't do it! You can't make me!"

Ignoring Bree's pleading, he strolls from the room without a second glance.

"What an interesting turn of events." Gray smirks as he lifts his glass to his lips. "This should be fun."

I close my eyes for a moment and try to take a steadying breath as I work through my options.

I expected to be leaving this room with a corpse, not a bride.

"Give us a moment," I ask Gray as I open my eyes and turn to look at Bree, my jaw aching as I clench it.

"Normally, it's tradition to wait until after you're married to fuck—"

The snarl that escapes my throat is enough for Gray not to finish that sentence.

I know he's just teasing her. We were taught better than to force ourselves on women or take advantage of them. I may never have considered marriage a real possibility to me, but I was always honest about my intentions. I never mislead any of the women I fucked.

But things have gone way out of my control, and I don't need the added mind fuck.

He shakes his head, chuckling to himself as he leaves the room, closing the door behind him.

I listen to the sound of my brother's retreating footsteps for a moment before I move to kneel in front of Bree, my eyes roaming her body as she stares down at me with nothing but hatred.

"Seems we're caught in a web, princess," I murmur, taking a finger and tracing it along her calf.

Fuck. Her skin is even softer than it looks. How is that even possible?

"I'd rather die than marry you," Bree hisses through her teeth.

"Perhaps." I'm delighted by the trail of goosebumps my touch leaves on her skin. "But my father is a very demanding man. If a marriage is what he wants, then a marriage is what he gets."

"I didn't peg Declan Burke, the Irish scourge himself, as such a pussy." Bree's cheeks flush. "Doing what daddy says like a good little boy."

"I'd watch yourself, princess," I murmur, trailing my finger up and along her thigh as I snicker at the name.

"The Irish scourge" is a nickname given to me by the Feds, back when they thought they had something on the Burkes. Of course, we'd gotten out of it, like we got out of everything else.

Her body tenses, and I glance up to find her focused on my movements. I smirk as her throat bobs, and a flush creeps along her chest.

"Remember who's in control right now. I wouldn't test my patience if I were you. I wouldn't want to do something I might regret..." My fingers trail higher, teasing her inner thigh.

"You're the one on your knees for me, Burke."

"I'm enjoying the view," I admit, letting my eyes flick down to her chest, the sight of her peaked nipples through the thin silk of her cami making my mouth water.

I can't deny Bree Murphy is hot as fuck, but that doesn't mean I want to slide a ring onto her finger and disappear into the sunset.

Bree's expression turns from one of hatred to disgust as she pulls against the restraints to no avail.

"The only way you can get a woman is by tying her up against her will? You're pathetic," she spits.

I wrap my fingers around her perfect neck and squeeze just hard enough that her eyes widen, and her mouth opens in a delightful little O shape.

Damn. The things I could do with that mouth...

"I suggest you keep that pretty little mouth shut," I snarl, my face barely an inch from hers. A waft of jasmine and vanilla hits my nose, and I bite back a moan.

"Do it," she gasps.

I squeeze a little tighter, our eyes locked.

"I think I'll take advantage of our wedding night first," I threaten before dropping my hand and standing.

"Fuck you!"

"See you at the altar," I head to the door and yank it open, only to find my younger sister Paige strolling toward me, a scowl on her face.

"What did you do?"

"You're needed in there." I jerk a thumb behind me.

She goes to retort but I storm past, not wanting to hear her disapproving comments.

How did I get in so deep?

Kidnapping Bree was meant to send a message to Niall Murphy, a warning not to mess with us. That we are ready for war.

And once he hears I've made his daughter my wife? There will be more than just my balls on the line. He'll come after my fucking head.

I'll be ready for him and all he has.

I'm just not sure if I'm ready for the hazel-eyed menace I'm about to marry.

2
—

BREE

These people are insane. Not just crazy, but like straightjackets-and-padded-white-rooms mad!

My father's words repeated to me throughout the year keep echoing through my mind. *"God knows I hope it never happens, but if you're ever behind enemy lines, remember one thing,* wean. *Keep. Your mouth. Shut."*

So, I didn't open my mouth when I was grabbed, just clawed and fought for all I was worth. I've broken a couple of nails and my fingers sting, and I'm otherwise none the worse for wear.

But I had to say something when that lunatic Patrick Burke made that crazy announcement.

Patrick Burke and his sons have lost their minds, clearly.

And it doesn't seem like there's a clear way out of this.

They haven't hurt me yet, so that's a plus at least.

I need to get out of here, escape, but I don't want to die trying.

So, I'm going to have to go along for now, bide my time, until something breaks. Because something always does. And when that happens, I'll run for my life.

When Declan leaves, a dark-haired woman comes in.

"Have fun, Paige." Gray empties his glass and walks out of the room, leaving me alone with the woman he called Paige.

She is older than me, but not but all that much, I don't think.

She comes up behind me and unties me.

When she is done, I slowly stand up, massaging my wrists and looking around studying my surroundings now that I can move. I'm not much of a fighter, but if I see an opening that doesn't kill me, I'm taking it.

She starts walking outside the room. "Come, please."

She waits by the door until I pass her, and she closes the door behind me, grinning at me brightly, taking my elbow and leading me down one of the halls.

"Who are you?" I ask, and Paige tilts her head as if confused.

"I'm Paige Burke, of course. From what I heard, I'm your new sister!"

Another, taller, lighter-haired woman comes into view. "And so am I. Your new sister, I mean."

She's long, lanky in a way that the petite Paige isn't, towering over me. She's statuesque, elegant, where Paige is cute and tiny. She smiles softly. "I'm Lara. The second oldest. Paige here is the baby."

Paige pouts. "I'm not a baby anymore." She looks me up and down, but not in a judgy way. More like she's gauging my measurements in an analytical way. "You look to be about the same size as me."

She takes my hand, and hers is small and warm, and leads me up the stairs. Lara follows close behind me.

I feel like it's on purpose, so that Lara can keep me from sprinting out of the house.

The whole Burke clan is fucking nuts, apparently. These two are acting as if we're new best friends. We are supposed to be mortal enemies. What is wrong with this family? Have they all lost their fucking minds?

"What are you, a size four? Six?" Paige asks.

"Something like that," I mumble, my mouth feeling like I've eaten cotton. I keep looking down at my cracked and broken nails.

Lara makes a displeased sound in the back of her head. "This won't do. I think I have some press-ons that you can wear. I know it's a little tacky, but I use them between nail appointments."

She disappears into a room, and I'm finally able to look around the mansion. It's a little bigger than my father's, probably fifteen rooms instead of our ten, and Paige drags me into a bedroom that's bigger than my own.

There's a four-post, king-sized bed with a pink canopy in the corner, and it's very clearly her room. A crystal chandelier hangs above us, and there's a portrait of Paige and a small dog on the wall.

She catches me looking at it and smiles sadly.

"That's Bouncer. He passed on when I was twelve. I'm so glad we posed for that portrait together before Da accidentally backed over him." She sighs, frowning. "Took me years to forgive him."

I want to open my mouth and scream, tell her I don't give a fuck about her stupid little dog or any of this, to just let me out. But I don't.

Relax. Go with the flow. Just wait it out and your chance will come.

I might be delusional, but that's what I'm doing now. I'm going along with the flow, so that I can strike like my cobra of a father later.

I take a breath.

This is not how I pictured my night when I got to bed six hours ago. My dreams and hopes are resting all on the chance that my father will come for me.

I would say my brother too, but he left the family, cut all ties with our father, so he won't even know if something happens to me. And if he does, he'll just think maybe I'm my mother's daughter.

No, stop that! This night is bad enough without having to think about that too.

God. I really am all alone now, aren't I?

Please, Daidí, *hurry up and save me from this fate that might be worse than death.*

I just have to focus on my breathing and try and make this as painless as I can for me.

"What kind of dresses do you have available?" I force a smile.

Paige beams back at me, sliding open a closet door to a huge walk-in closet with more shoes than I've ever seen. I have plenty of clothes and shoes on my own, but this is ridiculous.

Lara hurries into the bedroom, taking my right hand and filing my nails as Paige rustles through the dresses in her closet.

"You should shower, honey. There's fear sweat all over you," Lara says. "Let me finish filing your nails, and then I'll get you a towel. I know this isn't ideal, but it will all work out. I promise."

I blink at her, surprised that she cares.

"Thank you," I whisper, and Paige just keeps looking through her closet, humming, as Lara takes me to the bathroom.

"I'll give you some privacy," she says, but I don't miss

that she stays right outside. I can hear her and Paige as they whisper gibberish right by the door.

They're all crazy. Every last one of them.

I look in the mirror.

As far as kidnappings go, mine wasn't all that bad. Sure, it was scary, but Declan didn't hit me or anything, so there's no bruises. I just look sweaty and pale, like I've been through something bad.

I suppose I have.

I take in a shaking breath, suddenly fighting tears now that I'm alone.

Looking around the bathroom, I search for windows. And I find them... about six feet off the ground. And they're too small for me to climb out. There's also a skylight, but it's not like I can burst through there like Superwoman. It's about ten feet to the ceiling, anyway.

I guess I can't do anything but what they tell me to do, so I turn on the water and hop in the shower.

It's one of those shower walls, and I lean against the tile, letting the warm water cascade down my back.

I wet my hair, dragging my fingers through it to finger-comb it and finding knots. I had been sleeping when Declan grabbed me right out of my bed, so it's all messed up since of course it hasn't seen a comb or a brush since yesterday.

I get to shampooing and conditioning with clearly expensive products that I find in the bathroom. It smells like lavender and rosewater and just... clean. I don't know a better way to describe it.

I do feel better when I step out of the shower, and the towel is big and fluffy. At some point, Lara has opened the door and hung a big, pink robe on the hook.

I put it on after drying myself and towel-drying my hair

and slowly open the door, hoping against hope that they've left the room so that I can figure something out.

Of course, Lara is standing right there, taking my elbow with a smile and leading me to the bed.

I sit down on it, defeated, and she starts putting glue on my newly-filed nails. I'm wearing simple French tips, and that's the style of press-ons she's brought me.

As she does my nails, Paige grabs a dress that's on the bed and holds it up. She hums.

"This one is a size five, but I think you've got more hip than me," she muses. "And this ivory color will suit you so much more than the white Da wanted."

"Sure." I have no idea how else to respond. I'm trembling.

I've always wanted to get married. Always wanted a big, white wedding with all the trimmings. But I never imagined it would be like this. This was a childhood dream for me that has now turned into a nightmare.

"You'll look so beautiful," Paige gushes.

Lara, less exuberant than Paige, looks at the dress.

"Can we style it off the shoulder?"

Paige gasps. "Oh, my god. That would be perfect."

My nails have dried, and I look down at them. They honestly could have been done by my own nail tech.

"Stand up," Lara urges, and I do as I'm told.

Paige pushes off my robe and I stand there, fully naked, wanting to cover myself. But I don't.

I'm going along.

Relax, I tell myself, steeling myself for what will happen next.

But nothing happens. Paige just crouches to let me step into the dress, and she's right, it fits perfectly. She zips it up and it hugs every curve just like it should. I look down at it.

There are embroidered flowers all over it, and a slit up one side that shows the long line of my thigh.

Paige positions the straps off my shoulders, and smiles.

"You're so beautiful," she says, moving my wet hair out of the way. "Lara, get the blow dryer."

Lara does as her little sister says and starts to blow dry my hair as Paige begins to put on some light makeup.

So, we're really doing this. They're really going to marry me off to the Irish scourge.

"Declan is mostly nice," Paige says, and it's the first real mention of the wedding they've made, just focusing on dressing me up like some doll.

"He'll treat you well," Lara pipes in. "We'll make sure of it."

"This is crazy," I whisper, unable to hold back.

Lara shrugs. "It's unorthodox, I'll admit. But so much of our lives is. I think you'll agree?"

I suppose she's expecting some kind of answer, but I just stare at her.

"Not like you come from a family of saints." Paige chuckles.

There's a brief knock on the door just as Lara finishes blowing out my hair, and when I glance over at the mirror, I have to admit that she did a good job. Paige also made my makeup look really natural, and the green eyeshadow shows off the green in my hazel eyes.

"Come in," Paige calls.

Gray walks in, and I stiffen as his intense blues eyes zero in on me.

"You girls done primping?" His demeanor is so different. He still looks intimidating, but he has a bit of a smirk on his face.

Relax.

I stand up, although I can't imagine my face looks like I'm feeling anything but dread.

"I'll walk you down the aisle." Gray sticks out his elbow.

"Lovely," I mutter, but I loop my arm through his.

I take a breath. I just have to endure this until I can get away, and then my father will drown the city with their blood.

3

———

DECLAN

WHAT IN THE ABSOLUTE FUCK IS GOING ON HERE? My family have all gone nuts, and I don't know how it happened. When I suggested kidnapping Bree Murphy, I definitely didn't have any idea that it would go this way.

I thought we'd hold her for ransom, scare her, freak out Niall so that he would act. Da had seemed so into the idea, but now I wonder if he had these plans all along.

How the hell do I get out of this?

My sisters stand as if they're bridesmaids, both dressed in chocolate brown dresses that I suppose they just had hanging in their closets.

Unless the family planned this ahead of time? It took a couple of days before I was able to grab Bree, so maybe....

God, was this all planned behind my back?

I'm panicking, and I don't know how to hide it. I don't understand how this is happening, and why the hell I'm going along with it. I guess it's because I always listen to my da, no matter what.

I'm married to the life, married to doing exactly what

my father needs, and I never thought I'd be here. I certainly could have never imagined I'd be marrying a *Murphy*.

I'm wearing my best three-piece suit, in black, with a silk blue undershirt, and when Bree comes out into the foyer, she's wearing an ivory dress with embroidered flowers all over it.

And if I had to be honest, she looks stunning. She was a sight before, all sweaty and pale, but now she's one of the most gorgeous women I've ever seen with her long, auburn hair flowing down her back. There's a slit up one side of the dress and her shoulders are bare and the flashes of skin I can see are mouthwatering.

She has her small hand looped through Gray's arm, and her face is absolutely blank. There's fear in her hazel eyes, too, but also... she's tough. She hasn't cried, hasn't screamed or had any temper tantrums. There's something hard about her that intrigues me.

But did I want to marry her? No.

I can understand what my father is thinking, although it seems insane.

This *will* piss off Niall Murphy, maybe even more than holding Bree for ransom. He'll be out for blood after this. It will kill him to learn his daughter was taken from home and forced to marry under duress.

Gray walks her up to me, and as she gets closer, her hazel eyes blaze as she looks into mine.

She's not just afraid. She's *pissed off*, and I guess I shouldn't be surprised. I thought she'd just be scared, like everyone else I've ever put in that panic room.

As she gets to my side, Father Hannigan starts his spiel, and I'm barely listening. She's glaring up at me, making eye contact, and it's making my breath catch in my throat.

There's something very attractive about how angry she is, how it's overtaking the terror in her eyes.

"I do," I say, after Father Hannigan asks me if I'll take her as my wife, still shocked that this is happening.

When Father Hannigan asks the same to Bree, she stays silent, her mouth pressed tightly together, looking up at me.

My father clears his throat, looking at me intently, and there are four or five of our men standing behind him, at attention.

I lean forward, putting my mouth close to the shell of her ear.

"Say I do or there are eight men in this room that will end you."

She trembles, but only slightly.

"I do," she whispers. That's good enough for Father Hannigan, who is being paid handsomely for this impromptu wedding, and he finishes up his speech.

"I now pronounce you husband and wife. You may kiss the bride."

I lean down and press my lips against her mouth, chastely and coldly, barely tasting her cherry chapstick. A rush of arousal runs down my spine nevertheless, and I hate myself for it.

Why does she affect me so much? She is a *Murphy*.

Bree stands stock still, trembling slightly, but my father walks up to her.

"You won't be harmed," I murmur to Bree as I stand beside her. "Not as long as you do what you're told."

She doesn't respond, but her hazel eyes flash to mine, and they're full of rage.

Good. I don't want her getting any ideas that I give a shit about her or actually want this.

"I've invited a few people for the ceremony," my father

says, and I stare at him as if he's lost his mind, which I'm pretty sure he has. "You'll be polite."

I nod. It's not like I have a choice.

If this is what he wants, this is what I'll do, but I don't have to be happy about it.

I take a drink of champagne from a nearby table and offer one to Bree but she shakes her head briefly.

I sigh. "You can loosen up, you know? I told you that you won't be harmed."

"Forgive me if I don't believe you," she grumbles in a low tone. "You just threatened me to death if I didn't say yes to this scam of a wedding, so I'm not really chomping at the bit to be here."

"You were not doing your part, so I had to remind you of the consequences," I admit. "But don't worry. You're my wife now, you'll be fine."

She scoffs, but her stomach growls loud enough that I can hear it.

"I'm sorry we have been such dreadful hosts and starved you since you got here," I tell her. "You should have some crab cakes. Our chef, Marisol, is amazing."

She huffs out a breath. "How do I know it isn't poisoned?"

I roll my eyes and take a plate off the catering table. When Da had gotten all this set up, I don't know, but his ability to throw a party at a moment's notice is well documented.

I pop one into my mouth, taking my time chewing before swallowing. "See?"

She glares at me, but slowly takes the plate from me, taking a couple of small, polite bites before finally shoving the rest of it into her mouth.

I give her a half-grin. "It's good, isn't it?"

She doesn't answer, but she eats another.

I sip the champagne, telling myself not to overindulge. I just want to get the hell out of here, so I can be alone and process.

Lara and Paige whisk Bree away somewhere, and I have to admit, I'm grateful. Her staring holes through me isn't making me feel any better about this whole situation.

My father sidles up to me, smiling. "You're doing great, Declan."

I just glance at him. I don't mean to brood, but I can't believe he pushed this on me without talking to me about it first.

"I set up one of the guest rooms as a honeymoon suite," he comments, as if I'm supposed to be happy about this. "You'll have to take your new wife to bed pretty soon."

My eyes widen. "What? You can't expect me to force myself on her?"

My father scoffs. "Of course not. What kind of man are you that you can't seduce a pretty young girl? You're a looker, Declan."

"You've lost your fucking mind," I mumble, as low as I can, almost hoping he doesn't hear me.

My father's gaze goes sharp. "What did you say?"

"Nothing, Da," I sigh. "But I'm not going to—"

"I didn't say rape her, Declan. I said take her to bed," he barks, and I don't know what that *means*.

"Why are you doing this?" I ask him, unable to stop myself. "Why are you punishing me?"

My father looks at me, smiling softly. "It's not a punishment, son. I just know that you're the right man for the job. You have to consummate the marriage. We can't leave it open to the possibility of an annulment."

The job? What job?

Punishing Murphy? Punishing Bree? *Marrying* a Murphy?

I don't argue any further because my father has this look on his face, one I've seen before. That look tells me that nothing is going to change his mind. And when he has that look, you don't talk back.

I've known that since I was a little kid.

Paige, giggling and on her third glass of champagne brings Bree back to me.

"She's getting tired," she teases. "You should take her to bed."

Bree's hazel eyes snap to mine, and the rage in them is bigger than ever.

It's almost as if I can hear the thoughts running through her head challenging me to *just try it. Just you fucking try it.*

Paige bounces away, and I lean down to whisper to Bree, "I'm not that kind of man. We'll just go in the bedroom and talk."

"What do we have to talk about?"

I grab her by the elbow, with more strength than I needed, but not in a way that might hurt her or mark her in any way. "You'll go along with this, or Gray will be tempted to do something stupid. Like pull a knife on you."

Bree's eyes widen, but she doesn't break eye contact, and it makes me almost proud of her.

What am I thinking? She's the enemy.

I don't want this any more than she does, though, and so it does make me have pangs of sympathy for her.

I don't care that she's afraid. I just wish we weren't in this situation.

Gray walks by and whispers to me, "It's the guest bedroom by your office."

I take Bree's hand, leading her upstairs, and she jerks away from me.

"I'll follow you if I have to, but don't fucking touch me," she seethes.

I hold my hands up as if in defense, trying to fight a smile. I do like how feisty she is, I can't help it. I've always been attracted to strong women, and I'm impressed by how Bree is handling all of this.

She stalks up the stairs, right behind me, as I walk up them.

There's a chorus of jeers and cheers from the peanut gallery, and I look back with a grin, but Bree looks straight ahead, her face pinched and drawn.

I get it. If she is anything like me right now, she hates this. She hates *me*, and the feeling is mutual.

I walk into the bedroom, and she blinks at me, staring at the bed as I close the door.

"You have got to be fucking kidding me," she hisses. "You don't *really* think I'm going to sleep with you, do you?"

I shrug. "Stranger things have happened."

If looks could kill, I'd have my head exploded by now.

She brings her fists up in a fighting stance, spreading her legs apart. "If you're going to do this, you're in for a fight."

I laugh, holding up my hands. "I don't force myself on women. Not even dirty little Murphys."

"Then why are we here? Why are you going along with this?"

I stalk toward her. "You think I want this any more than you do? You think I want to be in here with *you*?"

"I don't know," she shoots back. "I have no idea who you are or what you want. I didn't even *recognize* you until we got here."

I scoff. "You didn't recognize the Irish scourge?"

She snorts. "You think so fucking highly of yourself."

"Damn right I do," I admit. "I've worked hard to get where I am."

Bree barks out a laugh. "You've worked so hard, just dribbling out of your father into your mother."

"Isn't that how you got here?" I sneer.

I keep stepping closer to her, but she doesn't back up, having whirled around to face me.

"You're no better than me," she accuses. "Just a spoiled little prince."

"You'd know, being the most spoiled little princess in the city," I drawl.

"You couldn't even find your own wife," she spit out. "You had to have *daddy* find you one."

"I told you," I say through gritted teeth. "I didn't want this, either."

"Then why are you doing it?" Her hands hang on her considerable hips. She's built like a brick shit house, and if this were solely about looks, I'd be all over her.

But it's not. She's a *snake*. A Murphy.

"What? Are you scared of daddy?" she goes on. "Are you afraid that he'll put you out, kick you out of the lifestyle he affords you?"

"He would never," I hiss. "But maybe that's what you're scared of. Maybe your daddy will drop you like a hot potato as soon as he hears that you're married to a Burke."

"That's what you want, isn't it?"

I give her a twisted grin. "Not at all, sweetheart. I want us to live happily ever after because that would chap your daddy's *ass*."

"He'll never allow this. It'll get annulled so fast it'll

make your head spin," she insists, but then I really notice her, and I smirk.

"Then why are you shaking?" I ask her. "You afraid I'll seduce you, princess?"

"Oh, *please*," she huffs out, but she hasn't moved, and she doesn't move at all when I put my hand on her waist.

"I think you like it," I murmur. "I think you like being told what to do."

"Just fucking try it," she says. "I'll kick you in the balls worse than I did this morning."

She's staring up at me, her hazel eyes full of anger and fear and... something I can't quite name. Something familiar.

"What are you doing?" she whispers.

"Nothing," I murmur. "I'm not doing anything. But neither are you. You're not pulling away."

"Maybe I'm afraid." Her voice is as low and as breathless as mine.

I shake my head. "I don't think you're the type to let fear rule you, princess. You've been angry this whole time. Ready to kill me. But now, suddenly, when I'm close... you don't push me away. Why is that?"

She looks up at me for an instant more, and leans up on her tiptoes, crushing her lips to mine, our teeth almost gnashing together. And then she closes her eyelids and groans.

Shocked, I flinch, but then she slips her tongue into my mouth, and I kiss her back, with a vengeance.

I push her backward, and her knees hit the bed before she falls onto it, and I cover her with my body.

What the hell are you doing? a voice in the back of my head says, but what my father wants and what my body wants are one and the same, so I kiss her again.

And the warmth of her mouth makes it that I'm not listening to my brain at all, just listening to my body as it takes over.

I just hope I'm not dooming myself.

4

BREE

As Declan kisses me back, I'm shocked that I started all of this. He's just so close to me and he smells so good and all day I've been *angry*, furious even, and it feels good to get the feelings out. Not to mention that he's an incredibly handsome man, deep blue eyes, broad shoulders, a sharp jaw with just the hint of stubble across it.

At first, I'd hoped to distract him, but as soon as my lips met his, it was like I couldn't stop myself.

He'd just been so close to me, and the anger in me had to go *somewhere*. And I thought, at first, I was going to hit him but then ... I did something completely insane.

The Burke crazy must be rubbing off on me. But I'm just so *pissed off,* and I want it out of me. I want a distraction, and Declan Burke is here and he's hot and he's all over me.

His breath feels hot against my neck before he kisses me there, and I moan as his teeth scrape across my flesh. The pain as he bites down hard shoots pleasure through me, and I arch my back, then gasp.

Declan's ripping the wide straps off my shoulders,

almost ripping my breasts out of the top and attacking my nipples with his tongue and his teeth, and the tug as he pulls his head up makes me soaking wet.

He grunts, pushing up the fabric to my hips, and there's so much of the dress he gets frustrated and just starts ripping strips off. Each sound of the fabric shredding makes my lower abdomen clench with need.

This isn't about love, and this is very clear as he finds me bare, groaning low in his throat.

"No panties? On your wedding night?" he teases, and I lean up, angry, clamping my hand over his mouth.

"Shut up," I tell him. "I'm trying to pretend you're someone else."

He glares down at me, ripping my hand away from his mouth. "After tonight, you'll never say that again. You won't be able to forget me," he taunts, and then he unbuttons his pants.

At some point during the night, he's discarded his suit jacket, so he's only wearing a tailored blue shirt, and the buttons are close to popping at his chest as he shifts to put my legs around his waist.

I spread my thighs easily, and when he slides his fingers through my lower lips, he finds me slick and ready.

I don't think I've ever been this hot, this wet, and I hate myself for it. I hate *him*, even as he releases his long, thick length from his slacks, taking himself in hand as he presses inside me.

I cry out, arching my back, wrapping my legs around his waist to bring him closer, deeper.

He leans over me, doubling over, and then a couple of the buttons on his shirt *do* pop, showing tantalizing glimpses of bronze skin.

I let out a grunt of sorts as I rip his shirt open, sliding my hands under it as buttons fly across the room and feeling his skin, palming across his nipples.

He gasps, his hips bucking involuntarily, and that's what I want. I want him deeper, want him *harder*. I want it rough, and Declan seems all too willing to oblige me.

He spears into me, bumping the edge of my womb with how deep he's going, and it aches but god, it hurts so *good*.

All the anger flows out of me and into him, and his blue eyes are dark with lust as he looks down at me.

"*Fuck* you," I spit out, and he gives me a wicked half-grin.

"I am, princess."

He fucks me harder, thrusting in and almost out of me, going so deep that it makes my eyes roll back into my head.

"Fuck," I curse. "Fuck, fuck, I'm going to come."

"Come all over my cock, princess. Want to feel you," he grunts, rolling his hips in a slightly uneven rhythm.

I know he's as close as I am, can feel him pulse against my walls. And when I finally reach my peak, I nearly scream, clawing my nails along his back. My press-on nails pop off, but I don't care.

I don't care about anything but how good he feels inside me. "God, don't stop," I moan as my second orgasm approaches, and when it hits, it hits like a freight train, and spots appear behind my eyelids.

After just a few more hard thrusts, Declan spills inside me, and then it washes over me.

What have I done? I've just consummated this marriage.

I open my mouth to curse him, to tell him how much I hate him, but Declan kisses along the side of my face, pressing his mouth against his teeth marks on my neck.

What is he doing?

He pulls out of me, panting, and when he does, I just know he's going to walk off.

Instead, he stands up and then crouches at the end of the bed, grabbing my ankles and pulling my legs over his shoulders.

When he presses his face into my sex, I moan so loudly I'm sure the whole huge household can hear me.

I'm already so sensitive, but he doesn't go easy on me, latching around my clit and pressing two fingers into me, fucking his come back inside as he laps at my clit.

I come again, crying out, and he hums against me.

"Enough," I whimper.

"Not yet," he murmurs against my inner thigh. "You can come again, princess. I know you can."

His praise slides pleasure through me, and it's almost painful, the ache I have in my lower abdomen.

I take in a deep, shaking breath as he continues to finger-fuck me and suck on my clit, and when I come, I gasp and whine, barely able to breathe.

Declan looks up at me with a grin, and he plops down on the bed next to me before throwing an arm around my waist. He's only there for a few moments, but it's strange, the way he holds me, like he's cuddling me.

Why isn't he just walking away?

"I'm going to shower," he mutters, and stands up, as if he's realized what he's doing.

He leaves the room, and I rub my hands across my face.

"What the fuck did you do, Bree?" I huff, wiggling out of the rest of my dress and letting it fall to the floor. I'm nude, but it's a little too late to be embarrassed about it. I feel a little sore, and I think I'll have fingerprint bruises on my hips after that session.

I can't believe I just did that. It's not that I've been

treated badly here. Just the opposite, especially since Paige untied me. And the sex was unbelievable.

But they are still the enemy, and I have to get the hell out of here.

I always thought that I'd get married for love, and now I'm married literally out of hate. It's depressing, and the long day catches up with me and tears finally slip down my cheeks.

I slither under the covers, covering my face with the pillow and trying to keep my cries quiet. After a few moments, my tears dry up, and I think about my family.

My brother is gone. He left as soon as he could. Said he wanted nothing to do with the family business or anyone involved in it. He calls, occasionally, just to check that I'm okay, but he hardly ever talks to Dad.

Sometimes, I wish I had his courage. I don't know that I could cut my father out of my life like that. He's always given me everything I asked for and more. He's always been a hard man, and he's been a little distant, even more when it comes to anything emotional, but he's always been there.

Especially since my mother left. She might have abandoned us, but he didn't. Many nights I was up crying with him holding me as I did.

He's my *father*.

And now I'm married to his enemy's son. What will he think of me?

Finally, I close my eyes, and I'm sure that I won't be able to sleep in such a strange place, but I drift off before I know it.

I wake up a few hours later, in an unfamiliar place, trembling. Everything crashes down on me, and I wonder if they've locked my door. I get up and walk to it, slowly opening it.

My heart starts to beat faster as the door opens easily.

The hallway seems empty, but I can't be sure.

I step out, bare-footed, trying not to make any sound. I can't stop looking around, my throat tight with fear, remembering Gray's look of pure hatred, and Declan's threats. From what he said, I'd assume men to be everywhere, guarding the estate, but at least upstairs, there's no one.

I creep to the staircase and the murmur of voices reaches me, coming from the far door. I can't quite make out what they're saying, but I think I recognize Declan's voice.

He's close. I'll have to be careful.

I slip down the stairs, silent as a mouse, heading toward the front door. As I'm about to reach it, Gray steps out of the shadows, the gold tints in his dark blond hair glinting in the light.

"Where do you think you're going?" He has a twisted smirk, and I can't help it, I squeak and turn, fleeing back up the stairs and into my prison, slamming the door behind me.

My heart is pounding so hard it almost hurts, and I rest against the door, chest heaving, for a long moment, afraid that he might come after me.

Declan said that I won't be hurt, but I don't trust any of the people here as far as I can throw them—which isn't very far.

My eyes fill with fearful tears, and I climb back onto the bed as I let them fall. I certainly can't cry in front of *them*.

My brother doesn't know I'm here, or he'd be here by now, but my father will come for me. I know he will.

I still remember the night my life changed forever.

"Wean," *my father says hoarsely, waking me from my slumber.*

He always calls me that. Child. One of the few Irish words I know.

I sit up, rubbing my eyes. "Daidí?"

"Your mother." He shakes his head. "She's gone."

"Gone?" Panic settles in my throat. "What do you mean, she's gone?"

At twelve years old, I was very close to my mother. She had always said we were twin souls. I didn't have other friends, not really. Well, maybe Yolanda Ricci, the niece of the head of the Ricci family, but to be honest, she kind of got on my nerves.

I was home-schooled by a tutor, and I couldn't really meet other kids my age unless their parents were also in the life. I was sheltered, but my father just wanted to protect me.

When Daidí gets closer to the bed, plopping down on it, the aroma of whiskey is strong on his breath.

"She's hurt?" My heart is slamming against my chest plate.

He shakes his head. "She just left us, wean."

Tears start to stream down his face. I sit on his lap and his arms wrap around me as we sit there and cry most of the night.

He told me she'd left a note, said that she wasn't ready for this kind of commitment, which seemed strange after twelve years of being a mother and fifteen of being a wife.

I never saw the letter. I never had to. My father would never lie to me.

Over the next few weeks, he drank too much, and I started helping out anyway I could. Sometimes trying to understand the books, others with phone calls and keeping his appointments.

He needed me, and I was more than willing to help.

We became united, a Murphy front, and we've been that way ever since.

I squeeze my eyes, my heart tightening with how much I miss my father. He wasn't always there for me like he had been that night. He has his issues with expressing emotions, but he has tried. I know that he loves me, and that is enough.

And now I'm stuck behind enemy lines, and what do I do? I sleep with the son of my father's greatest enemy.

I take in a shaking breath, trying to stop crying. Crying doesn't do any good, it just makes our eyes red and our soul a little lighter for a bit, my mother always said. I guess she was right, even if she ended up abandoning us.

I need to get some rest. It's the only way I can stay sharp and find my way out of here. So, I close my eyes.

When sleep overtakes me at last, oddly, it's not my father I dream of but my mother: her kind blue eyes, how her soft hands used to refresh my forehead when I was sick.

5

DECLAN

I slip out of bed while Bree is still sleeping, her soft snores in the air. She's *out*, and I can't help but find it a little cute how she's drooling on the pillow, which I slipped back under her head last night after finding her under it.

Cute? A Murphy?

I shake my head, throwing on a pair of jeans and a T-shirt, not worried about wearing a suit today. I just got married, after all, and if Da is going to make me do the ceremony and the consummation, he can damn well give me a vacation for the honeymoon.

I'm shocked that last night even happened, given how much Bree hates me. And she was the one who initiated. Of course, I wasn't going to say no. I don't make it a habit of saying no to beautiful women.

She may be a Murphy, but she's also drop dead gorgeous.

Besides, it's just sex.

I'm going to have to work out how to get around this, how to get out of this marriage, because love isn't in the cards for me. It never has been. And with a Murphy, it will never be about love. But still. A wife is a weapon to be used against you in this life, so I just need to convince my father that this is a bad idea.

But when this is all over, when we've been able to take down Niall Murphy, maybe we can get a quickie divorce. I'll make Da and Gray pay for every cent of it.

I walk downstairs, following the fresh scent of coffee in the air. Our chef, Marisol, has made muffins and some sausage, and I grab a muffin on the way to the dining room table.

She smacks at my hand briefly. "Wait for your father," she scolds, but I stuff a muffin into my mouth, grinning at her.

She shakes her head. "You always were stealing food."

"It's because your food is so good, Marisol." I hug her slightly with one arm.

She smiles up at me, putting her slender but familiar arm around my waist.

Gray's already at the dining room table, sipping coffee and eating a plate full of sausage. He's got a massive plate in front of him, and I wrinkle my nose, eating my muffin.

He narrows his eyes at me. "Sugar's not good for you."

My mouth full of muffin, I shoot my middle finger up at him, and Gray rolls his eyes.

We're always like this, at each other's throats in a playful way. It's different with our sisters. They need to be protected, but Gray and I? We've battled a lot over the years, getting into fistfights over something as simple as the last piece of cheesecake. I like to think we've grown up a little, but stuff like this makes me think differently.

He scoffs at me. "Childish."

I slowly raise my other middle finger up, grinning at him, and then Gray finally cracks, breaking into a laugh.

"How'd it go with your wifey?" Gray smirks, and I shake my head.

I'm not one to kiss and tell, even in this situation. But in reality, it'd been out of this world. I can't believe how good it was, how well she took me, how much she gave back.

"That good, huh?" Gray responds, but I ignore him. "I need you to come down to the warehouse."

I raise an eyebrow. "I thought I was on my honeymoon?"

Gray snorts. "Yeah, right." He finishes his sausage and stands, putting his coffee cup down on the table. "Come on. You're late."

I look down at my watch. It's only nine in the morning, so I'm not *that* late.

"You guys are really going to make me work the day after my wedding?"

Gray chuckles, walking out the door and expecting me to follow. I sigh, annoyed, but I follow him anyway.

When we arrive there, Jimmy Connor, one of my father's right-hand men, is already there, popping open crates of the shipments we've gotten.

Gray goes to him and claps him in the back. "Have we lost any to Murphy this month?"

Jimmy scoffs. "Not yet, but there's still time."

Niall Murphy, unlike my father, started his business outside of Ireland. He basically keeps things going by stealing from us, causing havoc and chaos, etcetera. Even when he can't manage to steal our shipments, he fucks them up somehow. He's a snake, plain and simple.

The warehouse is huge and abandoned, dust everywhere, the building dilapidated and nearly falling down. There are leaks in the ceilings and we have to be careful how long we keep our product there. Of course, we can't do renovations, or it would be suspicious, even though we own the business.

"What do we have today?" I ask.

"Thirty kilos of china white. Fifteen kilos of dust. Three hundred firearms."

"Pistols?"

"AKs," Jimmy responds. "All accounted for."

I hum. "Have you tested the dust? Last time they tried to pass off ten kilos of basically baby powder."

"Tested and pure," Jimmy brims.

He helps my father with arranging shipments and a few other things. He's Da's most trusted man, besides us, of course. Jimmy's a few years older than Gray, and he's been basically like a brother to us.

"So, things are going well?" I ask.

"I mean, for now." Jimmy raises his eyebrows. "Word on the street is that Murphy's pissed off. Out for blood."

I grin. "Good."

Jimmy looks at me, confused.

Gray shakes his head, but he's smiling, too. "You're obsessed with starting a war."

"I'm ready for a war," I insist. "It's about fucking time."

"I don't know what he's on about," Jimmy admits. "Thought he was too busy with his new strip club, Luxe."

"Speaking of that."

Gray turns to me. "One of his girls is waiting for you in the back."

I blink at him, confused. "One of his girls?"

"Just listen to what she has to say," Gray urges.

Why the hell would one of Murphy's dancers come to us, of all things? And why talk to me? My brother is next in line for the business, not me.

But I guess of the two, I have more patience to listen.

Anyway, I shouldn't look a gift horse in the mouth. If she has information about Murphy and his plans, then she's an asset.

I walk to the back office and open the door.

The girl sitting there, wearing a tube top, a short skirt, and a full-length fur coat, flinches as if I've burst open the door instead of gently opening it.

"O-oh," she stutters. "Mr. Burke."

"Call me Declan."

She looks to be about Bree's age, maybe younger. With a sweet, round, pretty face, she doesn't seem like the type of girl to work for Murphy.

"D-Declan," she says, her voice finally smoothing out. "I'm sorry to bother you. I'm Diamond."

I'm aware that Diamond isn't her real name, but it doesn't matter.

"What is it you need to tell me, *honey*?" I try to set her at ease.

She swallows hard. "Luxe is getting dangerous." She looks at her feet. "Mr. Murphy's taken a lot of the girls. He's forcing them into doing extras."

"Extras?"

She licks her lips as if her mouth is dry. "You know, *extras*. Prostitution." She nearly whispers that last word, as if it's a bad word.

I frown. "He's forcing girls to sell their bodies?"

She nods slowly. "Yes. A lot of us... well, we're reliant on...things."

"On drugs."

Diamond looks up at me, something suddenly sharp in her dark brown eyes. "Drugs that the Burkes supply."

I can't argue with that.

I spread my hands. "Well, if you're here for freebies, I can't help you."

"It wouldn't be freebies."

I know she's hoping for dust or some of that new china white we have, but I'm not in the business of giving dust away to all the pretty girls that come to me.

She seems as if she is thinking of approaching me, but her body just sags in the next second. "It wouldn't be free, because I'm giving you information."

"What do you want?"

A pang of sympathy for her rocks me for a moment. I know how girls get caught up in this life, and she looks so young…

"Just a gram." Her eyes are pleading, and her voice is getting squeakier. "Dust. I'm going to share it with the other girls."

I wince, not liking the sound of that, but what can I do? It's the life we live.

"All right," I say. "You can have it, if you give me something I can use."

"Some of the girls are under eighteen," she murmurs.

My eyes snap up to hers where I'd been looking at my hands.

"What?"

"Some of them are *young*, Mister. He keeps bringing them in, from all over the world."

"Sex trafficking," I nearly whisper.

I know that Murphy sinks pretty low, but I didn't think it was *this* low.

She nods. "He's getting a shipment in a few days. I was hoping that you could stop it."

She presses her lips in a thin line. "I know I'm just a junkie stripper," she says, and suddenly there are tears standing in her eyes. "But I don't like the idea of children getting pushed into this life."

"You're doing a good thing, Diamond." I stand up. "Listen, I'm going to get you to Jimmy. He'll give you the gram if that's what you want."

Her eyes light up, but then I pause, just standing there, looking at her.

"But if you want a way out," I say quietly. "Out for good? Jimmy can also take you to rehab. Change your name. Get you away from Murphy."

Diamond looks up at me and I hope the flash in her eyes is hope.

"You're a good man, Mr. Burke."

"Declan," I remind her.

"Declan." She smiles and stands up.

I lead her over to Jimmy, walking away so that I don't know if she chooses the drugs or the rehab because I think it would break my heart if she chose the former. It might make me think twice about what we do, and that isn't good for anyone.

I find Gray popping open crates and checking product, not testing it because none of us actually partake, but just checking to see that it's all there.

I tilt my head to the crate in front of him. "How's it look?"

He glances at me. "It's fine. Everything's here. It's almost a miracle."

"I've got something to tell you."

Gray frowns. "What is it? Don't tell me he is using underage girls at the club?"

"Not just at the club," I say. "Prostitution. He's bringing in girls from all over, making them work in the clubs, getting them hooked on *our* shit, and then pushing them into sex work."

"Jesus," Gray mutters. "What a piece of shit."

"Well, we knew that," I point out. "But there's a shipment in a couple of days."

Gray wrinkles his nose. "It fucks me up when you refer to people as *shipments.*"

"I know," I say. "But it's Murphy, not me. The girl that showed up, she's going to give Jimmy a date, time, and location. I want us to be there, intercept it."

Gray grins. "Well, why not? He intercepts our shit all the time."

"We offer them a way out."

Gray nods. "Of course." He pauses. "You know, this thing with his daughter, intercepting his girls... it really *is* going to be war."

"I told you, I'm ready." And I mean it with all my heart.

We haven't been able to take Murphy down because they have too many allies, and we never have had definitive proof that he's the one stealing our shipments and messing everything up.

Gray looks at me for a long moment. "I hope you mean that."

"I fucking do." My eyes narrow at him. "It's time to put Murphy out of business once and for all."

By the time we get ready to leave, I can't stand the curiosity anymore. I sidle up to Jimmy, and he glances at me as he closes all the crates, getting them ready for sale.

"Did she take the rehab pamphlets?" I ask. "Did she take the help?"

Jimmy smiles, but it doesn't reach his eyes. "She did, but she also took the dust. You've got a bleeding heart, *capo.*"

I sigh. It's not great that she took the drugs, but maybe, after a bender, she'll take a look at the pamphlets, too.

"I'm tough as nails."

Jimmy gives me a knowing smile.

He knows as well as I do that I have a soft spot for young girls, want to protect them. God even knows if Diamond is more than eighteen or nineteen. She needs protection, and she's clearly not getting it from the Murphys.

I keep thinking about poor Diamond's dark eyes as we leave the warehouse, and I think there's more than one reason to hate Niall Murphy.

6

BREE

I slowly wake up to someone bouncing gently on the bed, and when I look up, it's the dark-haired sister, Paige, grinning at me.

I jump and flinch, and then it all comes rushing back.

Oh. Right. I'm married to a fucking Burke, and his sister is here basically jumping on my bed like a little kid. Because they're all crazy.

Maybe I'm crazy too, given what I did last night.

"It's almost ten o'clock," Paige says in a whining voice. "It's time to get up. Marisol has made breakfast."

She stands and then looks down at the ruins of my dress on the ground.

"Oops," she says, wrinkling her nose. "Looks like I need to grab you some new clothes."

She disappears, and for a moment, I hope she won't come back and snuggle back under the covers. But of course, she's back in thirty seconds flat, throwing a huge amount of clothes on my bed.

"Take your pick!" she says, and then just stands there.

I squint up at her.

Her eyes widen. "Oh! I'm sorry. You must want some privacy. I'll be right outside."

Of course you will.

There's no mistaking that I'm still a prisoner, even if Paige is bright and bubbly.

She closes the door, and I stand up, stretching and yawning.

I go to the shower, realizing that all of these rooms must have a suite, or at least most of them.

Only this one is a bit bigger, and there are no hushed voices coming from the door at least.

I take a luxurious, long shower, putting my hair up. The smell of sex needs to be washed off, but my hair doesn't need the dryness that comes from washing it so often.

When I step out of the shower, I go into the bedroom and rifle through the clothes, picking through them to find something comfortable—a pair of high-waisted, white shorts and a comfy T-shirt with a graphic of the sun on it.

Paige is about my size, although the shorts stretch a little tightly over my ass. The clothes are high-quality, maybe better than what I have at home, so I can't complain there.

Paige and Lara have been kind to me, and it's not like anyone did anything to physically harm me so far, but I'm still on edge. I don't know what to expect next from the Burkes.

Taking a deep breath before sliding the door open, I hope that Paige has given up so maybe I can jump out a window or something.

But when it slides all the way through, she's leaned against the wall, looking at me, and I hold back the groan that wants to be set free.

"Breakfast will be cold," she says in a scolding tone, and starts down the stairs, clearly expecting me to follow.

And I do. As we go, I look around and try and get my bearings a bit more. When we get to the stairs, they are much longer than the ones at my father's mansion.

"I put a plate in the microwave for you," Lara says, sitting at the table as we enter the dining room.

"Thank you," I mutter, and sit down at the table, taking a small bite of a blueberry muffin. Sugar and tartness bloom in my mouth, and I almost want to moan. They really *do* have a great chef.

"I can't wait to show you the rest of the house," Paige says in a bubbly tone.

"She's probably tired," Lara pipes up. "Don't push her too hard."

"I'm not pushing," Paige pouts, looking at me. "Tell her I'm not pushy."

I can't help but let out a small laugh. I think, in another situation, I would have liked Paige and Lara. They have such opposite personalities, with Lara quieter and statelier and Paige so bubbly and sweet.

"Did you guys fight a lot as kids?" I ask.

Lara snorts. "Yeah, all the time."

"I'm not surprised," I mumble.

"What is that supposed to mean?" Paige says, still pouting, and Lara and I share a laugh.

I feel slightly lighter, my shoulders relaxing a bit, but I'm still on guard as we eat. I won't let their kindness sway me. They're still daughters of the enemy, and sisters to my forced husband.

If my goal is to get out of here, maybe they are the way to do it, but I can't risk getting attached or thinking at any time that I can trust them.

I'm on my own here, regardless of however well they might treat me, and I'll do well to remember that.

When we finish with breakfast, Paige leads me around the bottom part of the house. I look around, eyes wide and mouth ajar, at all the modern but comfortable-looking furniture, but then I see the ratty recliner with the peeling leather.

I pause, frowning. "What...is that?"

"Oh, God, that monstrosity." Lara groans. "That's our father's special chair."

"He keeps it because of Ma," Paige says.

I raise an eyebrow.

"He says that he and our mother used to sleep together in it when they lived with her parents back in Dublin," Lara explains. "He won't have a single thing about it changed."

I find myself feeling a little bad for Patrick. I know that his wife died in an accident, but he clearly isn't over it. How does someone get over a thing like that, though?

It doesn't matter. He's still the one trying to kill my father, destroy my family. Just because he misses his wife doesn't mean he's the good guy in this story. I mean, he had me kidnapped and married me to his son.

Lara leads me out to the terrace, and there's a beautiful garden all around it. Roses, lavender, honeysuckle, all the scents mix in the air and float by me on the breeze.

Looking all around me, I can't help the sense of peace that falls over me. "It's beautiful."

"All Ma," Lara explains with a wide smile. "But we keep it up. I do most of the gardening myself. Just don't trust anyone else to keep Ma's flowers alive."

Again, a pang of sympathy hist me, and I push it away.

The Burkes are the bad guys. They're evil and crazy, and I shouldn't like them.

We go past a small office, but neither of the girls makes much mention of it, so I assume it's one of Patrick's. Upstairs, they lead me past the area where Declan and I stayed and into the left wing.

"You'll have to pick out a suite." Paige grins. She is almost skipping as she goes.

"What, why?"

Lara nods. "Yeah, Declan's room is too small, and all the other rooms are technically guest rooms, so they're not all suites. You'll want a bigger space as a couple."

I want to argue, but I don't think it would do me any good. The Stepford sisters don't seem to have any clue what's going on. They act as if I chose this, as if I'm really their sister-in-law instead of a prisoner. As if Declan and I are a happily married couple and all of this is just normal.

I slowly trail into each of the suites. They are like little apartments.

The one I choose has a small kitchenette, a sitting room, the bedroom, a huge bathroom with a big clawfoot tub, and a huge walk-in closet like the one in Paige's room.

"It's perfect," Paige says.

It's beautiful.

But I don't say it. If I'd actually gotten to choose my husband, actually chosen for love instead of being forced, I'd probably be the happiest ever thinking I found my perfect home.

"And of course, we'll send the stylist right up," Lara says. "We'll let you get settled."

"What do you mean, the stylist?" My eyes widen.

"What do you think I mean? You'll need a whole new wardrobe," Paige says. "You can't keep wearing my hand-me-downs." She looks me up and down. "Besides, you'll have to get your measurements done, you have a lot more junk in the trunk than I do." She giggles, and I can't help but smile.

"Yeah, we're a little jealous," Lara admits. "We wish we could get a new wardrobe without Da freaking out about how much we spend."

"Thirty thousand a month isn't that bad, I keep telling him," Paige says.

Thirty thousand dollars? A month?

My breath catches in my throat, and I almost choke on air. I know that I probably spend a good deal, but thirty thousand? The Burkes are crazy but also loaded, it turns out.

"Melissa will be right up," Lara says, and she and Paige leave me in the suite to get settled.

I'm not sure what to do, especially since I don't have any of my things and am not likely to be able to get them, so I just sit on the bed, bouncing slightly.

The thread count on these sheets must be insane. Everything in this house is insane, including the people. But Lara and Paige are at least *good* crazy, and they make me feel a little less alone.

Instead of knocking on the door, a woman I assume is Melissa bursts right in, wheeling a huge clothes rack behind her. I have no idea how she got it up the stairs.

"Girly!" she says, with a heavy Slavic accent. "It's time to get you all dressed up."

She pulls a measuring tape out of her purse and quickly starts to take my measurements as I stand there, gaping at her.

"Ooh, you have Marilyn Monroe waist," she praises, and I laugh a little.

"Maybe Marilyn with a few extra pounds," I argue.

"You look wonderful, girly. Aunt Melissa will take good

care of you, don't you worry."

She's probably about forty years old, but she looks amazing, long, white-blonde hair, baby blue eyes. Maybe she's had some work done or maybe she's younger than I think, but either way, she looks great.

She flips through the clothes. "Pick out ten outfits." She tilts her head toward the rack. "At least for the week. I'll come back and bring more, but I don't think I have more than ten that will suit your figure."

Ten? For a *week?*

"What about pajamas," I ask meekly. "I really like pajamas."

She scoffs. "Pajamas, I have," she says, opening up a drawer at the bottom of the rack and revealing short and tank-top sets, lingerie, all manner of underwear and bras.

I pick out several items, throwing them on the bed, and eventually, with Melissa's help, I pick out ten outfits.

She snatches the last one back from me. "No white," she says, and I huff out a breath.

"What is wrong with me wearing white?"

"You don't have the complexion for it, girly. Yellow. You'd look good in yellow." She hands me a dress in yellow, and I have to admit, it looks better.

Melissa abruptly leaves after I pick things out, muttering about tailoring some new clothes for me, and I blink as she closes the door.

I feel like I'm in one of those princess movies, where an ordinary girl finds out she's royalty, but this time the princess is kidnapped, and all of this is against her will.

I slowly start to put up the clothes and change into a pair of tight shorts and a gray tank top, not wanting to continue wearing Paige's clothes.

After getting everything squared away, I look around at the cream-and-gold-colored walls.

It's pretty, the best suite that I've been shown, and I like the furniture. It seems more comfortable than modern, which I enjoy.

I walk to the right wing to Paige's room and knock softly on her door.

She opens it immediately, having changed into a bright blue cocktail dress, and she grins at me.

"Oh, you look...comfortable," she says, and it doesn't even seem like a slight.

I smile. "Just wanted to return your clothes. I don't know where the laundry is."

"We send it out, of course."

"Of course." We do, too, but I still wash some of my own delicates just so I won't have to wait for them.

Apparently, Paige doesn't do that. Doesn't seem like the girls lift a finger around here, which is a little enviable.

I help my father with the books and take phone calls for him sometimes. Of course, he doesn't tell me anything. There's no information I have that could implicate him, and I can't help thinking that's on purpose.

"I know this is hard on you," Paige says softly, and I look up at her, shocked.

"You do?"

She nods. "I can imagine how I would feel if Da did this to me. But Declan really is a good guy, deep down. He'll treat you right."

"Don't you understand why that doesn't matter?" I can't stop myself from being honest.

She shrugs. "I don't know. It's not *so* bad, is it? You have built-in sisters, and Gray is kind of a drag, but he's a good big brother."

I remember Gray's slate blue eyes, glaring into me when he told me in no uncertain terms that I had no choice in any of this.

"I'm sure," I drawl, but she seems to take it in stride.

"Finding love is hard." She sighs. "Maybe it's better if it's been chosen for us."

"Maybe, but wouldn't you at least want to make that choice for yourself? To choose to try and find it or ask to have it chosen for you?" I sigh. "You know what. Never mind. It's done, so let's just move on from this."

It's not that I disagree with Paige. I've had my bad experiences with men, and I know how hard it is to want love and a family and have that constantly out of your reach.

I've always wanted someone to come home to, someone to confide in, someone to just hold me when the world is falling apart.

Now, I'll never know that. I'll never have the chance to find my person. I'll never be truly free to choose love. Because along with my freedom, I've been deprived of a happy, loving future when my husband was chosen for me. A husband I only know from his less than stellar reputation. A husband I know nothing about. A husband who is my family's sworn enemy.

But Paige doesn't seem to get that.

"I should go. Think I'm going to take a nap."

She touches my hand. "It's been an ordeal, but it will be okay, you'll see."

I nod because I'm tired and I don't want to talk anymore. Making my way back to my new home, the suite, I crawl under the covers.

I try my best but sleep eludes me.

All I can think about is last night, how urgent and rough

the sex was.. I groan, flipping over on the bed, my skin feeling hot.

Maybe I need another shower. A cold one. Otherwise, it might sound like a good idea to do it again even if just to pass the time more quickly until someone comes for me.

7

DECLAN

I CAN'T STOP THINKING ABOUT THE NIGHT WHEN WE consummated our marriage. That was two days ago, and I haven't seen Bree since.

Paige insists on showing me the suite that Bree chose, and it is a great suite, probably the best one in the house since it's the only one with a kitchenette.

But I don't see Bree, except briefly in the halls. I'm sleeping in my own room because I get up so early for work lately. We're focused on intercepting the shipment of girls that Murphy's working on, and I don't want Bree to get wind of it.

I guess it's not like she can get word out to her father, but at the same time, I don't want to risk it.

And frankly, I don't know if I want a repeat of our wedding night either. It was too good and for my own sake, I should stay away from her.

Too bad that only lasts until dinner.

Bree's dressed in a yellow shift dress that stretches nicely across her ass and thick thighs, and I can't help but steal a few glances. Her auburn hair looks shiny and freshly curled, like she's the belle of the ball, but there's something wrong.

Her eyes... they don't seem angry anymore. Not really. It's almost like something's dimmed in those hazel eyes, and it makes my stomach twist.

It's the first dinner that Bree has attended, having always preferred to stay up in our room, and I never thought much of it.

Now, though, I'm a bit worried.

"Don't you just love Bree's new clothes?" Paige asks me brightly. She's had a couple of glasses of wine, and it just makes her even more bubbly.

"It's a beautiful dress," I agree quietly, but Bree doesn't even look up at me, picking at her lamb chops. I frown. "You don't like lamb?"

"I love it." Bree looks up at me, and an ember of anger burns in her eyes for a fleeting second, and I can't help but feel a little relieved. If she started being depressed, I think I'd feel almost bad about it.

But it shouldn't matter. She's related to Niall Murphy, so I shouldn't be feeling any type of way about her.

She doesn't speak much other than answering Lara and Paige throughout dinner, even though everyone else is lively. Hell, even Gray is regaling us with a story.

"Cillian and I were taking some... things .... from the warehouse," Gray says, laughing already. "We were in my SUV, and he kept asking if I'd pull over and let him smoke."

Lara shakes her head. "He needs to quit."

Gray nods. "Exactly. So, I tell him I won't, and then next thing I know, we're whizzing by a state patrol car. I had to have been going seventy in a thirty-five."

"Holy shit," Paige pipes up. "So, what'd you do?"

Gray laughs. "He put on his sirens, and I took off, taking

the back alleys back toward the house. I finally got rid of him, but it scared the shit out of Cillian."

I'm laughing but I keep glancing at Bree, and she's just sitting there, as if she's barely paying attention.

I can't hold back anymore, so I lean to her, putting my mouth closer to her ear. "What's wrong?"

She doesn't answer. Doesn't even react at all. As if I haven't said anything to her.

"Leave her be, Declan," Lara warns. "She's just having a bad day. Some days girls have bad days."

I grumble under my breath. Seems to me that Bree has no reason to be having a bad day. After all, I've given her everything that she could have possibly desired since she got here.

Sure, we got off to a rough start with the kidnapping, but she has everything she needs.

"If you want anything, all you have to do is ask," I tell Bree, and she looks up at me coolly.

"Is that so?" She narrows her eyes at me. "Then, I want to go home."

Gray snickers. "You should have seen that coming."

I huff out a breath, the growl, "You know what I meant. And you're being rude at dinner."

"Can't seem to help myself." She looks directly at my father. "May I be excused?"

Bree stands up.

My father raises an eyebrow at her before nodding. "Yes, of course. You don't have to ask."

She nods back and listlessly walks up the stairs.

I frown, excusing myself and following her, and my father throws me a wink.

"The best ones have fire in their eyes," he comments, but I don't respond.

He's right, of course, but I haven't exactly forgiven him for everything.

I open and close the door, and Bree's lying in bed, staring up at the ceiling.

I stand near the door, my arms crossed over my chest. "Why are you being so sullen?"

Bree's quiet for a moment. I think she's not going to respond, that the fire is dimming, and something like panic rises in my throat.

She sits up slowly, staring at me. "Sullen?"

"Yes. Sullen. Like a little child who didn't get her way."

"My way?" Her eyes widen.

Bree stands up, stalking toward me.

There it is.

The fire is back in her hazel eyes, and I have to admit, I'm glad. I'm pumped. That fire seems to have an effect on me.

"*None* of this is my way, Declan. You kidnapped me. You forced me to marry you. Then you fucked me, and you ignore me for two days?"

I bark out a laugh. "Ignore you? Is that what you're mad about, princess?"

"You think I'm mad about *that*? Are all Burkes this stupid, or is it just you?"

My own temper starts to stir, and I press my lips together.

"You've been treated well," I look around. "New wardrobe, nice digs... any food you could ever want."

She scoffs. "Oh, *please*. I'm a prisoner here. The fact that it is gilded doesn't make this place any less of a cage."

"You're not a prisoner." My eyes clash with hers. "You're family now, Bree. You're a *Burke*."

"In name only," she snaps.

I spread my hands, smiling. "So, you admit it?"

"Admit *what?*"

"That you're a Burke. That you have been treated well."

"I didn't say that," she snaps, pointing at me, poking me in the chest.

While she moves, that little shift dress is riding up, and my mouth goes dry.

"Sounds like you're finally accepting your fate." I'm doing everything in my power to piss her off because I want her anger. I want her hatred. I want *something* other than that despair that was so clear in her eyes.

"I'll never accept it," she insists. "I'll *never* really be your wife. I hope you know that. I'll never love you, Declan."

Who does she think she is? Like I'd even want her love.

Yet, as the thought crosses my mind, my chest tightens.

Her words sting a little for reasons I can't begin to understand, and when she points at my chest again, I grab her wrist, turning her hand inward and pulling her closer to me.

She gasps, her breasts bouncing against my chest, and I slide my arms around her waist.

"Maybe not," I murmur. "But you want me, and you can never take that away from me."

"Who says I want you?" she taunts, but her breath is coming shorter and shorter.

"Your body." I squeeze her against me. "Your heart, racing away."

"My body's a fucking traitor," she spits out.

I hum. "Yeah, I know how that feels."

And as my own body betrays the feelings I should have for her—disgust, hatred—I lean down and smash my lips against hers, our teeth nearly gnashing together in my haste.

She fights me for a second and then melts against me, sliding her tongue against mine, kissing me back hard and hungrily. Then she shifts, pushes me down on the bed, and I grin up at her.

"Can't wait to have it, can you?"

"Shut up," she growls, straddling me, bunching up her dress around her waist.

When I tug it off her, she's not wearing a bra, just a pair of nearly translucent panties, and I take a nipple in my mouth.

She arches her back, rocking her hips against my erection, and I gasp against her skin.

Bree reaches down between us, unbuttoning my slacks, reaching inside, and fills her hands with my cock

My breath catches in my chest.

"Fuck." I thrust into her hand, wanting her so badly it feels like I'm already about to explode.

I shove her panties to the side, thrusting into her.

Last time, her temper got her all hot and wet, so I hoped this time was the same, and I'm happy with how slick she's already, just like I thought.

"You want me," I taunt. "You want me so bad you're aching for it."

"I think you're thinking of yourself." She rocks her hips with a little smirk, the very first smile I've seen, and I can't breathe as she does a little lap dance, rolling her hips, shaking her ass, bouncing on me.

I grab hold of her hips, thrusting up beneath her as her hands slide across my chest, her thumbs flicking over my nipples. It sends pleasure down my spine.

"I do want you." Like I could deny it if I wanted to. "But at least I'm man enough to admit it."

"God," she moans. "God, please, I'm going to come."

I pull out of her, throwing her down on the bed as I pull her panties down to her knees, and she gets up on all fours, spreading her thighs, not bothering to take her panties all of the way off.

I love the way she looks, spread out for me, glistening in the light.

She's shaved almost bare with just a landing strip, and looking at her makes my mouth water. Part of me wants to press my face into her pussy, taste her, inhale her musk, but my dick is aching for her, and I want to be inside her so badly I don't think I can wait.

"You're so fucking hot. So wet and tight," I moan. "Your perfect ass."

I shouldn't be praising her, but I can't seem to stop.

She rolls her hips back against me, and I guide myself into her, riding her hard.

She buries her face into the pillows, and I wrap my hand around her hair, pulling her face up.

"Nuh-uh, princess. I want everyone to hear how well I'm fucking you."

She cries out as I continue thrusting. "Please, please, please."

"Please what?" I slow down even though my balls are already drawing up.

"Please make me come," she begs, and I grab hold of her hips, dropping her head, and fuck her hard and fast, angling up to get to her deepest parts.

She moans out my name when she comes, and between that and the way she clenches around me, I can't hold back anymore. I spill inside her, groaning out her name.

Bree gasps, collapsing as I pull out of her, and I slowly shift her so that I can put her under the covers, lying next to her.

I'm panting, and Bree's still lying face down.

"Just because I want you to fuck me doesn't mean I like you." Her voice is muffled by the pillow where she buried her face.

I chuckle. "All right. Fair enough."

She twists on the bed, turning over and frowning at me. "What's that supposed to mean?"

I shrug. "I said, fair enough."

Bree frowns wider. "You're not supposed to agree with me. That's weird. Don't do that."

"Don't do what?" I laugh. "Don't agree with you? Ever? Seems like that's an unrealistic ask."

"I don't like it," she mumbles, and then she turns over, facing the wall.

I want to slide an arm around her, just instinct, I guess, but she scoots as far away as she can.

I sigh, standing up to undress.

Paige and Lara have had my things moved into this room except for a few suits and some clothes in my old room, which is nearer the office.

I undress and throw on a pair of sweats, just because it's a little chilly in the room, and slide back under the covers.

She's snoring softly by now, and so I sneak an arm around her waist.

She doesn't stir at first, but then she pushes back against me, wiggling to get closer, and I can't help but break into a smile.

This is bad. Like, really bad.

8

———

BREE

The line between reality and dream is blurring as kisses are planted along my throat. They feel so good. I want to melt.

My eyes flutter open to Declan, his mouth soft against my skin.

"What the hell are you doing?" There is no real fire in my voice and I don't move away from him.

I should. I should even want to. My head is screaming at me to move away, but I can't seem to make myself.

"It can't always be screaming and hate sex, Bree. I want to show you how much I can make you feel. It doesn't always have to be angry."

"With you, it does," I argue, but I tilt my head back to give him more access.

Argh. My body *is* a traitor, just like I said last night.

He traces his fingers along my bare shoulders, and when I turn to look at him, his eyes are dark with lust.

It's still dark out, so it must be in the wee hours of the morning.

"How much did you have to drink at dinner?" I ask, and Declan chuckles.

"Not much." He trails his fingers down my abdomen, now, and I start to tremble. "Now. Will you let me show you how good I can make you feel?"

I look up at him, still worrying my bottom lip between my teeth, and he thumbs it out of my mouth.

I shouldn't be doing this. I should fight him off, tell him to leave.

"Thought you didn't force yourself on women."

Declan freezes.

"If you don't want this, I'll go right now." He removes his trailing fingers from my stomach.

I miss his touch instantly.

"I do want it. And I might be damning myself, but I want you."

His eyes burn through mine. "Are you sure?"

"Yes." I nod, and my voice lowers. "Please, don't stop."

It's just... a distraction.

What else am I supposed to do stuck in this room all the time?

Looking into my eyes, Declan trails his hands lower, to my thighs, slipping down the negligée I'd picked out earlier. The silk against my skin feels so good, I couldn't pass it up.

Some part of me had thought this might happen again, even wanted it. I just didn't want to admit it to myself.

He bunches the negligée around my hips, sliding his fingers slowly under the fabric over each hip, tugging my panties down to my ankles.

Then he lifts my right leg, kissing along my calf as he slips the panties off me.

Instead of lowering my leg back to the bed, though, he

loops it around his shoulder, and then my left leg around his other shoulder, settling between my thighs.

Oh god, Is he going to—

"Ah!" I cry out as he presses his face against my sex, sliding two fingers into my entrance and finding me slick.

He murmurs something against my inner thigh, kissing it and making me feel lightheaded. He licks it, pumping his fingers in and out of me, sucking and probably leaving a mark.

I'm trembling all over, wanting more, wanting him to latch around my clit, but he doesn't, instead licking *around* it, touching every part but it.

I whimper.

"What's wrong, princess?" He lifts his head slightly.

"You're teasing me," I accuse, but my voice comes out shaky.

"Not teasing," he says. "Just working you up. I want you to be sensitive when I sink myself inside of you."

"I'm already so sensitive."

He laughs softly, his breath hot against my sex.

"You are. You're lovely."

Lovely? That's not a term I'd ever expected him to use.

He finally starts to lap at my clit, and I rush near the edge of my orgasm as he keeps pumping his fingers in and out, curling them up just like I need.

"I'm going to come," I breathe out, and then he finally latches his lips around my clit, working the flat of his tongue against it.

I cry out, putting my hands in his thick hair and pulling slightly, and Declan moans against me, the vibration just making my orgasm last longer.

I open my eyes as I come down, and he licks his lips slowly, moving his hands up to my hips.

"I left marks on you," he says, almost mournfully, and then he moves his lips there, kissing and touching the sore spots as if in apology.

I tilt my neck up, needing his mouth on me there. "On my neck, too."

He chuckles. "Those I meant to leave, princess. Want everyone who sees you to know you belong to me."

"I don't belong to you," I rasp out, but he still has his fingers inside of me, pumping slowly as he kisses my hips, my stomach, eventually my throat.

I'm going to come again, and soon, but then Declan slips his fingers out of me.

I whine, "Wait." I'm breathing hard.

"Poor baby," he croons. "Can't think of anything but coming on my fingers?"

He's right, but I don't want to say it. Instead, I shut my mouth, looking up at him with pleading eyes.

"Maybe one more," he teases, and then he rams three fingers into me, making me arch my back and close my eyes, seeing spots of light beneath my closed lids. I'm catapulted into my second orgasm, bucking my hips and crying out Declan's name.

"Look at you," he murmurs. "You look so pretty when you come."

He strokes my hair with one hand as he slowly pulls his fingers out of me, and I whimper at the loss, feeling empty.

"Don't worry, princess." His tone is low. "We're just getting ready for the main event."

Declan pushes down his boxer briefs, freeing his thick, long length, and covers me with his body. My mouth is all-but watering as I look down at him, and I impatiently wrap a hand around him, guiding him into me.

Declan hisses in a breath, chuckling as he rolls his hips, thrusting deeper into me.

I gasp in a breath, already so sensitive from my other orgasms.

"God, I'm going to come so soon," I whisper, and Declan grits his teeth, thrusting into me in a steady rhythm.

"Me, too." His voice is strained. "Watching you like that... it drove me crazy."

"Yeah?" I ask breathlessly, rolling my hips up to meet his thrusts.

"Yeah," he says. "You don't know how beautiful you are."

It feels good, being praised by him, and my body is alight with pleasure.

It's only a few more thrusts before I come again, nearly screaming and digging my nails into his shoulders.

Declan gasps and moans, pumping into me deeply before pulsing and spilling inside me.

He kisses along the side of my face as we pant and try to catch our breath. It's oddly sweet, and part of me wants to push him away.

He's not as bad as I thought. Maybe he's not such a bad man, but I'm still a prisoner here. He is still the enemy.

Even if I don't mind, and maybe even want, the sex between us, I don't want to be here. I don't want to be married to him. I want to be free to make my own choices.

When Declan pulls out of me, I assume he'll go straight for the shower, but he doesn't, plopping down next to me, staring up at the ceiling.

I tremble, cold, and next thing I know, he's pulling up the covers around me to tuck me in.

"Maybe we should talk," he murmurs, close to my ear, kissing my temple.

I stiffen. "Talk about what?"

Declan shrugs. "I don't know. Get to know each other. Not like either of us wanted this, but we're stuck, aren't we?"

"Stuck." My tone's flat. "I guess. What do you want to know?"

"You don't have siblings, right?"

"I have a brother, Rory… But he's been estranged for years now. Could hardly wait until he was eighteen to leave the family business behind. So, it was me and my dad after my mother left, and my dad never wanted anyone else."

Declan snorts.

"What is that supposed to mean?" I ask, angry.

"I've just heard otherwise, that's all. I've heard he gets around that strip club he owns."

"Well, those are just stupid rumors." I'm sure my father hasn't been completely celibate ever since my mother left, but I don't think that he's been with anyone long term.

"Maybe." Declan shrugs. "There's a lot of those floating around this community."

"Wiseguys gossip like a bunch of old hens."

Declan barks out a laugh. "They kind of do. Especially the older ones."

"Like your father?"

"And yours." He glances over at me. His eyes really are remarkable, darker blue in the moonlight.

I nod. That's fair enough. "What about you? Did you always get along with your siblings?"

Declan laughs out loud. "God, no. Gray and I used to fight like cats and dogs. And Lara, she used to try and dress me up like one of her little dolls, before Paige was born."

I grin, looking over at him. "God, I'd love to see that."

He groans. "Don't tell Da, he'll bring out the photo

albums." He pauses while I laugh, and then continues. "Did you ever get lonely without your brother there?"

"Nah. I had friends. Besides, I kind of liked being the only one around. I love my brother, but as the oldest, he was sometimes under the impression he could boss me around. Spoiler alert, no one can."

"Spoiled." He grins.

I giggle, and then close my mouth, realizing that I'm acting like a schoolgirl with a crush.

What is wrong with me? I need to focus on what's important–trying to get out of here.

But... making friends with Declan may be just the way to grease the wheels enough. Maybe, if he thinks I'm into him or something, he'll lower his guard.

Against my better judgment, I'm already halfway to friends with Paige and Lara. So why not try?

"Your mother?" I murmur, and Declan's face shutters, his emotions unreadable.

"I don't talk about my mother."

I nod. "I don't like to talk about mine, either."

He glances at me but doesn't say anything.

I'm losing steam here. I need to get him back on the friendly side. Mentioning his mother was obviously a mistake.

I flip over on the bed, looking at Declan with a devious smile.

He raises an eyebrow. "What are you doing?"

I shrug. "Nothing."

I slide my hand under the covers, slowly wrapping it around his cock.

He draws in a sharp breath. "Doesn't feel like nothing, princess."

"You showed me how good you can make me feel," I murmur against his neck. "Let me do the same for you."

I slowly pump up and down his length, and he thickens and plumps in my hand, his breath growing shorter.

Then I slide under the covers, spreading his thighs and licking across his testicles before taking him into my mouth.

I do gag a little when I take him further in, but that only seems to make him pulse more on my tongue.

He lets out a low groan, almost a growl, putting his hands in my hair.

I think he's going to push, but instead he just tugs, guiding me in the rhythm that he wants.

I suck in, hollowing my cheeks, and Declan lets out a string of curses that seem to be in Gaelic.

"Jesus, fuck, Bree," he moans. "If you keep that up, I'm going to come."

I scratch my fingernails down his thighs to encourage him, loving how heavy he feels in my mouth, and then he explodes, sending come down my throat.

I keep pumping him with my hand and swallow every drop before pulling back up and grinning at him.

"Where did you learn to do *that*?" he asks.

"Wouldn't you like to know?" I smirk, and he grabs me around the waist, pulling me down on top of him and kissing me passionately.

He slides back down my body, making me come a fourth and fifth time with his hands and his mouth before sliding back into me.

Daylight is fading already before he's done with me, and I'm sore and exhausted enough to cuddle up to him, my head on his chest.

I slip into sleep before I even know what's happening.

I wake up in the middle of the night, after a dream

about my mother, a few days before she left, and there are tears on my cheeks.

I walk downstairs to get a glass of water, and Lara is up, sitting with a cup of hot tea.

"Couldn't sleep?" she asks, and I nod, pouring myself a glass of filtered water and sitting across from her.

"What about you?"

"Lifelong insomniac." She gives me a wry smile.

I smile back, and with her, it's not forced.

If I'm honest with myself, I haven't been forcing smiles with any of the Burkes, not even Declan. Am I developing Stockholm syndrome or something?

I sit there across from Lara, trying to figure out what it is I'm feeling, and finally, she cocks her head, looking at me.

"Penny for your thoughts?"

"I don't know if you want to hear them," I mumble.

"I promise you that I do."

I sigh. "I'm just thinking that it's not so bad here."

She smiles. "I thought you might feel that way." She pauses. "And you're feeling worried *because* you don't hate it here?"

"Actually, yes." I sip my water. "I spent so much time at the beginning thinking of ways out..." I trail off, not wanting to give away that I'm still thinking about it. Except now, it's different being here somehow.

"But now you don't want to go?"

"It's not that I don't want to. It's that... being here is just not as bad as I'd thought."

"Because we don't feed you bread and water?" she teases. "Or keep you in a room with just a bucket?"

"Something like that." I chuckle.

"Paige and I tried to tell you that Declan isn't such a bad guy."

"He's not, but he still drives me crazy."

She laughs out loud, and the sound echoes in the large kitchen. "That'll never change."

We chat for a bit longer before I head back up to the bedroom. When I slide back into bed with Declan, he instantly rolls toward me, putting his arms around me.

I feel warm and safe and almost like home.

This is supposed to be my enemy. I can't feel like this. What the hell is wrong with me?

9

———

DECLAN

The way that Bree acted two nights ago confuses me. It's not just the sex. From the first time I touched her it was clear she was as into it as I was. So, that's not the problem. The problem is everything else.

The way she wanted to know more about me, how she cuddled up next to me.

What is she trying to pull?

I can't deny that she's better this way than depressed like she was at dinner the other night, but it's so different than her fiery anger that I'm a little concerned. Especially because this side of her pulls me in even deeper than angry Bree.

Fuck me. I don't have time to muse about it. It's time to meet with Niall Murphy and finally take the next step in my master plan. I can't wait.

My hope is he tries to start a war immediately so that I can take him down with a bullet between his eyes.

Gray is coming with me, of course, and there's a light in his blue eyes I haven't seen in a while. He loves shit like this, and usually, I don't. But Niall Murphy is different. It's personal between us, and I can't wait to see the look on his ugly face.

"You ready?" Gray grins.

I grin back. "I was born ready."

We're taking Sean and Finn O'Toole, two of our guys. They're fraternal twins, one is blond, and one is dark-haired. They are massive and it's even more clear when they pile into a second car as Gray and I take one of his convertibles.

It's about a twenty-minute drive out to Niall Murphy's place, and I frown when we pull up at the gates. "How do we get in?"

"Oh, I called ahead." Gray's still grinning. "He called me every name in the book, but I told him we had information about his daughter."

Good. He'll already be angry. Maybe it'll spur him to do something stupid like try to shoot one of us.

I pull up to the intercom and it buzzes immediately.

"Aw, he didn't want to talk to us," Gray says with a decidedly evil cackle, and I smile back as we drive up to the main house. It's a bit smaller than ours, but no less opulent.

The doors are covered in wolves, the Murphy family crest, and it's a bit tacky, if you ask me, even though they seem to be carved from marble.

Sean and Finn pull up behind us and get out, adjusting their suits. We look like a bunch of mobsters today, all wearing suits as if we're going to a wedding.

Or a funeral.

The door opens before I can ring the doorbell, and a truly giant man stands there, glaring down at us.

"It's the Wolfhound," Gray whispers, seeming awed.

The man has close-cropped red hair, a full but well-kept ginger beard, and he towers over me by at least three inches, which is crazy since I'm six-foot-two. He's as wide as he is tall, almost, his shoulders barely fitting in the huge doorway.

"I had an appointment with Niall." Gray seems calm, but there's a hint of nerves in how he's holding himself.

The Wolfhound, otherwise known as Cormac Ryan, Niall Murphy's childhood friend and his right-hand, doesn't speak, and it's no wonder, because from all the rumors, he's mute.

He turns to lead us into the foyer, and grunts, gesturing for us to sit.

We do, and Gray bounces his leg. I put my hand on his knee to stop him, giving him a hard look. Sean and Finn continue to stand.

I look around. The wolf theme is a big deal to Niall, it seems, because they're everywhere—there's a blanket covered in a wolf pack draped over the back of the couch, and there are marble carved wolves howling in the corner. I'm surprised there isn't a taxidermized one sitting in the middle of the room.

I look up to a crystal chandelier not unlike ours above my head. Someone starts stomping down the stairs, and Gray and I both stand in unison, expecting Niall.

Sure enough, it's him. His dark hair is mottled with silver around the temples and his hairline. He's around Gray's height, about six-foot, and he's got a generous beer belly hanging over his suit slacks. His eyes are a deep green, almost like the green in Bree's eyes.

Where are all the photos of her? It seems like Niall lived in this big house by himself all his life.

I know that isn't true, and yet there's no suggestion that Bree even exists at all.

She's supposed to be the apple of his eye, isn't she?

"Where the hell is my daughter?" Niall barks out as he steps too close to me. I don't back away, looking at him.

"She's safe in our bedroom."

Niall's eyes nearly bug out of his head.

"You better start explaining," he orders in a near roar.

"Didn't you hear? We got hitched." I smile from ear to ear. "She's very comfortable in her new mansion. Wouldn't think she'd want to come back here."

"Bree would never marry *you*," he spits. "What did you do to her?"

"Nothing she didn't want done." My grin is wicked, and Niall grabs me by the collar, slamming me up against the far wall.

I laugh, and Niall punches me right in the nose. It stings pretty bad, but I'm still laughing because this is exactly what I wanted. He's taking the bait.

Sean and Finn pull him off me, and he's so red in the face I'm almost afraid he's on the verge of a heart attack. Man, he's so mad.

"Not now, I don't want to have to kill my father-in-law." I taste blood on my teeth from my nose. "Or do I?"

"You can't kill me," he growls. "My men will shoot you five times before you hit the ground if you try."

"Maybe you're right." I shrug. "But maybe I'll take that chance."

I reach into my suit pocket, and the sound of hammers pulling back clicks from upstairs. His men have their guns trained on me.

But instead of a gun, I slowly bring out a copy of the marriage license, handing it to Niall.

"You'll see that everything's in order. It was a good Catholic wedding, don't worry."

"What have you done to her?" He fights Sean and Finn's hold to no avail.

He's a snake of a man instead of the wolf he wants so badly to be, and I know that he'll find a way to try and hurt me if I stay here long enough.

"What do you want out of this? What possible reason do you have for forcing my daughter to marry you?"

I grin. "Maybe I just wanted to piss you off."

Niall wrenches away from Sean and Finn and adjusts his suit, taking in a deep breath. His cheeks are flushed red, but he seems calmer.

"That's not the reason, and you know it."

"It's part of the reason," Gray drawls, and I nudge him playfully with my shoulder.

"Maybe so. But the real reason is this—you've been going around town doing whatever the fuck you want for too many years, Murphy. It stops now."

"What stops?" He smirks, the snake, as if he doesn't know.

"Stealing our shipments, for one. For another, and the most important–Trafficking. Especially minors. You stop taking girls off the street."

"Or what?" he sneers.

"Or maybe your pretty little daughter doesn't have such a good time."

"You wouldn't." He looks right at me, his brows knitted together.

"I don't have to hurt a hair on her little head. But I *can*. And I will. If you don't stop."

Niall doesn't say a word, his cheeks growing redder and redder.

"We'll be in touch, Murphy." I walk toward the front door, the rest of the guys following me.

Gray whoops, slamming his fists down on the dashboard when we get into the car. "That was so much fun! But he did get you pretty good."

As he pulls away, I sniffle, tasting blood in the back of my throat. "Worth it."

"Let's go home and get you cleaned up and then go out for drinks."

I blink at him.

Gray isn't one for partying. In fact, he is the farthest away from a party person as can be. Usually all business. But I guess we do deserve a night out after all this.

"All right." I nod. "Where are we going?"

Gray grins. "Where else? Paddy's Pub."

I snort.

Paddy's is a local place, run by Irish guys just like us, first generation immigrants. The only people who ever go there are gangsters and thugs, but I suppose that is what we are too. Those are our people, and Gray likes to be around our people.

"But you still need to change shirts. I've got an extra shirt in the trunk if you prefer," he says.

"Yeah, thanks. I'm sure Paddy won't mind if I come in with a little blood on my face."

Gray laughs, clapping me on the shoulder. "Hell, he'll probably buy you a drink."

I park in the back at Paddy's, going in through the emergency exit which is supposed to have an alarm but doesn't.

I head straight to the bathroom and strip off my shirt, looking in the mirror at the damage.

My nose doesn't appear to be broken when I move it around with a wince. It's just sore.

I splash water on my face and use some paper towels to clean the blood off, sliding on Gray's shirt and just depositing mine in the trash. This isn't the first time I've done something like this at Paddy's, but it's been a long time.

And it's been years since I've done it with Gray.

I'm so tired of shit like this. I'm tired of violence, of blood, of getting punched in the face or splitting my knuckles doing it to someone else.

Sure, my beef with Murphy is as personal as it gets, but at the same time, I'm just ready for this stalemate to be over. If it has to end in war and blood, so be it. At least it'll be over.

My mood has dropped but Gray seemed excited to go out, and I'm not about to pass that up. Gray is the least outgoing of all my siblings, even Lara, and when he wants to tie one on, I'll always be there.

Besides, if I get him drunk enough, I can take videos of something stupid he does and use it to blackmail him. A smile spreads across my face at the thought, and I exit the bathroom and head into the main bar, the music booming.

Paddy decorates in an unusual way, taxidermy animals all over the walls. A squirrel, a panther, and a moose are the most unusual ones. Especially since there are no moose anywhere in this area. And Paddy isn't even a hunter, so I'm not sure what went through his mind when he put these things up.

There's also stolen road signs, including a yield sign, hanging above the bar. Then, behind the register, there's a "bad check" photocopy with various faces and names on it. Some of those faces and names are currently in this bar right now since Paddy is too forgiving.

Gray stands at the bar, holding a beer and grinning.

"What are you boys celebrating?" Paddy's hair has gone completely silver as has his beard.

"Can't exactly say," Gray says. "Just know it's big."

Paddy nods slowly. "First beer on me, then."

Gray hands me a beer.

I sip it but he puts his hand on mine, forcing me to chug it. I indulge.

Gray's in a good mood, and maybe he'll dance the Riverdance on the pool tables again so I can film it this time.

"Bottoms up." I hold back a belch, and Gray cheers, chugging his own beer.

A couple of hours later, the room is spinning, and Gray has already given me the show I yearned for and more. Those poor pool tables have some crazy tales to tell. The whole thing is securely in my video files, just waiting for the right moment. It's been a good night.

I look at my watch. Shit. It's late!

I wonder what it'll be like with Bree tomorrow since I'm probably staying out all night. Will she be worried? Jealous?

I can't deny that I can't wait to find out.

Part of me is hoping that she is jealous, that we have a big argument about it. It feels like I'm running out of reasons to hate her. And that's dangerous.

I never thought I would have a relationship, someone to come home to. I always thought I'd be married to the life, no room for anyone. Now, it's like it's all I can think about.

Gray nudges my shoulder.

"What are you thinking about?"

My new wife, as always lately, it seems.

But what I say is, "How good it felt to put Niall Murphy in his place."

I smirk, and Gray brays out a laugh, handing me another beer. I mutter a curse under my breath and take a sip, despite my better judgment.

The bartender is drunk from the shots we've been

pushing on him, and he sits on the bar, playing the guitar and an old Irish ditty.

Gray finishes it in a sing-yell and claps me on the back so hard I almost fall over.

"Isn't it time to call it a night?" I'm slightly nauseous.

Gray's eyes widen at me. "Are you even Irish?"

I continue to drink my beer, sitting down and listening to the off-key music from the bartender.

My chest is heavy with this longing, something strange. I think I miss Bree.

I miss my wife.

What does that mean for someone like me?

10

____

BREE

Declan didn't come home last night, or if he did, I didn't see him, and I feel pretty strange about it. We haven't talked about fidelity, although I've always been of the mind that wedding vows are wedding vows. I don't care that most mobsters have mistresses, that's not what I want for my marriage.

But I don't want this marriage at all, right? Except, while I'm stuck in it, I want him to respect me. To not be with other women. So, I'm not sure how to approach this.

We're getting ready for dinner, and I dress in a pair of high-waisted shorts and a blue blouse, looking casual chic, while Declan wears just a button-up shirt and a pair of tailored slacks.

It's strange how all the Burkes always dress for dinner, how they always have things to say to each other. It's not like that at my house. Hell, I can't even remember the last time my father and I broke bread together. He's always so busy, and I am, too, keeping up the books and making appointments.

We live separate lives, and sometimes I feel more like a

secretary or one of his employees than his daughter, but that doesn't mean we don't love each other. Right?

I watch Declan sweep his hair back from his face, slicking it back in the mirror, and I frown slightly.

"Where were you last night?"

He stiffens, which doesn't exactly fill me with confidence, and keeps looking in the mirror.

"Why do you care?"

I scoff. "Because you didn't come home?"

He turns to look at me, half-smiling. "You jealous, princess?"

"Do I have a reason to be jealous?"

Declan grins wider. "No. I just find it cute that you are."

I let out a sigh of relief. "So, this... this whole marriage thing, we're faithful?"

"You fucking better be." His face is serious, his brows drawing together, and his smile fading.

I laugh. "I'm pretty much trapped here. Not even sure where I'd meet someone."

Declan keeps frowning. "Do you want to meet someone?"

I shrug. "I guess not. I've got everything I need for the moment."

"For the moment?"

"I mean, you can't expect this to last forever." I let out a long breath through my nostrils.

Declan keeps frowning, but then Paige knocks softly on the door.

Declan calls for her to come in, and she pops her head in. She's got her hair curled, and it makes her look even younger than she is.

"Marisol says to hurry up, dinner's getting cold," she says brightly, and then starts off down the stairs.

I begin to walk out into the hallway, but Declan catches me by my wrist.

"I'm serious, Bree. You belong to me, now. I won't stray, and neither will you."

I pull out of his grasp. "Not like I have a choice."

I wouldn't stray if I could. This might have been forced on me, but as soon as I said the vows, they became mine. But I'm so confused because I don't want him to stray either. The thought alone makes my chest hurt. But why do I care?

I have no interest in anyone else, and though this just seems like a new set of prison bars, I'm not sure if the circumstances were different if I wouldn't choose him.

I'm angry and frustrated, and I need to get away from Declan for a bit.

I leave our room and walk down the stairs after Paige and into the dining room, sitting down in my usual spot next to Lara, Paige sitting on the other side of her.

Declan comes down, his face blank and serious, and he sits next to me.

The only member of the Burke family who isn't here is Gray.

I guess Patrick sees me looking over at Gray's empty seat because he comments on it.

"Gray's taking care of some business."

I look over at Declan. He's the second-born, so I guess he doesn't have a direct line to everything about the business. I don't, either. My father doesn't share business with me, except for numbers, and only because I have a good head for it.

"I was thinking." Patrick's voice jolts me out of my thoughts.

"Don't do that." Paige giggles. "That's probably what I smell burning."

"Nothing's burning," Marisol chides, eating at the end of the table. She often joins us, too. The Burkes seem to be kind to their staff, which again, is unusual.

My dad treats them as the help and nothing else. He says with as much as he pays them, they deserve it.

I've always been kind to our staff, but it's strange to see the whole family treating them well, almost like they're part of the family.

"Very funny, *a'stor*," Patrick says with a chuckle. "But I was thinking how Declan and Bree didn't get a real honeymoon."

A honeymoon?

I look down at my food.

Why does this whole family act like I chose this instead of being forced into it? Why would I want to go on a honeymoon?

"Where were you thinking, Da?" Paige is almost jumping up and down on her seat. "I can help Bree pick out some new clothes to take with her."

"How about Nevada?" he suggests. "Declan likes Vegas."

Las Vegas is one of the few places in the country I haven't been. My father always called gambling a waste of time, but I have to admit, I've always wanted to try it.

I look up at Patrick. "I've never been to Las Vegas."

"Then it's perfect!"

"Is it?" I look at him. "We all know how this marriage came to be."

Patrick smiles, reaching over to pat my hand. "I still think you could have some fun in Vegas, especially since you've never been. Just a week." He looks over at Declan.

"Besides, I have some work for you to do out there. I need you to relay a few messages to John Renno. I've already booked you two at the Four Seasons. You leave tomorrow afternoon."

"You would have me doing work on my honeymoon?" Declan smiles. "All right, Da. Vegas sounds good."

"I'm paying," Patrick insists.

John Renno.

The name doesn't sound familiar, but I file it away in my brain, hoping that it might come in handy later.

Patrick looks at me. Maybe he is waiting for me to respond.

"Does it really matter if I say yes or no?"

Patrick shrugs. "No."

I sigh, turning to Lara and Paige. "Fine. What do I pack?"

Paige squeals. "Da, can I be excused?"

"Not yet. You've barely taken a bite of the lasagna that Marisol slaved over a hot stove for. Sit down and eat. And stop your bouncing."

Paige pouts but relaxes into her chair, sullenly starting to eat.

Declan and Patrick talk about Vegas, where we'll be staying, when he's supposed to meet Renno. I listen just enough to put some details away with Renno's name.

Maybe, in Las Vegas, there will be an opportunity for me to escape. I may have accepted my lot in life to some degree for now, but I don't accept it forever.

I'm going to make my own choice about who I marry, dammit. This is just a deviation from the plan.

I finish eating, and then Paige asks again if she can be excused, and Patrick nods. Lara stands, too, and we go up the stairs to my bedroom.

Paige bounds ahead of us, giggling.

"Vegas is so fun, Bree, you have to try the slot machines!"

"Declan will love that." Lara laughs, and I smile, unable to help myself.

The girls don't have that much to do with why I'm here, even though they seem to accept it, and so I can let loose a little bit with them.

When we get into the bedroom, Lara grabs her purse and brings out a little fifth of vodka, top shelf.

I stare at her. "Lara?"

She shrugs. "Hey, the guys get to drink after dinner, why not us? Besides, they'll be busy for a couple of hours while we pack."

Paige gasps. "This is why you're my favorite big sister."

"I'm your only big sister."

"Still."

Paige grabs the fifth and takes a swig, passing it to me.

I shrug and drink a little, grimacing, before handing it to Lara.

Paige is already rifling through my closet, throwing all my shorts and dresses onto the bed. "You'll need something formal for a dinner or two, and of course, that killer string bikini you picked out."

"Don't forget regular clothes, Paige, she can't wear a bikini or an evening gown to everything." Lara gets up and puts a large suitcase on the bed, folding my clothes and putting them inside, leaving the evening gowns out to be stored separately.

"You should pick out your own lingerie." Paige wrinkles her nose. "I don't want to think about that."

I chuckle and stand up, digging through my dresser

drawers and picking out a few things—including a teddy that I haven't worn yet.

"Keep Declan away from the Blackjack table," Lara warns. "He always loses way too much money."

"Not always," Paige pipes up. "There was that one time he came home with thirty grand."

"He left with fifty grand," Lara points out, and Paige snorts out a laugh.

Fifty thousand dollars?

Just for gambling?

My father would never allow it. But I guess the Burkes have more money than he does. He's always saying they take up too much of the territory.

I look at Lara, then Paige. "He's not very good at Blackjack?"

"Oh, he's extremely good." Paige shakes her head. "But he plays until he loses, that's the problem."

I smile a little, thinking of Declan having the gambling bug. It doesn't seem like him, but then again, I don't know much about him.

Maybe he was right the other night, suggesting that we get to know each other. Maybe this honeymoon will be a way to do that.

"Has Declan always liked gambling?"

Lara shakes her head. "He used to be against it, but back then, Da spent a lot on the races. When Declan discovered cards when he was fifteen, he never looked back."

"Yeah, he was gambling well before Vegas," Paige says.

I try to imagine him at a poker table with smoke in the air and drinks in glasses, looking up over his cards at the crowd. It's kind of hot, actually.

A lot about Declan Burke is kind of hot, and that's the problem.

I've got to keep my head in the game. Keep my eye on the prize. All those sports metaphors, or whatever. What matters is that I just have to focus on slipping away, getting ahold of my father so that he can come and pick me up. There's got to be a way out of this.

It's not like divorce is illegal. I just need to get far enough away from Declan to file the papers.

Maybe gambling is the way to do it.

"Did he get into trouble a lot when he was younger?" I ask.

Paige smiles, "God, all the time. He was a lot more rebellious than Gray." She pauses, looking at Lara. "And you'll never believe who the rebellious one was between us."

"Lara?" I gasp, shocked, and Lara takes another pull from the vodka bottle, winking at me.

I have to admit, the Burke family is fascinating. They have such interesting personalities, and such intriguing pasts.

I want to know more about all of them, not just Declan.

But why? I'm getting too wrapped up in all of this.

Sure, I've got whatever I ask for, except for freedom, and Declan has been kind to me, for the most part, and amazing in bed. Paige and Lara act like my real sisters, and Gray stays pretty far away from me.

Even Patrick treats me like his daughter-in-law.

But I have to remind myself I'm still not here of my own will. As charming as the Burkes may be, I need to get away. I need to be free to make my own choices.

As Lara and Paige pack my things, I start planning a way to escape in Vegas. I won't be so guarded there, and I'll even be outside for a while. This is a chance I can't miss out on.

After an hour, we're all tipsy, but I'm all packed, and Paige hugs me impulsively at the door. I hug her back, and Lara does the same.

"We'll miss you around here." Paige pouts. "But have the best time."

"I will." I wave as they walk away.

Declan walks up to me, putting his arms around my waist after nodding goodbye to his sisters on the way by.

He pushes me inside or room, and all thoughts that aren't him fade away.

I can't think of anything but his mouth on mine, his hands on my hips as he pushes me down onto the bed.

This is bad. This is so bad.

I should push him away. I should tell him that I'm still mad at him, but the way he slides his fingers down my abdomen makes me shiver, and it seems to drain all the annoyance out of my body.

"You're so beautiful," he murmurs. "Who thought Niall Murphy could make such a beautiful daughter?"

"Don't talk about my father right now," I mutter, and he laughs against my mouth.

"Very well, princess. Let's not talk at all, aye?"

He pulls off my pajama pants, pressing into me since I'm bare beneath, and even though there hasn't been much buildup, I cry out at the pleasure of the stretch rolling through me.

Declan stares down into my eyes as we make love, and I know I should look away, but I can't seem to bring myself to. It's too intimate and my chest feels tight, and when it's over, he rolls over and draws me into his arms.

He's asleep before I know it, breathing evenly against my throat.

This is becoming my new normal, having him in bed with me every night. It feels so comfortable and right that it scares me.

Because in the back of my head, I'm still planning a divorce and an escape.

But his arms feel more like home than any place I've ever been.

I'm so screwed.

11

DECLAN

We take Da's private jet to Vegas, and Bree's eyes widen.

"What? Your father doesn't have a private jet?"

"He does." She sits down in one of the plush chairs. "But he only uses it for business. I've never been on it."

"This is still business." I shrug.

"Of course," she mutters. "How could I forget?"

I look at her, smiling. "You almost sound disappointed."

"Well, I did expect we could have a little fun." She buckles up her seatbelt as the pilot announces that we're about to take off.

I reach into the cabinet behind me and pour a glass of champagne for her, handing it over before pouring my own.

"Don't worry, princess. We're going to have lots of fun."

She sips the champagne, looking straight ahead.

It's about a three-hour flight, so once we're in the air, I put my hand high up on her thigh.

She looks up at me, having finished her champagne. "You trying to ask me to join the mile high club?"

"And what if I was?" I unbuckle her seatbelt, and she

looks at me for a moment before climbing into my lap, straddling me.

She rocks her hips forward, and I start to harden beneath her immediately, groaning against her throat before kissing her there.

"Only one rule," she murmurs. "You gotta let me be on top."

"I've never minded a woman on top." I grin, and she scoots back on my thighs, reaching between us to unbutton my slacks.

She frees my cock from my pants and pumps it up and down until I hiss, putting my hand on hers.

"Were you going to blow like a teenager?" She giggles.

"Maybe." I smirk. "But I wanted to be inside you first."

I bunch her dress around her hips, tugging aside the crotch of her panties so that she can seat herself on top of me. She does. So slowly that I'm sure she can feel every inch.

Bree lets out a long moan as she gets me to the hilt, and I grit my teeth to keep from thrusting up into her like I want. She wants to be on top, so she gets to be in charge.

Bree's up for it, though, bracing her hands on my chest and bouncing on top of me. The slick wetness of her walls and the way her breasts bounce in my face get me close to the edge quickly, and I grab onto her hips to slow her movements.

"Wait. Just a few more minutes."

She whines, trying to rock her hips. "But I'm so close."

"Me, too." I grab onto her hips, moving her on top of me slower, at a steadier pace.

"Oh," she breathes. "Oh, that's good."

"So fucking good." I kiss her neck, biting down on the

base of her throat. She moans, bucking her hips, but I keep the rhythm steady.

She comes around me, pulsing, in just a few more strokes, and I only last a few more after that, my orgasm hitting me like a freight train.

Bree breathes heavily and leans down to kiss me, slow and sensuous.

I chase after her lips when she pulls away, smiling, to go to the bathroom.

I watch her walk away, her hips swaying, and I want to grab her and kiss her again, but I restrain myself.

It's strange, really. This could almost be a real marriage if it weren't for how things started. And more and more I'm finding I wouldn't mind that one bit.

WE STOP IN FRONT OF THE FOUR SEASONS. "WHAT DO you want for dinner?" It isn't until she looks up at me that I can see how tired she is, bags under her eyes. I guess the trip has really worn her out. "What about room service?"

She smiles. "I just want to be in a bed. I plan to live there until tomorrow."

I laugh. "Sounds good to me, princess."

The valet takes the car, and the bellhop takes our luggage, so all I have to do is check in before we head up the elevator.

She leans against me as we get to the top floor, the penthouse suite, and I kiss the crown of her head.

Our things have arrived before us, and Bree walks in and promptly falls face down on the bed, groaning.

"Oh, God, it's so comfortable."

"It should be, with as much as this place costs."

She turns over, looking up at me upside down on the bed. "Isn't your dad paying?"

"He is, but I've booked this penthouse myself."

"Let me guess. Business."

I laugh. "No. I usually come to Vegas for pleasure."

"Oh yeah. I heard you like Blackjack."

I turn and blink at her. "My sisters told you that?"

She pretends to zip her lip and lock it with a key, and I chuckle.

"My sisters talk a lot. I'm used to it."

"Are you going to teach me to play?"

"You don't know how to play Blackjack?" With where she comes from, I'd assumed she did.

Bree shakes her head. "My dad doesn't like playing cards."

Funny, that. Because he probably got caught cheating.

But I don't want to start a fight. Bree's been considerably better the last couple of days, maybe excited for the vacation. I haven't told her that I brought Sean and Finn O'Toole, knowing that she'll hate the idea of being watched. But she needs someone to protect her while I'm away taking care of business. I have a couple of things to do while we are here, and the first order of business is meeting up with John Renno and his friends.

The things I have to say to John can't be done over the phone, but I'm surprised Da didn't want to come himself. Maybe he's really pushing this marriage thing.

I have to admit, I like being a married man, so far. Even when she's mad at me, it's good to have someone to come home to. Good to have someone I can go head-to-head with before sinking myself into her.

It's not about feelings, though. It can't be. She's still

Murphy's daughter, and this is supposed to be just a means to an end.

Besides, it's not like this is going to last forever. It's just until her dad is gone because once this war is over, so are me and Bree. We'll get a divorce and go our separate ways.

It's not like she wants me anyway, regardless of what these weird growing feelings inside me want to make me think, and I'd never force myself on a woman.

I just want her to be happy, and as long as this marriage lasts, I'll do my part, but soon she'll have her freedom back to choose who she wants to be with. And that won't be me, for sure.

That makes my blood boil, and I can't understand why.

It's not like I have feelings for her or anything. I'm just getting used to her, I guess.

I have to admit, though, that I'm enjoying her company.

I watch as she stands up, muttering as she unzips her dress.

I raise an eyebrow, and she snorts out a laugh.

"No funny business. I'm just uncomfortable."

"Change into your swimsuit. We'll go down to swim after dinner."

"Aren't we supposed to wait?"

"I was a lifeguard in high school—that's just a myth."

"Ooh la la," she drawls, going into the bathroom to change.

I frown. I wanted to see her naked body, but I guess there's plenty of time for that. I'm still mostly satisfied with what happened in the plane, so I don't push.

The room service comes while she's changing. She's ordered some seafood, and I ordered a steak.

My mouth is watering from the smell as the bellhop wheels it in, and I throw him a hefty tip. He's about to exit when Bree walks out of the bathroom, wearing what appears to be navy blue dental floss.

I gape at her, how her breasts spill out of the top, how her hips nearly hide the strings. It's a thong bikini, too, so her perfect ass is on display.

I look over at the bellhop, and his eyes are nearly bulging out of his head.

"Get the fuck out," I say in a low tone, and he all but sprints out of there.

Bree giggles, plopping down on the bed, and the rest of her jiggles as she does so.

"Jesus Christ. You're not wearing that to the pool."

"And why not?" She pops a shrimp into her mouth.

"Because you might as well be naked, that's why."

She tilts her head. "What, can't handle a little friendly competition?"

"There is no competition." Anger rushing through me. "You're my wife."

She just hums, and I realize that short of locking her in the room, I'm not going to win this one.

"Fine, but you stay near me."

She rolls her eyes. "I'm not something you can just own, you know?"

"You are mine. I do own you," I remind her, and her face flashes with something I can't quite name. Hurt? Anger? A little of both?

"I know. My life is not my own." She turns glum, and I want to kick myself. Why would I mess it up? We've been getting along so well.

Bree and I eat in silence, and finally, I let out a long breath.

"Look, I'm sorry," I say softly.

"For what?" She looks at me.

I lick my lips. "For being a possessive asshole."

She barks out a laugh. "Well, thank you, I guess? Never expected you to apologize."

"I might have to apologize again. I can't make any promises with you wearing *that*."

She laughs again, and it seems less forced, more genuine. "I'll stick close to you."

"Thank you." I smile, hoping that I've gotten her out of her bad mood.

Two hours later, Bree and I are swimming in the pool with a couple of cocktails on the pool edge. She breathes out a happy sigh and floats on her back.

Thank God, there's no one else at the pool, so I don't have to worry about men staring her down and undressing her in their minds. I don't want just any asshole to see my wife like this.

She looks unbelievable, though, and I want her so badly I can't wait to get her back to the bedroom.

She floats, looking up at the tall ceiling of the indoor pool. "When do you have to do your work?"

"Not until tomorrow."

She smiles, sitting up and treading water, eventually swimming back over to me and looping her legs around my waist.

I hold her up with one hand on the small of her back, wanting to kiss the water beads off her chest and throat.

But in the end, she swims away from me, getting out of the pool and grabbing a towel.

I frown at her, still treading water. "Where are you going?"

"Your sisters told me I had to hit the slot machines."

I laugh, following her back to the room.

We get dressed and again, she goes into the bathroom, as if I haven't seen everything she has to offer. It's a bit annoying, but if it makes her feel better, so be it.

I dress in a button-up shirt and a pair of jeans, not wanting to stand out too much. It's possible that some of the bouncers still remember me from when I was in my early twenties.

I certainly hope not.

Bree comes out of the bathroom wearing a cocktail gown, deep green with sequins all over it, and it brings out the green in her eyes. It falls just a few inches above her knees, but it's backless with a plunging neckline.

"God, did you only bring clothes that make you look like a supermodel?" I ask, only slightly irritated.

She laughs, tilting her head back with the force of it, and the sound of it makes the room feel brighter.

She takes my arm, slipping on a pair of black stilettos, and follows me out of the hotel room down to the ground floor, where we get into my car and head to the casino.

"We can spend the night here, if you like."

"Yeah? Spend the night at Caesar's Palace? I'd love to."

Bree sounds excited, almost like a little kid, and I can't help but smile at her.

"Whatever you want, princess."

"I want to learn Blackjack."

I snort. "I don't think they'd like it if I taught you all my tricks on the floor, but you can watch me play for a bit."

"And then we can go to the slot machines?"

I nod, putting an arm around her waist and leading her into the casino.

It's huge, of course, lights everywhere, the slot machines

whirring and dinging and bells ringing. It's raucous at this time of night, too, and Bree's eyes widen as she looks around at the marble floors and each table.

I take her slowly to the Blackjack table, and she stands next to me as they deal my cards. She looks at the cards with me, humming in the back of her throat, and when I win four rounds in a row, the dealer starts to look a little antsy.

I hold up my hands, stepping away. "Just a lucky streak."

"Do you cheat?" Bree whispers in my ear, and I clamp my hand over her mouth.

"No, but you don't say that in a casino." My tone is low, and she closes her mouth, going silent until we make it to the slot machines.

"I still have no idea how to play Blackjack," she says. "But I know how to play slots."

I laugh and sit next to her, ordering us a couple of drinks. She has a taste for Moscow Mules, it turns out, and I'm more of a beer and wine person.

She pulls down the slot arm and frowns. Then I put her arm back on it, rolling it again with her, and it pays out two hundred dollars, spitting quarters everywhere.

Bree squeals and takes the ticket claim, and I take it to the cashout area. I've won ten grand myself, in four hands, and with her two hundred, we have more than enough to entertain us.

"How about this—we use this to gamble with for the rest of the trip, and whatever we win, you can keep?"

She looks up at me, her eyes wide. "Really?"

"Really." I lean down to kiss her temple, grinning at her exuberance.

She grabs my face and kisses me.

I grab her around the waist, kissing her back deeply, and when she starts to melt against me, I pull away.

"Tease," she accuses, but then I put her against the wall of the elevator, kissing down her throat, popping a nipple into my mouth through the fabric of her dress.

As soon as we enter our room, I pick her up and fuck her right there, against the wall, and when I carry her to bed, she puts her head on my shoulder.

My heart starts to race, but I tell myself it's just the excitement of the night.

She wakes me up when she gets out of bed, stretching, walking naked to the bathroom.

I watch her go, loving the way her ass and hips jiggle, but when she returns, she's dressed in a pair of shorts and a blouse.

"What's on the docket today, hubby?" she asks, only the slightest hint of sarcasm in her voice.

I sigh. "Unfortunately, today I have to do a little business. But you'll have some company."

"Company?"

I take her to the front door, putting my fingers in my mouth and whistling loudly.

Sean and Finn O'Toole come out of their rooms, standing in the hallway and waiting for instructions.

"Oh, Jesus," she mutters.

I look down at her. "I know you're probably not happy about this, but someone needs to keep you safe while I'm gone."

"Someone needs to keep me prisoner while you're gone, you mean."

I close my eyes.

I knew this wouldn't last forever.

"I'm sorry, princess—" I start, touching her hand, but she wrenches away from me, sticking out her hand.

"If you're going to leave me all day with these thugs, you're going to pay for it."

I smile and put a stack of bills in her hand. She's right. This is the least I can do. This is our honeymoon after all and I'm leaving her behind for a few hours.

I wish I didn't have to, though. Yesterday was the closest we've ever been, and it felt better than I ever dreamed it would.

Her hurt just now when she realized she was staying with the twins pierced my heart deeper than it should be possible.

As she puts the money away, part of me is proud because it is almost as if I'm being the man I should be as a husband. I'm taking care of her.

And my damned traitorous heart skips a beat.

I grab her around the waist, pulling her to me, and she fights just for a moment before melting against me when I kiss her deeply.

"I'll see you soon." I let her go.

She stumbles a little, pouting,

I head toward the elevator, smiling, hoping that maybe she is starting to enjoy being with me just as much as I enjoy being with her. And that is a dangerous thought.

My smile fades when I realize what I have ahead of me, and I take a deep breath.

I am so fucking tired.

12

——

BREE

"You guys could at least let me make conversation," I say to the twins as we walk back to the hotel after hours shopping and touring all I could.

As I go, I take it all in and I wonder if I can talk Declan into coming with me to tour other places. Walking around Vegas is so much fun!

Wait. Why am I wanting to spend more time with Declan? It's not that I'm falling for him. It has nothing to do with that. He's just been a good distraction, that's all. And since the twins are keeping me from escaping, he's the only distraction I have.

That and shopping, but I've done that for so long now that my feet and calves ache, even though I'm wearing flats.

"Sorry, Mrs. Burke," Sean mumbles, and I look back at him.

"You can speak?"

Finn laughs. "We both can, ma'am." It comes out, in his Irish brogue, like "mum."

"Good to know."

They follow me up to the hotel penthouse, bringing in

all my things. They start to leave, but I stop them. "Hey. Do either one of you know how to play Blackjack?"

That's how thirty minutes later, I'm sitting cross-legged on the floor with two Irish mobsters who outweigh me by about a hundred pounds together, playing Blackjack.

"Hit me," I say, and Sean looks at my three cards incredulously. "Just hit me," I growl, and he slips me a card.

I groan, seeing that I went over.

"That's your problem," Finn says, throwing down his cards—a King and a nine. "You keep worrying about getting twenty-one. Instead of trying to make twenty-one, just get as high as you can without going over. Most times, you'll win the hand that way."

"Let's play again. Finn, you deal this time."

We play for a while longer, and finally, I start to beat Sean.

I narrow my eyes at him. "Are you letting me win?"

He grins. "Guilty."

I throw down my cards. "I'm gonna beat Declan at Blackjack if it kills me."

Sean laughs. "You won't beat Declan, dearie. He's a card shark, you know?"

"He is?" I have to admit that I suspected, given his sister's stories. "Does he cheat?"

He shakes his head, frowning. "Never. Irishmen don't cheat."

My father does.

I don't know why I thought that. He's cheated here and there at small games that we played, but I don't know if he does it in business. I don't like thinking that way about my father, and I shake my head to clear it.

"When will Declan come back?"

Finn shrugs. "It's getting dark. He should be back soon."

As if on cue, Declan comes in the door, stumbling a bit, and I look up at him. He frowns, seeing me sitting on the floor, and Sean and Finn scramble up.

"What's this?"

I kick the cards so they scatter as I stand up. "We were just playing Solitaire."

"Isn't Solitaire a solo game?"

Finn and Sean exit the room, and Declan kicks off his shoes, falling onto the bed.

"You smell like wine."

Declan nods. "Let's just say John and his friends like their booze," he mumbles.

"How'd it go?" I climb into bed with him, and he shrugs.

"It was fine. I was just relaying some messages, but James was not the most in the most attentive mood."

I frown.

"Never mind. John's friends left before I did, and John Renno and I were able to finally get everything sorted after a few more glasses of red."

"Well, you'd better sober up. We're going back to the casino. Plus, I'm hungry."

"You can order room service," he groans, but I shake my head, bouncing on the bed just to annoy him.

"No, it's our honeymoon, and you're going to take your wife to dinner and gambling. We leave tomorrow, right?"

"Tomorrow *evening*. And we've already switched hotels to Caesar's Palace, what else do you want?"

"I want you to take me to dinner and the casino," I repeat stubbornly, and he opens one eye, looking up at me.

"Okay." He gives me a half-smile. "I'll go wash my face."

I cheer, going to the closet to bring out my other evening gown –a black one with a slit up the side.

I put it on while he's in the bathroom, sliding on a pair of heels. I wince. My feet and ankles are starting to get sore from wearing heels, but it's worth it for how good I look.

It's worth it for the way that Declan looks at me when he gets back out of the bathroom.

He hums, putting a hand on the small of my back as we leave. He's still wearing a suit, although he's discarded the jacket so he's just in a shirt and vest. He looks amazing, though, because it's tailored tightly around his trim waist, showing off the broadness of his chest.

We head down to the restaurant, and they seat us right away.

I look over the menu, which has no prices, but at this point, I don't care. I have enough money stashed in my purse from shopping to gamble all night.

Declan orders a chicken salad, and I raise an eyebrow at him while I order steak and lobster.

"Don't want to overwhelm my stomach," he admits. "I had quite a lot of wine."

I laugh. "How drunk are you?"

"There's not two of you, so I guess I'm doing okay."

I smirk at him. "Well, I need to drink a bit to catch up, then."

But Declan shakes his head. "One of us should be alert."

I pout. "All right, fair enough."

Declan doesn't order a drink either, just water, and I order ginger beer, wishing I could have a Moscow Mule.

When the food arrives, he picks at his salad.

"Are you sure it went okay?"

"Yeah, it was fine." He smiles. "I guess I was worried I'd come back and you'd still be mad at me."

"Mad is kind of an understatement to how I feel about you, Declan."

He shrugs. "Well, I thought we were making some progress."

"We were." What's the point in pretending? I'm getting more comfortable in this whole situation. If you go along with something long enough, you can get used to anything.

"Then let's not let it be ruined." There's an edge of pleading to his voice.

I smile. "All right. That's why I wanted to come out, you know? I thought we could spend a little more time having fun before we go home."

"I am having fun with you." He looks away and then back at me.

"Me too," I murmur, before biting into a piece of melt-in-your-mouth steak.

Declan seems to rally after a couple of glasses of water and food, and we go to the casino after we leave the restaurant.

I take his hand, leading him immediately to the Black-jack table.

"You're playing against me?"

I grin. "Sean and Finn taught me how to play. What, you scared I'll win?"

He snorts and puts down money on the table to bid.

I get a face card but then so does the dealer, so I narrow my eyes.

"Hit me," I tell the dealer, and wonder of wonders, he gives me an ace. I try my best not to let it show on my face, and Declan bets against me.

The dealer takes a hit and stands at twenty, while Declan is at nineteen.

I show my card.

"Blackjack, for the lady!" the dealer says, pushing the chips toward me, and I cheer.

I've won about ten thousand dollars since we were the only ones in the round.

I grab up the chips, cackling.

Declan puts a hand on my arm. "That was just beginner's luck. Let's go again."

Three hands later, I've lost all my money and another three hundred dollars, and I'm flagging. Other people have come to the table, and Declan is fleecing them for all their worth, but I start to see the casino workers kind of watching us.

I stop bidding and head over to Declan, placing a hand on his arm and gesturing to the guards standing around.

"That's it for me," Declan says, winning his final round. The crowd boos, but Declan grabs my elbow in one hand and his winnings in the other and swiftly takes me to cash out.

As we wait for the money to be counted, guards are still eyeing and pointing at us, and my heart starts to race.

Declan grabs me and the bag of money and we start to jog toward the elevator. When we close the doors, the guards head our way.

My heart is beating out of my chest. "Are we in trouble?"

"Not if they don't catch us." Declan winks at me. "I'll call the twins, get them to grab our things."

"Where are we going?"

"Back to the Four Seasons."

"But...your credit card—" They have his card on file at the hotel.

He grins. "Not mine, sweetheart. I don't book under the Burke name. That's trouble waiting to happen."

"*You*'re trouble waiting to happen," I murmur, but I am so turned on right now I can barely stand myself.

I've grown up among mobsters and thugs, but never a card shark. This is exciting, and I can't deny that it's making me hotter and hotter.

We go to the parking garage instead of upstairs, and Declan makes the call to Sean.

"Grab our stuff, meet us at the Seasons." He hangs up.

Sean is apparently trained not to ask questions.

Declan and I grab his car at the valet, and he takes off when we get inside.

We make it back to the Four Seasons without delay, and I grab his hand while we're inside, dragging him to the hotel room.

"Text Sean to keep our stuff until tomorrow. Tonight, I want you to myself."

"Oh?" He raises an eyebrow, but by the time we get into the room, I can tell that he's exhausted. It's nearing two in the morning, and he's been working all day.

I don't believe he simply talked to the Rennos, especially since he seems to be favoring his right shoulder.

"Maybe we should just sleep tonight." I try to take deep breaths and calm myself down, and Declan groans.

"I'm sorry, princess. It's just been a long day."

"I can see that." I unbutton his shirt and pull it off him.

He winces, and sure enough, there's a huge bruise on the back of his right shoulder blade.

"Just relaying information, my ass."

"You know I can't tell you everything I do."

"Didn't say you had to. But you should tell me when you're hurt," I insist. "I never would have dragged you out."

"You had fun, didn't you?"

I unbutton his slacks, and he steps out of them when they fall on the floor.

I turn and let him unzip my dress. It pools on the floor, and I'm wearing a teddy underneath, a dark green one that I think shows off my eyes.

"This is just mean." Declan pouts as he looks me up and down, and I laugh.

"You're too tired for sex. And to tell you the truth, my dogs are barking from all the shopping."

"It's like a real honeymoon." He chuckles. "Everyone always does too much."

I laugh, pushing him down in the bed and crawling on top of him. It isn't sexual, though, just wanting to touch him, and he drags his hands along my shoulders and my bare arms.

I kiss him softly, sliding over to the side of him so I don't put weight on his bad shoulder.

He turns onto his good side, putting his arms around me and pulling me close.

I turn to kiss his cheek, and he's already nearly dozing.

I have to admit, today has been a dream, and it feels safe in his arms.

I had this plan to save money from gambling to get away from him, but I can't keep myself from enjoying his company and just being here. I've just been acting like this is a real honeymoon.

I've been acting like a real wife, and it's scary.

Do I have feelings for Declan? If I do, is it just some kind of weird reaction to spending so much time together?

I've got to get my head together. Why doesn't he feel like the enemy he is supposed to be? Why do I feel more like I belong with him than I ever felt since my mom left me?

13

DECLAN

I wake up before Bree and get into the shower immediately, trying to clean off the sweat and dirt from yesterday. I told her the truth when I told her that I was only relaying messages to Renno, it was his men that didn't get the memo.

But there is still something I need to do. And it's the last thing I want to do in my honeymoon, but this was a last-minute assignment Da threw at me.

And I'm already so tired. I just want this all to be over, but as long as people keep disobeying my father, I'll have this kind of thing to do.

I kiss Bree on the forehead before I leave. It's barely daylight, and she doesn't even open her eyes.

I walk down to Finn's room. Sean will be staying to protect Bree. Finn's a little bigger than his brother, and more intimidating looking with his close-cropped dark hair, where Sean's is long and reddish blond.

He's Irish coming around a corner, but Finn isn't. And I don't want us to be recognized. As soon as Ronan Sullivan sees us, he'll know he's caught, and he'll fight like the cornered animal he is.

Finn comes to the door immediately, freshly showered and wearing comfortable clothes—just jeans and a T-shirt. I'm dressed similarly. We need the element of surprise.

"How many?" Finn asks as we head down to the valet.

"Two, maybe three," I tell him. "Sullivan works in small groups."

"Do we leave any of them alive?"

I shake my head solemnly. "They knew what they signed up for when they sided with a thieving rat."

Finn nods. "Where are we meeting them?"

"We're going to surprise them at the warehouse. They should have had a shipment last night—guns, probably AKs. They won't be loaded, so they'll just be armed with their handguns."

"He's skimming off the top?"

"Enough that Da couldn't not notice."

Finn whistles. "Your da lets a lot slide."

I think sometimes Da lets *too* much slide, but that's Gray's problem, not mine. Gray's going to inherit everything, not me. I don't think I'm built for this life, really, built for this amount of violence.

We head to the warehouse, and I park a couple of blocks away.

We step out of the car, and I start walking with Sean as if we're just going on a morning stroll. The drop-off was supposed to be at daylight, so they should still be at the location.

I catch sight of a few crates as we get closer, and I grab Sean and pull him behind them. I draw my gun, and Sean follows suit as we walk up closer, hiding behind the crates here and there.

There are two guys laughing and taking things from crates as Sullivan supervises next to them.

One's a young guy I've never seen before, couldn't be more than twenty.

Fuck.

I hate killing kids, even if they're technically adults. But this kid knew what he was getting into. And if you work with the Burkes, you don't break your word.

I come out from behind the crates and shoot the kid in the head, giving him a quick death, before Sean shoots the other guy next to Sullivan, another man I don't recognize.

Sullivan's eyes bug out of his head, and he drops to his knees, clasping his hands together in front of me. "Please, boss. *Please*, don't kill me, I'm sorry. I got five kids, I—"

I shoot him point blank, and his body slumps to the floor.

"Jesus," I mumble, looking over at Sullivan's body twitching. "Wish we could've brought Sean."

"You're telling me." Finn shakes his head and goes to search their pockets. When he finds some car keys, he tries them and one of them is an SUV.

He gets one of the tarps laying around the warehouse floor, putting it in the back of the SUV and throws the bodies inside. I help him with the last couple, looking into the kid's dead brown eyes and wanting to vomit.

I have killed so many by now, I should be numb when I kill anymore. It's like after the first time, the second time, the third—it should start feeling like a chore instead of taking a life.

It doesn't. I still feel each life I take as a slice of my soul being torn away.

Finn and I drive to the Escalade, and he drives the SUV as I follow behind.

We leave the bodies rotting in the Nevada desert, and I take the chance to change my shirt, burning the bloody one. Before starting the engine, I look down to make sure there's no stray droplets on my skin.

We drive to an area that is notorious for crime, where we know the car will disappear from our hands soon enough and leave it with the keys inside in plain sight.

By the time we drive back to the hotel, I'm exhausted all over again.

I check in with Sean, to be sure that nothing happened.

He cracks his jaw in a yawn as he opens the door. "She's been fine. Stayed in the room. I think she's still asleep."

I nod tightly. "Good."

"How'd it go?"

"It's handled."

I don't want to think about it anymore, about the way that kid's brown eyes stared lifeless at me. How he never even got to beg for his life.

All I want is to get back into bed with my wife. See for myself that she is there. That she is real.

Sure, it's terrifying to think that she's the one person that can calm me down, and she's Niall Murphy's daughter, but right now, I'm just seeking comfort, craving her touch.

I push away all the fear as I head into our room and climb back into bed with Bree.

She hums, turning toward me, and she tucks her face into my good shoulder. "Where did you go?"

"Nowhere important," I tell her, and she mumbles something incoherent and presses herself into my arms.

It's the first time she's initiated this kind of contact, this kind of intimate contact that isn't sex, and it makes my heart skip a beat.

"Is it time to go?" she asks, and I draw in a breath.

"Yes," I murmur, some part of me wishing we could stay here forever, in this little bubble, and I could pretend that I didn't just kill three men and leave them to rot in the Nevada sun.

I could pretend that I'm really on my honeymoon, with a woman who loves me instead of one who I started having feelings for but merely tolerates me.

Bree yawns, flipping over to wake up, and then she heads to the bathroom.

I rub my hands across my face, knowing that I have a long trip ahead of me.

Bree and I head to the private jet, Sean and Finn drive to the airport to fly first class.

"Why don't they ride with us?" she asks.

"It's our honeymoon," I tell her, and she smiles slightly. It doesn't quite reach her eyes.

I know she knows that something happened today. She's not stupid. After all, she grew up in this life, too. She knows that I have blood on my hands, just like her father.

Even though I'd like to claim I'm nothing like him, that's one thing that we do have in common.

The plane ride back seems longer than the plane ride there.

"You look ready to be home," Bree muses.

"I am," I admit. "It's been a long trip."

"I actually had a great time."

I smile at her, and she leans her head against my shoulder.

"I did, too," I utter, and she takes my hand, squeezing it.

My heart clenches in my chest.

What is this feeling? Guilt? Pity? Is it just because this is the kind of marriage, the kind of life I've always secretly wished for?

It's not real. It'll never be real.

Real or not, though, her nearness comforts me on the trip home.

When we arrive home, there's barely time to put the bags down before Gray and my father whisk me away.

I wave slightly at Bree as she gets carted off by my sisters, and she waves back.

My father sits me down, and I wince a bit as he puts his hands on my shoulders.

"Did you speak to Renno?"

"Of course I did. After one of his men tried to dislocate my shoulder," I drawl.

My father laughs at my pain. "You should've known not to sneak up on them."

"Yeah, yeah."

"What about Sullivan?"

"Took him out. Me and Finn. They're in the desert."

My father nods. "Good job, Declan. I knew I sent the right man."

Gray scoffs. "You only sent him because I don't have a cover to go to Las Vegas."

I look up at Gray. Is he jealous?

I wouldn't be surprised. Gray's always been kind of the golden child of the Burkes, but lately, my father has been taking up a lot of time with me and giving me a lot of work. It's not that Gray couldn't do most of what I do—he just wouldn't be good to have a marriage as cover. He's just not the marrying type.

I never thought I was either, but having Bree makes me rethink things. Having a wife has been more fun than I imagined. You have a smart, funny, beautiful woman to come home to, and if you feel up to it, she'll argue with you, and you can have hot make-up sex.

What more could a guy want?

It would have been nice to be able to choose it, but I have to admit, I don't think I ever would have chosen someone as great as Bree. The way she makes me feel should really terrify me, and it's starting to.

It's not just that she's a warm body. It's because it's *her*, because she's bright and funny and sassy, and I *like* her. Love is a different story, but I definitely like her, and that's enough to make me feel a little panicky.

"How was your honeymoon?" Gray smirks at me.

"I won fifty thousand dollars."

He chokes.

"Did you get thrown out of the casino again?" my father asks in a scolding tone.

"No, Da."

Just barely.

"Don't go thinking you can get the gambling bug again," my father warns, and I smirk.

"Wouldn't dream of it."

"Good, because I bought off enough casino thugs to finance a college education."

Gray snorts out a laugh. "I was more asking if you consummated your marriage?"

"That would be none of your business," I mutter, and Gray brays out a laugh.

"That's a yes, isn't it? You dog."

My father claps me on my good shoulder. "Good job, Declan. You're doing great, boyo."

"Thank you." The praise makes me feel a little awkward. I'm not all that used to it. Gray's usually the one getting praise. "I think I'm going to nap before dinner."

I stand up and walk into the foyer, hoping to see Bree,

but she's off somewhere gossiping with my sisters, most likely.

I drag myself up the stairs, feeling more exhausted than I ever have in my life, and I wish Bree was there to cuddle with me.

What?

What am I thinking?

I don't need her to fall asleep.

After an hour, I huff and roll over, just wearing a pair of gray sweats after I'd dressed down to bed, and I walk out into the hall, going over to the wing where Paige's bedroom is.

I rap softly on the door, and Paige opens it, frowning.

"What are you doing here? You've had her all week."

Bree stands up.

"What is it?" She looks concerned.

"Can't sleep without you." Fuck. I sound like a sap.

Paige squeals, "That's so *cute*, Declan."

"It doesn't mean anything," I insist as Bree leads me back to the bedroom, waving goodbye at Paige and Lara. "It's just been a long time since I slept alone."

"I know." Bree's being kind to me, and I'm barely keeping my eyes open I'm so tired.

She puts me into the bed, cuddling up next to me, fully dressed, and once I can breathe in the rosewater scent of her hair, I instantly relax, drifting off into sleep.

By the time I wake up, it's time for dinner, and Bree is dressed in a nice, white shift dress that shows off her slight tan.

I groan. "I don't want to dress for dinner. Just bring me a plate."

Bree tsks. "You know that your father likes us all to have dinner together. Put on some pants."

She throws a pair of slacks on the bed, and I grab them and slide them on, as well as a t-shirt she throws in my direction.

I'm not dressed *nicely* for dinner, but so what? I'm jet lagged.

Gray starts to cheer and wolf whistle as we come into the dining room, and I can't help but laugh.

I'm getting used to this being married thing, and I hope that Bree is, too.

Maybe that should scare me, but it doesn't.

Should I be worried?

14

———

BREE

Gray's wolf whistles make me blush and laugh.

"We're married, it's not like it's scandalous," I argue, sitting down at the dinner table, and Gray grins.

"Was it all chaste and pure, with half your clothes still on?" He's clearly joking, but I'm not about to let him get away with that.

"Sometimes, we managed to get all our clothes off," I tease back, and Paige makes a face and Lara dramatically gags.

"Sorry." I chuckle.

"I hope you two had a good time," Patrick says. "I heard that you did some gambling."

"Oh yeah! I learned how to play Blackjack! Sean and Finn taught me."

The two men in question must have gone home, because they're nowhere to be found.

"She beat me a couple of hands."

Patrick laughs out loud. "I knew she was a little spitfire."

"Not like she comes from good stock," Gray mutters, and Declan gives him a death glare.

Just when I was starting to feel at home here, feel accepted, Gray has to go and ruin it. He's the one member of the family who I can't quite get a read on.

He doesn't outwardly hate me, mostly teasing me the way a big brother would, but he clearly still thinks of me as lesser, as someone that shouldn't belong to the Burke family.

"Neither do you," I shoot back, and Patrick stares at me for a long moment before he bursts out into raucous laughter.

Looking over at Declan, he looks furious at his brother and oddly proud of me for talking back to Gray.

"She's good." Patrick wipes tears of mirth from his eyes. "Very quick, aren't you, girl?"

"I do my best. My mother always said I was bright" I flush slightly at Patrick's praise.

I've never received a lot of praise from my father. He often tells me I'm pretty, pretty like my mother, but since my mother left, I've never known if that was a compliment or a slight.

"There's something I've always been curious about," Patrick says quietly, and I look up at him, my good mood fading.

"What? You can ask me anything."

"Your mother," he starts. "What happened to her?"

I stare at him. "That's really none of your business."

"You said I could ask you anything."

"I don't like to talk about my mother. Do you like to talk about your wife?"

Patrick's face goes suddenly blank. "Fair enough."

Now everything's awkward, and I guess I've made it

that way. I just don't like to tell everyone that she abandoned me when I was a kid.

Declan puts an arm around my shoulders. "Bree won a lot at slots, too," he says, even though I'd only won that first little bit.

"I told you the slots were amazing!" Paige says. "Lara won fifteen grand in one pull once."

Lara beams. "I did. It was that big one, you know, the one right by the door? They say it never hits, but it certainly hit that night."

I smile and listen, nodding, as they tell me about their last Vegas trip. It's fun to hear their stories, and eventually Patrick loosens up.

"You want to hear the one where Declan got arrested?"

Declan chokes on his wine.

"Da—"

But Patrick continues, "He'd won nearly eighty thousand at Blackjack. And I keep telling him, boyo, go around the tables. Different dealers. They'll think you're cheating. But he wouldn't listen. So, what do you think happened?"

I look at Declan, grinning and remembering the night that the guards came after us.

"They accused him of cheating?"

"Absolutely! Threw him in the casino jail, but the cops didn't have any proof, so they let him go. He was banned from Caesar's Palace by twenty-one."

"Then how did we—"

"An alias, princess."

"What's your alias?" I ask, and then blink. "Do *I* have an alias?"

"Eliza," Declan answers. "And I'm James."

"James and Eliza." I giggle at the strange sounding names. "What about our last name?"

"Smith."

I burst out laughing at the absurdity of it.

"Mr. and Mrs. Smith? Really?"

"I told you it was hackneyed," Gray pipes in, and I'm laughing even harder as Declan pouts in my general direction.

It's a fun dinner, and we're all laughing and talking until dessert is over.

Paige clears her throat. "I have an announcement to make."

All eyes turn to her.

"So... um... I want to find my own place."

"What? Absolutely not!" Patrick is so red I'm waiting for fumes to come out of his ears.

"Come on, Da. I'm an adult, but most of the time, I feel like everyone around here forgets. I just want to try it. Please? On a trial basis?"

"Paige..." Patrick sighs. The silence around the table is so heavy it is almost palpable.

"Dad, I need to know if I can survive out there without being sheltered all the time. Please!"

Gray's phone rings. When he looks at it, he excuses himself from the table, walking into his father's office.

"We'll talk about this another time. I really need to think about it, Paige. I promise I'll look at it with an open mind." Patrick excuses himself, as well, and then it's just me, Declan, and the girls.

"Well, that went well."

Lara sighs. "You did kind of dumped it on him, what did you expect?"

Paige just shrugs. "I don't know. I just wanted to get that over with. But now I need a sisterly sleepover," Paige whines. "Are you in, Bree?"

My heart melts for her. She considers me a sister?

"Not tonight, Paige," Lara hisses.

"Why not?"

"Because they're just home from their honeymoon. You heard Declan, he can't sleep without her."

"I can," Declan argues in a mutter, but I look at him, wondering if that's true. "Besides, I'll be up for a while. Took that late nap."

"Maybe I'll come hang out for a few hours?" I suggest. "And then go back to bed late at night."

"Aren't you tired from your trip?" Lara asks.

I shake my head. "No, I fell asleep with Declan. I feel kind of wired."

"Good." Paige grins. "Let's do makeovers and look at houses and watch movies."

Lara smirks. "Horror movies."

Paige pouts. "Okay, but only slashers."

"Fair enough."

I look back and forth between the two of them, having a hard time keeping up with their conversation. They seem to nearly be telepathic, knowing what the other is thinking.

Paige and Lara stand up, and I walk with them, looking back at Declan who's now eating my portion of dessert.

I smile at him, and he smiles back, and my heart seems to skip several beats.

I've got to get it together. It's like I've forgotten about my plan to get out of here. In Vegas, I got so caught up in Declan and all the attention that he was giving me that I hadn't even thought about escaping.

Now I'm back in this admittedly beautiful prison of a mansion, and I'm having a sleepover with his sisters. That apparently think of me as a sister too. At least Paige does. And I love that.

What am I doing?

My head's all messed up. Half of me is still angry about the way this came about, but the other half—it's like I'm actually *enjoying* myself.

I let out a long breath and follow Paige and Lara.

They're not going upstairs, though, but down toward the pool house.

"Are we going swimming?" I ask, and Paige laughs.

"No," Lara says. "You'll see."

"Da gave us special permission to take you here," Paige says excitedly, and we walk past the pool house into a building I've never noticed before. I guess I've been so much in the main house, I didn't realize the scope of the estate.

Lara uses a keycode to get in, and when the lights come up, I look around with awe.

It's like a movie theater. There's a projector in the back, and a an actual cinema screen on the far wall. There's also a bar, foosball tables, pool tables, and a couple of arcade games. It's less ornate than the main house, more comfortable, almost like a den with lounge furniture that's focused on comfort more than aesthetics.

"Wow. What is this place?" I look around in wonder.

"It's Da's den." Paige bounces like a little puppy.

I can't help but smile at her.

She touches everything as she goes by as if she is showing affection. "We haven't been allowed in here since Kael and Declan nearly wrecked the place in high school."

"Who's Kael?" I can't help myself from wanting to know more about Declan.

"Declan's best friend," Lara explains. "He's been out of town for a while."

Huh. I didn't know Declan *had* a best friend. I've never seen him hang out with anyone but his family and his father's men. I guess everyone has friends, but I never thought about a mafia boss having them. I assumed that Declan was too focused on work to socialize.

"What do we do first?" Paige wears a slight look of annoyance on her face, and I wonder what that's about, but decide not to ask.

We're having fun, and I don't want to bring up anything that will stop that.

She heads over to the bar area, pulling out various bottles of liquor.

"Da usually has his own bartender." Lara sounds almost disappointed.

"I can make drinks." I walk behind the bar. "I do it all the time for my father and his friends."

Paige raises an eyebrow. "Your father doesn't have staff?"

I shrug. "A maid, a cook, things like that. But he doesn't hire many people for that kind of thing. He likes to keep to himself." I grin as I take out a martini shaker. "What'll it be, ladies?"

"A dirty martini." Lara smiles. "Extra olives."

"A sex on the beach!" Paige claps her hands.

"Coming right up."

I hum as I put the two fairly simple drinks together, shaking one in each shaker and pouring the sex on the beach over ice and the martini chilled in a martini glass.

I make myself a vodka tonic and then slide the drinks over to the sisters.

Lara takes a hesitant sip, and her eyes widen. "Paige, this is delicious!"

Paige gulps half of hers before gasping. "You're so talented!"

I flush. "Not really. It's just something I've been doing since I was about twelve."

"I could never make a drink this well." Paige pouts. "Da doesn't even like the way I pour his scotch."

I snort out a laugh. It's pretty hard to mess up pouring scotch, but since Paige is so bubbly and a little scatter-brained, it makes sense. Usually, people like that annoy me, but not Paige. She's just cute, like a little sister.

Like a sister-in-law, I remind myself. *A forced sister-in-law, no less.*

And if she moves out, it might be easier to remember that.

My smile wants to fade but I keep it on, not wanting the girls to know about the dark cloud that has descended over me. It's easy to forget that these people, who've been so kind to me, also kidnapped me. It's easy to forget that Declan isn't my chosen husband, and this isn't my chosen family.

To be honest, it kind of hurts to think about.

Ever since I was twelve, it's just been me and my father. And he never gave me much affection or praise, just expected me to do well without much guidance.

A family, a normal one, is something that I've always craved, and the Burkes are just that—a real, loving family. The thing I've always wanted.

"Penny for your thoughts," Lara says quietly, and I glance at her, blinking.

"Oh, it's nothing," I mumble, looking down into my drink.

"Let's watch a movie!" Paige suggests, and twenty minutes later, Lara has made us popcorn, and we're sitting with our feet up on one of the big couches, looking up at the giant screen. There are theater-style seats in front of the projector, but Paige insists these are the best seats in the house.

She turns out to be right. We squeal at all the scary parts of the slasher movie we put on, a part six of something. It's cheesy but the gore is extreme, and Lara can't stop laughing at Paige hiding her eyes.

I can't keep the grin off my face. I've been having a wonderful time the past couple of weeks, probably more fun than I've had in years. Between the fun and the alcohol, I'm not even thinking about Declan or how confused I am by the Vegas trip.

By the time the movie is over, and we looked at a few house options for Paige, we're all a little tipsy, and we decide to take a dip in the pool.

I'm floating, face-up, wearing one of my new bikinis, when Paige cannonballs into the pool, spraying water everywhere and knocking me off balance.

I sputter as I come up, but I'm laughing, and Lara helps me to the edge of the pool.

I look at the clock, and I'm shocked to see it's nearly two in the morning.

"I should get to bed," I announce, wrapping a towel around myself.

"Gotta get back to hubby," Paige teases with a grin, treading water as Lara sits down on one of the lounge chairs.

I scoff, but my cheeks flush. It's true. I do want to see Declan a bit before he falls asleep, and I may already be too late.

I say my goodbyes and thank them for the wonderful night, heading into the main house and walking upstairs to the bedroom.

When I open the door, Declan's sitting on the bed in his

boxer briefs, the sheets tangled around his legs and bare, tight abdomen. He leans back against the headboard, and he's reading a book that he holds in one hand.

My breath catches in my throat as he looks up at me with a soft smile.

"I'm gonna grab a shower." I pause with my hand on the doorknob of the bathroom. "You'll be awake when I get out?"

"If that's what you want, princess," Declan croons, and I don't know if he's serious or if he's teasing me, so I huff out a breath and go into the bathroom, turning on the water as hot as it will go.

I close my eyes as the spray hits my back.

Maybe part of me hopes that Declan *will* be asleep when I get out.

Then, I won't have to deal with the complicated way I'm feeling about him.

15

DECLAN

Bree comes back from her girls' night wearing a too-revealing bikini, and I can't keep my eyes off her. She doesn't seem to notice, though, heading for the shower, and if I hadn't just showered myself an hour ago, I'd join her.

I missed her while she was gone, and I hate myself for it. I don't know why I've been so attached to her recently. I suppose it's just the time we've been forced to spend together. I've never spent every night in my own bed with a woman, and I have to think that's the reason that something in me aches when she's not around.

Because it can't be anything else. I don't have feelings for her.

Sure, I've never felt this way before, never longed to see someone after a hard day, never craved a woman's touch the way I do hers, but this isn't real. None of this is real.

I still want out of this marriage, don't I?

She always says this place is like a prison, and in a way, this marriage is my prison. I can't go falling for the warden.

I'm about decided to go into the shower and seduce her, fuck her rough and dirty, remind myself that the hot sex is the only real benefit I get out of this marriage, when Bree comes out.

Her auburn hair looks darker because it's damp, falling in curls around her face and down her back. My breath hitches in my chest when I look at her, fresh-faced and clean. She's gorgeous. That's half the reason I feel strange about her, surely. Because she's probably the most beautiful woman I've ever seen, and I'm a normal, hot-blooded male.

But it isn't lust that makes me reach out for her, tug her down onto the bed while she has a comb in her hand.

She squeaks, like a little mouse, and it makes me chuckle.

"Let me do it." I take the comb from her hand.

She frowns. "I am perfectly capable of combing my own hair."

"Shut up, I'm trying to be nice." I position her between my legs, her back to my chest.

She's only wearing a towel, and her damp skin against mine makes need clench in my lower abdomen.

"Since when are you nice?"

"Since always." I hum as I drag the comb through the ends of her hair, and then the middle.

Bree scoffs, but she doesn't move, and I smile as she settles back against me.

"How do you know to start at the ends?"

"I do have two sisters, you know?"

"I have a hard time believing that nannies didn't do the hair brushing."

"Sometimes," I say. "But there was a time when Paige wouldn't go to sleep at all unless me or Gray brushed hers out. Her curls could be difficult, and she wouldn't let the nanny touch her with a ten-foot pole."

"That's actually kind of sweet," she murmurs. "Rory would *never* brush out my hair."

I chuckle. "What can I say? I've got a soft spot for Paige."

"Everyone does," she agrees.

"Even you?"

"Especially me." She shifts, turning to look at me, and I take her chin in my hand and turn her face so that I can get to the baby hairs at her temple.

"Paige is easy to love."

Bree goes quiet, as if she doesn't want to continue the conversation, so I change the subject.

"Did you have fun in Vegas?"

She's still silent for a long moment but then she finally answers, "Yes."

"Me, too. I never thought of Vegas as a honeymoon spot, but it turned out all right."

"Have you ever thought about honeymoon destinations?"

I shrug. "Not really. I never thought about getting married."

"I did," she whispers, a hint of sadness in her voice, and I feel a pang of guilt.

"What did you imagine?"

"A white dress. My father walking me down the aisle."

"He doesn't seem like the type of man to do a daddy/daughter dance," I comment, and she pulls away from me, frowning.

"Why do you always have to shit on my father?"

I sigh, rubbing a hand across the back of my neck. "Look, I don't want to fight."

"Shocking. You always want to fight."

"That's not true," I argue. "You're the one who has the sharp tongue, you know?"

She twists around to look at me, smiling slyly. "Last I heard, you liked my sharp tongue."

Lust rushes through me, and I drag my lip between my teeth before grinning at her.

"I can think of how to put it to good use."

"That's what we're good at, isn't it?" There's something in her voice that isn't quite anger, isn't quite lust.

She turns, climbing into my lap, and her towel falls away, revealing her perfect, perky breasts.

I groan low in my throat as she rocks her hips against mine, the only thing separating us the thin fabric of my underwear.

I harden immediately beneath her, and I put my hands on her breasts, palming across her peaked nipples.

She lets out a long, moany breath.

I lean forward to kiss her, catching her lips with my own, sliding my tongue between them.

She licks into my mouth, hesitantly at first, and then more passionately, bracing her hands on my shoulders as she rolls her hips.

The slow friction of her wet heat is maddening even through the fabric, and I growl, biting down on her lip as I twist, putting her on her back.

Bree's legs spread immediately, and I put a hand on each of her thighs, pushing them further apart and looking down at her.

"So slick already," I murmur, moving one hand to cup her pussy, pressing my thumb against her clit.

She hitches out another moan, arching her back.

"Declan, please." She rocks her hips forward for more

friction, and I chuckle, moving my thumb slowly across her bundle of nerves while she writhes beneath me.

I kiss along her neck, sucking and biting down to leave marks all across her skin. I want to mark her for good, mark her mine.

She starts to shudder as I move my thumb faster, nearly vibrating it against her, and I know she's coming when her cry cuts off into a long groan that comes deep from her chest.

"That's it, princess," I murmur. "Come for me."

"Ah, ah, ah," she grunts out, unable to make words, and she's so sexy that I'm straining against my boxers, literally aching to be inside her.

But all I can do is watch her face, her eyelids squeezed shut. The arch of her back, the lines of her stomach, the little pouch just below her bellybutton, soft and feminine and absolutely gorgeous.

She's like a lustful goddess, keening out her pleasure, and I remove my hand from her, shoving down my boxer briefs and freeing myself to the cool air.

I stand fully erect, precum dripping from the tip.

But I grit my teeth when I guide myself into her, holding myself back as she clenches around me through the aftershocks of her orgasm.

I want to make this last, want her to come around me again and again.

Usually, it's because that's a stroke to my ego, to my sexual prowess, but right now, with Bree, it's different. It's because I want to please her, want to watch her face as she lets go and submits herself to me.

Her pink lips part as she pants, rocking her hips as I stay still inside her.

I ignore her undulating hips and lean down to kiss her, slowly, deeply, pulling away to look into her eyes.

"I want you to always know who's making you come, princess," I tell her. "Eyes on me."

She mewls, nodding her head for good measure, and then I start to move. I roll my hips, fucking her in long, even strokes that make an orgasm build up achingly slowly in my abdomen and balls.

I could fuck her hard and dirty, which is what I originally planned, make us both come, but some part of me wants this to last. Some part of me wants her to just fall apart beneath me. I kiss her once more but then pull away and her lips chase mine.

"You look so beautiful like this. *Bellissima.*"

"I'm so close, Declan," she whimpers. "I'm going to come again."

"Go ahead, baby. Come all over my cock, show me how good you feel."

Bree struggles with keeping her eyes open, but she listens, keeping her eyes on me, and it's like I could fall into those hazel pools, swim there all night as the green in her eyes grows more pronounced with lust. Her skin is hot beneath mine, our abdomens slapping together when I thrust into her.

Fuck, I'm close.

Not yet. Stay steady.

I want to *ruin* her, want to ruin her for any other man, want her to be mine forever, to *want* to be mine forever, and if I wasn't so close to the edge, that line of thinking might scare me. As it is, though, I grunt out her name, keeping my strokes as even as I can, given how close I am to orgasm.

"Oh, fuck," she curses, her voice low and raspy. "I'm coming, Declan."

I can feel that she is, her orgasm giving her a full-body reaction as she claws at my shoulders. The sting makes me moan, makes me start to move faster despite myself.

She's clenching around me like a vice, and she feels like heaven.

My orgasm is coming and nothing short of a natural disaster is going to stop it, but I keep up my slow, long strokes as she shudders all over, mumbling nonsense as she throws her head back.

I groan and kiss her deeply when I start to come, fucking her through her orgasm and mine, and when it's over and I pull out of her, I feel an odd sense of loss.

It seems that Bree does, too, because she whines and clutches at me.

I chuckle, finding it cute, but instead of lying down next to her, I slide down her body, kissing her abdomen, licking into her bellybutton, spreading her thighs with my hands.

"Again?" Her eyes widen.

"Two isn't enough." I kiss her inner thighs, biting down on the sensitive skin, and she cries out.

I wonder how she'd look with my hickeys marring her pale inner thighs, and I start to lick and suck in different spots.

Bree moans, putting her hands in my hair.

"You're teasing me," she whines, and when I look up at her, those pink lips are in a heart-shaped pout.

My heart skips a beat. I've got to bury myself in her so that I won't think about how that pout makes my breath catch in my throat, won't think about how much she affects my soul and not just my body.

Something like panic threatens to overwhelm me, so I press my face against her hot, slick sex, tasting both of us together when I lap at her clit.

Her inner thighs are already trembling.

"It's too much. I can't!" she cries.

"You can." My words come out muffled against her skin.

I slide my middle and ring finger inside of her, pumping in and out, taking my time, tasting her clit, her inner lips, her entrance.

I stimulate her everywhere I can reach, and she's nearly screaming by the time she comes again, pulsing around my fingers.

I thought by now I'd already be half-hard, but I'm not. I'm content just to pleasure her, wiping my mouth with the back of my hand and loving the way her taste lingers on my tongue.

Bree pants as she looks up at me, her hazel eyes blown with lust as she tries to catch her breath.

I lie down next to her, feeling satisfied, and dare I say it? Happy.

I don't think I've ever felt this happy, this content. It's like there's nowhere else in the world I'd rather be.

"At least we're good at something," she mumbles against my chest, nuzzling against me before biting me on the right pec.

I jump, yelping. "Ouch! Okay, shark tooth."

She looks up at me, giggling. "Did you just say shark tooth?"

"Yeah, you know, like in that kid's dinosaur movie."

"It's not shark tooth, you dummy. It's *sharp* tooth." She lets out peals of laughter that are contagious, and I join her.

When she calms down, she snuggles tight against me, pulling the sheets and duvet over both of us.

"We *are* good at this," I answer, but I think she's already asleep because her breath is steady and even against my skin.

Her head is on my chest, and I'm glad she's asleep so she can't feel my heart beating too hard.

That certainly hadn't gone the way I expected it to. My plan was to fuck all of these confused feelings out, channel my anger at her father, at this whole situation. But I don't feel angry at all. It's the opposite.

I stare up at the ceiling, thinking that fear and panic are going to send a cloud of despair over me, but instead, I just feel comfortable and tired. It's nearing daylight, after all, and I have Bree next to me.

I don't think I've ever fallen asleep so quickly in my life.

I'm doomed.

16
———

BREE

It's been a few days since Declan and I had sex. And it was even more confusing than the Vegas trip, to be honest. It was like he was making love to me instead of just fucking me, and I have no idea how to deal with the feelings it brings up.

Now it's Monday, and once again, Declan is out. In fact, this happens every Monday like clockwork.

Maybe this is something I can use to escape. It might be the only way I could get past him.

Gray isn't here on Mondays either, so they might be doing jobs together.

The sisters are almost always home, but often Lara will be in her room and Paige will be out with friends, especially now that she is looking for a place to move out.

Usually on Mondays, I don't see a single family member until dinner, when everyone comes together again, just like they do nearly every night.

They work together, eat together, and live together, and although occasionally I'll see Declan and Gray butt heads, it's not that serious or that often.

I can't imagine living in a household like that. I love my brother Rory, but he also drove me *crazy*, and we often argued while he was living at home. I know he loves me, and we are closer now, but I also know that he prefers to have nothing to do with our family business. I haven't seen him in so long now. Over a year.

My brain keeps telling me to formulate a plan, to run, escape, but my heart is saying something else entirely. My heart is saying that I may be falling in love with Declan Burke.

And what does that say about me? Have I developed some kind of odd Stockholm syndrome? He literally *kidnapped* me and forced me to marry him.

There's something broken inside me, evidently. Because otherwise, who would start falling for their captor?

And deep down, I know that Declan and his family plan to hurt my father. Maybe even kill him.

How can I want to be with a man that wants to harm my father?

He may not be the world's best dad, but he's been there for me, and since Rory moved out and distanced himself from my father and the business, it's just been me and him. He needs me. And without my mom, and my estranged brother, he's all I have.

Declan and his family talk about him like he's some kind of terrible person, akin to a monster. But he loved my mother so deeply, and I believe that he loves me and Rory, too, in his own way. He can't be a monster. Can he?

If I could just get a message to my father, I know that he'd come for me. That'd he'd save me from this place. And even though my feelings about the Burke clan have changed slightly, I still miss my family. Especially while Declan is away.

So, on Tuesday night, when Declan is finally home, it's time to take the first step in my plan.

I arrive at dinner before everyone else, basically because I have nothing else to do. It's not like I get to go out with my girlfriends or visit my brother or anything. I'm just stuck in this house. I spend most of my time either in the bedroom or at the pool. I'm developing a tan from swimming so much in the open air.

I stay mostly quiet at dinner, just forcing a smile when Patrick cracks a joke or Paige talks about the houses she visited that day. Apparently, she has narrowed her choices down to a couple already.

Declan keeps watching me, his brows furrowed.

I stand up before dessert. "I'm not feeling very well. May I be excused?"

I can feel Declan's eyes on me, but it's Patrick that I address.

He nods distractedly, deep in conversation with Gray, before looking up briefly at me. "Go on, sweetheart. I hope you feel better."

Declan stands, too, not asking to be excused, just putting his hand on my lower back, leading me up the stairs.

"What's wrong?" he asks close to my ear as we walk up to the bedroom, and I shake my head.

"Nothing."

He frowns harder, his generous mouth turning down at the corners. "Don't lie to me, Bree."

I huff out a breath. "Why shouldn't I? You lie to me all the time."

"What are you talking about?"

"You say I'm not in a prison," I whisper, sitting down on the edge of the bed. "You say that I'll be well taken care of—"

"And you are," he interrupts. "But yet, you keep sulking."

I bite my tongue at the sharp remark that comes to mind at his choice of words. I have to stay calm, or I'll never be able to convince him to let me talk to my father.

"It's my father's birthday tomorrow." I'm not actually lying. It's true. My father turns fifty-eight tomorrow, and we usually have a big celebration. I wonder if Rory will show up this time, since I won't be there. In fact, I wonder if Rory even knows or cares that I'm not home. Will he help my father save me? Or does he think I brought this upon myself when I refused to follow him out of this life?

I hope they are working together to bring me home.

Except for that pesky part of me that is an absolute fool for Declan Burke. I push that part down, deep inside me so that I can do this.

"Oh." Declan blinks. "Is that all?"

I glare at him. "Well, it's not like I can call him up and tell him happy birthday."

"You can write him a letter, send a card or something." Declan shrugs. "As long as I get to read it, and you don't give out any information, we have no problem getting it to him in time."

My eyes widen. I wasn't expecting that at all. I was expecting maybe a quick phone call from a burner phone. This is so much better.

I throw my arms around him, hugging him tightly, and he chuckles, turning his head to kiss my cheek.

"If I had known a card makes you this happy, I'd have let you send him one a long time ago."

I smile. "You'll have it delivered on time?"

"Today." He smiles, as if he's done some big favor for me. And in a way, I guess he has.

Declan takes me into his office, handing me a sheet of paper and various pens in different colors.

"Just in case you want to draw some balloons or something," he mutters, like I'm a little kid making a card for her dad. It's kind of cute.

I smile. "Thank you."

He nods, leaving the room and giving me my privacy, and I stare down at the blank page for a long time. I'll have to word this carefully.

My father and I have a code. We always have, since I was little, because he was paranoid that anyone would read something important. This code has been engrained in me ever since I learned how to write and even more when I started helping him with the books on business matters.

A different person's name for each day of the week. Thursday is Tony, Saturday is Salvatore, and so on.

I know exactly what to say so that he'll know when to come for me.

Yet for some reason, I have a hard time putting my pen to paper.

What if my father comes and saves me? What happens then? Will my father want blood?

My breath catches in my throat when I imagine something happening to Declan *or* my father. I don't want any of the Burkes to be hurt, but I know my father, and he can be vengeful. Ruthless.

I have to get out of here.

Just because Declan isn't the Irish scourge people made him out to be doesn't mean that I should stay in a forced marriage. Maybe if things were different—maybe if we'd met and fallen in love, maybe if I'd *chosen* this...

I can't think that way. I have to focus on the present,

and on my future, and I'll have no type of future being trapped here with the Burkes.

I draw in a sharp breath and force myself to start to write.

Daidí,

I'm doing okay. I am well taken care of.

I hope you are okay too.

How's Molly? Give her a big cuddle for me and tell her she's a good girl.

There. This will be enough to let him know Monday is the best day.

Are you having a good birthday? How is your back? You need to rest it more often, especially after your injury.

And this will let him know to be careful and bring backup.

Take Molly on a long walk as a surprise from me.

I love you and happy birthday.

Even though being here has felt more like home than I ever felt with my father, I do miss him.

I reread it and sign it.

It's short and sweet and enough to let him know I'll be waiting.

I don't think Declan will have any qualms about delivering it or sending it.

Everything in the note is somewhat true. Except Molly died eighteen months ago from old age.

My palms are sweating, the hair standing up on the nape of my neck.

What if he knows? What if he suspects?

And why do I feel awful about this? Don't I want to be rescued? Because I sure keep thinking I don't need to be.

I am doing the right thing. Right?

I can't overthink this, so I draw a few balloons in the

corner and a big birthday cake on the bottom along with a few hearts, using the multicolored pens that Declan brought me.

Just as I'm finishing up, he knocks lightly on the open door before walking back into the office.

"All done?"

I nod slowly, standing up and handing him the letter.

His eyes scan it quickly, and he glances back up at me.

"I didn't know you had a dog."

"Had her since I was a teenager." I had Molly all my life, a little thing who jumped all over me when I returned home from school or from being out. I do, in fact, miss her. And my father really does have a back injury, so maybe Declan won't think anything is amiss.

He smiles. "That's cute. What kind?"

"Cocker spaniel," I say. "She's an old lady now."

Declan nods, something sympathetic around the corners of his mouth. "I had my own dog, Slick. He was a puppy when I was born."

"Oh?" Guilt washes over me.

"Yeah, he died when I was a teenager," Declan says tightly. "Poison bait."

I swallow hard. "I'm sorry."

"It's okay." Declan shrugs. "I took care of the bastard who did it."

Fear rockets through me.

Would Declan take care of me just as easily as whoever killed his dog? As much as I'm feeling toward Declan lately, I need to remember that he's the Irish scourge, that he has a reputation for brutality.

What will he do to my father if he comes after me?

Part of me wants to lunge forward, take the note out of

Declan's hand, throw it away. But then he'd be suspicious, and I'd never get another shot to get a message out.

"This all seems fine." Declan turns to the door and whistles, putting two fingers in his mouth.

The sound is so loud I wince.

One of the twins, Finn, if I remember correctly, comes to the door, raising his eyebrows.

"Yes, boss?"

"Deliver this to Niall Murphy," he says. "And be quick about it. Bring a reply if he sends one."

Finn looks down at the note, which Declan has slipped into an envelope.

He nods and leaves the room, and Declan and I are left alone.

"Is this your office?" I ask dumbly, wanting to change the subject so I can stop feeling so guilty. I have no reason to feel that way, after all. I am a prisoner here, and everything I'm doing is just to save myself.

Declan nods. "When I was sixteen, Dad gave it to me and moved his office to the end of the hall. The other one was bigger, anyway. Gray has an office downstairs."

"This house has so many rooms," I murmur, looking around the office.

There are books everywhere in the wraparound book-shelf, some of them are law books, but most of them seemed to be autobiographies and fiction—mystery and science fiction, mostly.

I walk over to the bookcase, fingering one of the more well-loved titles.

"You like to read?" Declan asks.

"Sometimes," I agree. "Mostly girl stuff."

He snorts. "And what's girl stuff? I like a good bodice ripper from time to time."

Declan walks up behind me, putting his hand over mine and dragging it to a lower shelf, and sure enough, there's a series of Victorian romances.

"You can't be serious," I mutter, taking one of them out and looking at it, mouth ajar.

It's full-on bodice ripper, like he said, too, with a huge drawn man on the cover wearing a flowy tunic and a woman with heaving bosoms in his arms.

"There's nothing like Victorian era sex," Declan says, almost as if he's defending himself. "I mean, think of all the clothes they had to remove just to do it."

I laugh, turning to look at him, and he's smiling at me. His eyes are so tender.

My heart feels like it might fall out of my stomach.

What have I done?

17

DECLAN

Bree has been in a weird mood ever since I sent that note to her father. She seems nervous, in a way, and I wonder if her and her father have a more strained relationship than I'd thought.

Usually, I'd be suspicious about her sending a message, but it read just like a normal family birthday card.

Nevertheless, Finn knew to make a copy before he left and I plan to read over Niall's reply word for word, to be sure that he's not sending her some kind of plan. I know that a lot of our kind speaks in code, but she'd only mentioned her brother and her dog.

Having my own experience with Slick, I can understand missing your childhood pet. I miss Slick every single day. He was a big American Pitbull, and he had a vicious bark, but he'd never bite a soul unless I ordered him to. He was good with Paige when she was a baby, rolling around on the floor with her.

The day that he'd gotten ahold of that poison bait had been one of the worst days of my life. The day after, when I found out who did it—one of my father's rival's sons—had been the bloodiest.

There's a reason they call me the Irish scourge.

When Finn brings me the reply, just before dinner, it's just a single sheet of paper. I read over it, and it's simple and doesn't seem to contain any plans. I'm still suspicious of Niall, but I honestly can't see any kind of code emerging. I make a copy and leave the office.

I walk into the bedroom. "Your father replied."

Bree jumps at the sound of my voice and freezes where she's been brushing her long, auburn hair.

"Did he?"

I hand her the letter, and she reads it out loud.

"Wean,

I am so glad to hear from you. Just having dinner tomorrow to celebrate my birthday. Thank you so much for your sweet birthday wishes. I miss you so badly.

Molly misses you most of all, though! She howls and barks twice a day, around the same times you used to walk her.

And don't you worry your pretty head about my back. I'm as strong as an ox and twice as mean.

All my love,

Daidí."

Bree's hands are trembling slightly when she clutches the letter to her chest.

"Thank you, Declan," she says in an almost whisper. "This means a lot to me."

Her hazel eyes are wet and full of some emotion I can't quite name when she looks up at me.

I give her a soft smile, running my hand over her hair before taking the brush from her, and start brushing it. She's looking at me in the mirror, almost as if studying me.

"Do I have something on my shirt?" I look down with a frown.

"No," she blurts, looking away and flushing. "It's just that you look handsome today."

I grin. "Thank you, princess. You always look beautiful, too."

I lean down to kiss the crown of her head, and there's a little pep in my step as I walk downstairs for dinner.

Bree follows shortly, wearing a green shift dress that shows off her hazel eyes. She sits next to me, giving me a small smile.

We're the only ones at the table.

"I guess everyone else is late for dinner," I comment, and Bree nods, seeming almost shy.

What's going on with her? Maybe she's just overwhelmed by finally getting to communicate with her family.

My father and Gray come down next, chatting in hushed tones about something, and I frown as Paige and Lara trail in, as well.

"What's going on?" I ask in a low voice when my father sits at the head of the table, next to me.

"After dinner," my father barks, and I want to roll my eyes, but I know better.

My father hates talking about business at the table or talking about anything remotely negative. Dinner time is family time, and he's always enforced that.

"Fine," I mutter, and take Bree's hand under the table.

She squeezes it, and my heart skips in my chest.

I've really got to deal with these growing feelings for her, but if I'm honest with myself, I don't know how to. Every part of me wants her, all the time, wants her happy and safe and....

Loved.

I've been loath to even think about those three little words, but it's getting more and more serious, and it's not like I can talk to Gray or our father about it. Hell, even if I talked to Paige and Lara, they'd just blab to Bree. I certainly don't want her to know that I have feelings for her.

What if she doesn't feel the same way?

I look over at her, but she's focused on Paige, chatting idly about this house she fell in love with. A brownstone house with four rooms and a gym in the basement.

"Maybe now I can have that chihuahua I always wanted." She is bouncing on her seat.

I squeeze Bree's hand. "Did you know Bree has a dog?"

Bree freezes, stiffening up, and I pat her thigh.

"Molly," she says quietly. "She's my old lady."

"How old?" Gray asks. "Lara had a cat once that I swear was almost as old as she was when it died."

Lara laughs. "Poor thing. He ended up getting hit by a car, too. Didn't even die of natural causes."

"And he'd lost all his hair. He looked like one of those weird Sphynx cats." Paige giggles.

"Hey, leave Jack alone," my father interjects. "He was a good cat."

"Da used to *hate* cats," Paige explains, and just like that, Bree seems to have been brought out of her strange mood.

It makes sense that she just misses her family, so I have to cut her some slack.

"Yeah, he told me if I brought home another stray cat, he'd make me sleep in the basement with it," Lara says with a laugh.

"And he did, too." Gray chuckles.

I laugh along with them, and Bree's smiling. It makes me happy.

"Molly's almost seventeen," Bree tells us. "But I'd rather hear the story about Jack."

"Jack be Nimble, we called him," my father says, sounding sentimental. "He used to scratch all over the furniture, but he would also bring me my slippers."

"A cat?" Bree's mouth hangs open before she shakes her head. "There's no way a cat brought your slippers."

Lara brings out her phone, showing Bree a series of pictures of Jack carrying my father's slippers, up until he was old and hairless.

"That's so crazy," Bree mutters. "I didn't even know cats could do tricks."

"Oh, he expected a piece of steak after each time," my father says, chuckling. "And then he started bringing them to me at all times of day, not just after dinner, just to get that treat."

"I miss him," Paige whines. "I don't know why you wouldn't let me get a chihuahua. Maybe when I move, I can get one."

"He'd be a little ankle-biter," my father says. "No more pets in the house. Feel free in yours, but don't bring him here."

"But we have such a big yard here!" Paige complains.

Gray frowns. "If you bring your dog here, I'm getting my own dog."

My father throws up his hands, but he's still smiling. "It's like I've still got a bunch of kids in the house."

After we sober a bit and dessert is on the table, my father clears his throat, clinking his fork against his glass to get our attention.

"I need a family meeting after dinner," he says. "We have some business to discuss."

Bree starts to stand up and excuse herself, but I take her hand.

"You're part of this family now, too," I whisper, and she sits back down.

"Should we just talk over dessert?" Gray asks.

Da sighs. "You know I hate business at the dinner table, but fine, just for tonight."

Bree sits quietly while Gray starts to talk.

"I know this subject might be a little sensitive given our company," Gray starts, giving Bree a side look. "But Niall Murphy has intercepted yet another of our shipments."

Lara groans. "Isn't this the third one this month?"

Gray nods. "Exactly. So, I think, personally, that it's time to take him down."

I can't help looking over at Bree, and her hazel eyes are wide and wet.

"May I be excused?" Her voice breaks, but my father shakes his head.

"No, Bree. You need to hear this."

She stands up, knocking her chair over as she does so.

Fuck. I wish that my father and Gray had waited to bring this up.

Bree is still fragile from getting the letter from her father, from missing his birthday. But it's too late now.

"Why are you even doing this? Why did you all kidnap me to mess with my father? What is the big *deal*? You're just rivals? So what? My father has half a dozen rivals in this city."

"I wish it were that we were just rivals," my father murmurs. "Sit down, *a'stor*. Listen to the story, and you'll see that there's more than meets the eye."

"What does that even mean?"

I look over at Bree.

Could she be innocent? She lives with the man. There is no way she doesn't know, is there?

Deep down I could avoid falling for her because I could see her as a bit of a monster. Not as much as her father, of course, but still.

But what if I'm wrong?

Because if she doesn't know, she's innocent, and in her eyes, *we're* the monsters.

"Please stay," I tell her, but she storms out of the room.

I stand up quickly and follow her, catching her at the base of the stairs and grabbing her by her elbow.

"Don't touch me," she hisses, and tears roll down her cheeks, each slicing a piece of my heart. "I can't sit here and listen to your plans to kill my father."

"You don't understand," I say fiercely. "You don't understand what he's done."

"What could he possibly have done? What could he have done that is so bad that makes you want to take him away from me?"

I look down at her wet cheeks, the way her mouth is parted and turned down at the corners. I just want to take her into my arms and comfort her. But I can't. She has to know the truth.

She told me that her mother left, and taking away her father too does seem cruel—or it would, if he hadn't done the things he did.

Bree needs to know what kind of man her father is.

"Go and get yourself together." I tilt my chin up the stairs. "Then meet us downstairs, in the living room. We'll be waiting."

Her bottom lip trembles as she glares up at me. "You can't make me listen to this."

"I can. I can and I will, because you need to know, so

just listen to me, Bree, okay?" There's just a note of a pleading edge to my voice.

She will listen to the truth, one way or another. But I really don't want to have to tie her to the recliner.

Bree swallows hard and stalks up the stairs.

I sigh, going back into the dining room.

My father looks at me expectantly.

"She's coming downstairs in a few minutes. I told her we'd meet her in the living room." I pause, looking him right in the eyes. "I want you to tell her everything."

"Everything? Even—" Gray starts, but my father holds up a hand to stop him.

"All right, son. I'll tell her everything. If you're sure."

"I'm sure. She needs to understand."

Gray frowns, and Paige's eyes are filled with tears. Lara shoulders slump.

I think everyone, even Gray, hates that we have to tell her this.

Lara puts an arm around our baby sister, and Paige sobs into her shoulder before pulling away.

"Don't break down, *a'stor*," my father warns. "This isn't our burden. It's hers."

"It's ours, too," Lara interjects. "But we'll try to keep it together."

My father nods.

"I'll make sure she's there," I grumble, and walk upstairs, waiting outside the bedroom door.

Strange, gagging noises reach me. Is she throwing up?

My heart drops.

I hate this for her. I really do. If I was told my father did the things Niall Murphy did... well, I'd be devastated.

The door swings open, and Bree stands there, her makeup washed off, her eyes red and puffy.

"I'm ready," she rasps, and I put my hand on the small of her back and lead her down the stairs.

I guess I really must care for her, because I wish I could shoulder all her pain, make it so she never finds out about this, about what a monster her father really is.

I wish I could take her pain and make it mine, and what is that if it isn't love?

18

BREE

Walking into the living room, Declan's hand on my lower back feels half like support and half like he's forcing me forward. I'm still so conflicted about my feelings for him and the rest of the Burkes, and now I'm terrified of what they're going to say.

I know that my father is a criminal. Hell, so am I, just based on how I've kept up the books.

Declan and Patrick, Gray and Lara, even Paige—they're all in the life too. So, why is it that my father is so hated?

I can't imagine it being anything but petty issues with shipments or something like that—but what if it's worse? What if it's something.... unforgivable?

The very fact that I'm worried about it means that I'm aware my father is capable of it. I was just never forced to face that fact.

I keep my tears at bay, walking downstairs, and the Burke family seems to have been waiting for me.

Paige and Lara share the big chair in the corner, cuddled up together. Paige looks upset, tucked into her older sister's body. Patrick sits in the recliner, and Gray is on the couch, his blue eyes downcast, which is weird. Declan sits next to Gray, leaving me on the other end of the couch, watching Patrick.

Patrick keeps my gaze, not looking away.

"This is a long story, *a'stor*, so sit tight," he drawls.

I nod, keeping eye contact even as tears threaten at the backs of my eyes.

Declan keeps his hand on my back, rubbing small, comforting circles.

"I guess it starts back in Ireland when the Burke clan started up. My father and my grandfather before me lived in Dublin, and it wasn't until I took my young wife..." His voice falters, and he takes a deep breath. "The mother of my children, of course, to America, that the trouble started."

I frown. I know for a fact that my father isn't first generation Irish, so the Burkes are older than the Murphy clan.

From the way my father talked about them, I guess I thought that the Murphys were more established than the Burkes.

But just that is no reason to hate my father. I assume there's more.

"The Burke clan started up in this city much like we had in Dublin," Patrick continued. "I'm not saying that we were saints, God would strike me down if I did. But we stayed away from two things: kids and women. I even had cousins that dabbled in prostitution, but when it became forceful, I forced them to stop... with any means necessary."

I gulped.

Patrick Burke is a dangerous man, especially if he went after his own cousins for prostitution.

"My father has never run girls," I say, and Patrick raises an eyebrow, smiling bitterly.

"Is that so, now?"

I frown, standing my ground. "He's never brought any girls around the house, and I've been there for several shipments."

"Shipments he stole from us?" Gray asks, and Patrick gives him a hard stare.

"It's not the time, Gray."

Gray hangs his head, and puts his hands in his lap, seemingly chagrined.

"Your father runs *young* girls," Declan murmurs. "Underage. I recently spoke to one of them, and we're trying to help them get out."

I gasp. "You're lying."

But some part of me knows that he's not. There's money coming into the household that shouldn't be, that isn't explained by guns or drugs. But young girls? Underage?

I can't believe it. Don't want to believe my father would stoop so low.

"I wish I was, princess." Declan brushes a tear I didn't know was running down my cheek.

"Maybe he fell in with the wrong people," I say shakily. "Maybe—"

"He runs it," Gray says flatly. "He's been running it for years. We've kept it under control, trying to intercept shipments of women, but we can't be everywhere all the time."

I look at Gray, and then Patrick, and then Declan. All of them are stone-faced, serious. They are not gloating. Not having fun with this.

They're not lying to me.

I take in another shaking breath. "There's more, isn't there?"

Declan puts an arm around me, drawing me close.

Patrick squeezes his eyes shut and then opens them

again, and when he does, there are tears in his piercing gray eyes.

"I wish that that were the end, *a'stor*," he utters, and I find my heart going out to him.

I don't even know what he's going to say, I couldn't predict it if I tried, but I can see the pain lining his face.

Paige starts to sob softly, and Lara strokes her hair.

Even Gray looks down, his shoulders slumped. He runs his hand through his head and the longer hair on top gets a bit disheveled.

"My wife was in a car accident," Patrick starts, his voice raspy and gruff. "Maureen." He gestures to a picture of a gorgeous brunette hanging on the wall, her head thrown back as she swung a baby around.

"That's me," Gray says roughly, and I smile a little.

"She's very beautiful."

"Was," Declan bites out.

"When we found out that Niall was running young girls, letting God knows what happen to them, we retaliated. There were losses on both sides," Patrick says.

"I'm so sorry," I gasp.

Patrick holds up his hand. "Save your sorrys, *a'stor*. You'll need them for the end."

Declan took in a shaky breath, rubbing his hand across his face.

"After the first few battles, we thought we'd made a mark. We thought that your father would stop stealing our shipments, trying to recruit our men. We thought for sure that he'd stop running girls. And I suppose he did, for a few years." Patrick pauses and looks right at me. "I believe it was around the time you were a child."

I nod. I know that my father did take a break from crime for a while after my mother left, that he'd stayed home with me a lot, but I didn't know exactly why. I thought he was just grieving my mother leaving.

"Maureen was on her way to the market," Patrick starts, and then a sob hitches in his chest and he stops, taking in deep breaths to get himself together.

Part of me wants to reach across and take his hand, but I don't. My shoulders are stiff. It's like I'm frozen solid. I can't feel anything—not the tears running down my face, not fear or panic or sadness. Nothing.

I'm just numb.

It almost feels like I'm watching this scene from outside my body, as if I'm floating somewhere on the ceiling and watching Patrick break down.

"I'll do it, Da." Declan reaches across to pat his father on the back, and Patrick nods.

Declan turns to me, and there's such pain on his face it would tear me in two, if I wasn't somewhere on the ceiling watching. If I was back in my body, this would hurt.

"My mother was on the way to get groceries. We didn't have Marisol before Ma passed. She did all the cooking, all traditional, shepherd's pies and soda bread, things like that. She loved cooking for us." Declan pauses and pinches the bridge of his nose with his fingers, as if he's trying to stop tears.

His eyes are wet, anyway. "She never made it there."

"She was t-boned by a Rolls Royce," Gray states. "You know anyone who drives a Rolls?"

I frown. "No."

But a memory comes to my mind. A fleeting one. And I try to grab it. It's...

"My father..." I gasp. "He used to own one, years ago."

"Want to take a guess why he got rid of it?" Declan asks, bitterness clear in his voice.

"No. No, that can't be." I shake my head, and suddenly I'm slammed back into my body, and the world is full of emotional pain. "He wouldn't."

"He did, *a'stor*," Patrick whispers, as gently as he can. "There was video evidence, but we could never see his face. We knew that he'd arranged it, even if he hadn't done it himself. The man behind the wheel drove away, left Maureen there, bleeding to death in a car that, after capsizing a few times, landed wheels up but was completely destroyed." Patrick sobs now, dropping his head into his hands. "We couldn't even have an open casket."

"Why?" I whisper. "Why would he do that?"

"He hates us." Gray sounds almost frustrated, as if it should be simple. Obvious. "He wants what we have, and he's been trying to get it for decades."

"But your *mother*?" I gasp, and suddenly, I can't *breathe*.

I bolt upright and then stand, pacing around the room and wheezing, trying to breathe through what feels like a pinhole in my throat. "Innocent girls... *children*..."

I want to scream they are lying, but memories flow of things I hadn't noticed before, and the picture forming in my head is a dark one.

Oh god. My father is every bit of the monster that the Burkes think he is.

Paige stands, coming to me and putting her arms around me, and I sob against her shoulder, and she sobs against mine, both of us coming away with wet shirts.

"It's not your fault, Bree," she whimpers. "You didn't know."

"I'm a Murphy," I almost spit my name, looking over at Declan with tears streaming down my face. "How difficult it must have been to marry me. How disgusted you must have been."

Declan looks shocked, his eyebrows raised. He stands up, frowning. "No, princess. I'd never be disgusted by you."

He tries to put his arms around me, but I wrench away, bolting for the stairs.

Declan follows, but I slam the bedroom door in his face, panting, trying to get air that doesn't seem to be coming into my lungs.

"You know I can open the door," he warns, but I brace my back against the closed door, squeezing my eyes shut against the burn of tears.

"Please don't," I whimper. "If you ever cared about me, *don't.*"

"Bree," he starts, and then he's quiet for a moment. "I'll be right outside when you need me."

Something slides down the door.

Is he actually just sitting on the bedroom floor in front of the door?

It doesn't matter. I can't come out. If I could, I'd climb out one of these windows, and if I didn't fall to my death I'd move far, far away. Away from Declan, who deserves better than the daughter of a monster. Away from the Burkes, who deserve better than such a stupid woman for their family member.

Away from my father, the monster himself.

Underage girls... sex trafficking... the death of a mother...

He's responsible for all of it. And if I'm honest with myself, I know the sex trafficking is still going on. Ever since he bought that strip club, there's been more money coming in than makes sense.

"Will you let Lara in?" Declan asks through the door, jolting me out of my thoughts. "I just want to make sure you're okay."

"Okay," I sniffle in a small voice. "Just Lara."

Paige would be too much right now, and Gray barely tolerates me. I can't even look at Declan, knowing what my father has done to his mother.

That Rolls Royce hadn't been traded like my father said. It had been covered with Burke blood.

My stomach churns, and I run for the toilet, retching, as Lara enters the room.

She rushes to me, holding back my hair as I throw up what's left of my dinner.

"I'm so sorry you had to find out this way," she murmurs. "Especially just after you wished him a happy birthday."

I freeze.

God, I hadn't even considered that. I've sicced my father on the Burkes, and they didn't do anything wrong. Kidnapping me is the *least* they could do after what Niall did to them.

And considering who he is, the lies he hid from me, I think the Burkes actually saved me.

I'm having a hard time even thinking of him as my father anymore, and now I'm wondering what else he lied about.

Did my mom really leave? What made my sweet mother run from him and leave me and my brother behind? Could he have done something to scare her away?

Have I been living a lie my entire life?

I throw up once more before my belly is empty, and Lara cleans my face with a cold towel and helps me sit back against a wall.

"Just give me a sec," she says. "I'll deal with Declan to keep him away."

I nod, not trusting myself to speak.

She leaves for a minute, and I can tell he is not happy.

"She needs me!"

"She needs *time*, Declan."

Eventually, the bedroom door closes, and she comes back and leads me to bed, pulling the covers over me.

Lara's right. I need time. I need time to try and figure out how to warn them that my father is coming. If he was willing to kill their mother over a turf war, God knows what he'll do to Declan for kidnapping me.

And I don't think I can think about my father killing Declan. The man I'm falling for. The man who must think I'm as much of a monster as my father.

And he's right. I've ruined everything. I used to think of myself as a princess, being captured and waiting in my tower for someone to save me. But now I realize they took me away from a huge lie, a toxic situation that I never would have known I was in.

Or maybe I'm not the princess at all.

Maybe I'm the dragon.

19

DECLAN

I SPEND THE NIGHT IN THE GUEST ROOM, AND IT'S ALL I can do not to go to Bree in the middle of the night.

I don't sleep.

It's not her fault that her father is the way he is. It's not her fault that she didn't know.

God, I think I am in love with her.

What am I going to do? She probably hates me for telling her what her father has done, probably hates me for kidnapping her.... Do I even deserve to want her love back?

The next morning, she isn't at breakfast when I go down, and I stand up from the table, huffing out a breath.

Lara reaches up and touches my arm. "Don't."

"I have to check on her." I need to make sure she is okay.

"I'll do it."

"But I need to see her."

"You don't need to see her. You *want* to see her. She doesn't want to see you."

I let out a long breath. "But... she needs to know that I'm thinking about her."

"She knows." Lara pats my hand reassuringly and walks

up the stairs. I watch her go for a moment and then start to pace around the kitchen.

"I'm coming with you and Gray next week," my father's voice comes from the open kitchen.

I glance over to see him eating a piece of bacon, walking into the dining room.

"You're coming with us?" I ask, surprised and for once, distracted from thinking about Bree.

He nods. "It's time I made an appearance."

My father isn't one of those bosses who makes everyone do his dirty work. He likes to be with his men, to be in just as much danger as he's putting them through. I respect him for that.

"Are you sure?" It's been a while since Da has been in the shit, as we call it, and he nods.

"I'm sure. Monday."

We always do our visits on Mondays, so I'm not surprised.

"All right, Da."

"How's your girl?" he asks with a twinkle in his eye.

I sigh. "I don't know."

"She's got a lot to think about, boyo. Don't push too hard." He claps me on the back as he walks away, back into the kitchen.

Marisol laughs at something he says.

I smile a little. I've always thought that Da and Marisol should start dating, since she's single and childless, but I guess that'll never happen.

He's still married to Ma, in his heart, and I can't blame him for that.

They'd been so in love.

I still remember a day when they'd been dancing. Ma giggled as Da swept her off her feet, kissing her throat, and little me stood in the doorway, watching, covering my mouth with my hand.

I wanted to laugh. I wanted to cry, and I wasn't sure why.

Now I know what that feeling was.

Longing.

I'd wanted, even at six years old, what my parents had. I'd wanted someone to dance with in the kitchen, someone to come home to.

And now that I had a taste of it, of what it could be, I want it even more. Want *her* even more.

But now, after all the blood that's on my hands, after being the Irish scourge for most of my life—do I even deserve a woman like Bree?

Lara comes back downstairs, and I instantly go to her, meeting her at the base of the staircase.

"She's going to be okay." She pats my shoulder. "But you've got to give her some more space, Declan."

"I don't know if I can do that," I admit, frowning. "I need to see her."

Lara smiles. "I guess maybe you're not so against the idea of marriage anymore?"

I sigh. "Just... call me if she needs me," I say, not wanting to get into it with my sister, of all people.

I need to talk to *someone*, but it can't be Lara. She'll tell Paige, and Paige will tell *everybody*.

Bree doesn't come down for dinner that night, and all of us are a little subdued after last night's conversation.

When I excuse myself from the table, I go right to the bedroom, feeling silly for knocking on my own bedroom door.

"Yes?" Bree calls.

"Can I come in?"

She pauses, and for a moment I think she won't let me in, and my heart drops.

Then the door swings open, and she stands there in a fluffy pink bathrobe, her eyes puffy and red-rimmed.

"Oh, princess," I murmur, walking inside, and she steps back as if she doesn't want me to touch her.

I put my hands up in defense. "I just wanted to see you. I can leave if you want."

"Don't want you to leave," she mumbles, climbing back into bed.

"You need to eat something," I say gently. "Can I get you some soup from downstairs? It's cream of chicken with wild rice, Marisol's specialty."

"I don't want to eat."

"I know, baby, but you have to." I sit on the edge of the bed and when I reach out to smooth the baby hairs from her face, she wrenches away.

"How can you stand to touch me?" She draws in a ragged breath. "How can you stand to even look at me?"

"Bree, you're not your father."

"I have his blood," she says stubbornly. "I have his eyes, his stupid chin." She rubs at her face, as if wanting to rub away the resemblance, which is remarkable.

I've never met her brother, Rory, but if he looks as much like his father, they'd probably look like twins.

"You don't have his black heart." I climb into bed with her, pulling her into my arms even as she protests. Eventually, she relaxes against me, her back against my chest, her baby hairs tickling my jawline.

I don't say another word, but she falls asleep. If her night was anything like mine, she needs it.

With her body next to mine, I can relax for the first time since dinner last night.

Soon, I drift off too, and we sleep in each other's arms.

***

Monday seems to come quickly. Bree is still a little quiet, but she's better, engaging with Paige and Lara, almost back to normal. I think she's finally accepted her role here, that she's part of the family.

As much as I hadn't wanted it at first, I have to admit that I'm over the moon about it now. I want Bree to be a part of my life, and I'm trying to come to terms with that.

I knock on Gray's door, and he groans in response. I raise an eyebrow, grinning.

Is there a girl in there?

I throw open the door and Gray's alone, looking pale and drawn on his bed.

"What's wrong with you?"

"I had gas station sushi last night after a pitcher of beer," he says, gagging, and running to the bathroom.

I laugh out loud. "You should sit this one out, brother."

He throws me a thumbs up, hunched over the toilet, and I walk to my father's office, knowing he'll already be up and ready to go.

I'm wearing a suit because we have a few people to offer protection to today.

Da is in his office, fully dressed and standing behind his desk.

"Gray is... under the weather."

Da laughs. "I knew he would be. He and Cillian went out last night."

I chuckle. My friend can really raise hell, so I'm not surprised. I am, I guess, a little surprised that Gray went along with it, but he's been letting loose a little lately.

And it's a good thing too because he needs it.

"It's good to see him letting his hair down," Da says, and I nod.

We head out in my father's Escalade, driving to the south side to collect some payments. All goes well and everyone is happy—or alternately, terrified—to see my father out and about.

"It's been too long," Jimmy Connor says as we approach one of our warehouses. He's got a new shipment of both dust and guns, and he wants us to do our usual check.

"It has." Da pulls Jimmy into a quick hug.

Jimmy beams at him.

All of my father's men worship him like a hero, and I can't say I'm much different.

I think about Bree, and my heart goes out to her. My father has done some things neither of us are proud of, but deep down, I know that he's a good man. Bree cannot think the same about her father, not anymore.

I feel a little guilty for taking that blissful ignorance away from her, but it had to be done. She won't talk about it, instead chatting about idle things, and I can understand that she needs more time to process.

We haven't made love since that first night it went from fucking to more, and I don't want to push her, but I'm starting to get sexually frustrated having her near naked in my bed every night.

But for her, I'll wait as long as it takes.

I must be staring off into space because Jimmy snaps his fingers in front of my eyes.

I blink. "Shit. Sorry."

"He was thinking about that bonny new wife of his," Da says with a low chuckle.

"No, I wasn't," I blurt, although he's caught me red-handed.

"You were," Jimmy pipes in, laughing. "That's fair enough. I was at the wedding, and she's a real looker."

My cheeks start to feel hot, and I hate it. I don't blush or get embarrassed easily, but something about talking about Bree like she's really my wife...

"What do you think about her?" Jimmy asks. "Is everything going okay?"

"Fine," I mutter.

My father's looking at me as if he has something to say. I finally roll my eyes and look at him.

"What is it, Da?"

"You have feelings for your wife."

I scoff. "Is that so crazy?"

"Nah." He shakes his head. "She's a good girl. Bonny but also sweet, and that's important."

"You're not upset?"

"That you have feelings for your own wife?" His eyes widen. "Of course not."

"But she's a Murphy."

"Having Murphy blood doesn't make you a monster," he points out. "It's the heart that does that, and hers is as white as his is black."

We make our way to the crates and shipments.

Before we can crack even the first one open, my father stops me, holding up his hand to his mouth to make sure I'm quiet.

I freeze, holding the crowbar, and Jimmy does, too, looking to where my father's gaze is, staring at the front door.

Surely, no one would try to come in the fron—

Gunshots ring out, and I yelp and hit the deck.

Jimmy and my father follow suit, bringing out their guns as I chuck the crowbar and draw my own.

The crowbar hits a man square in the eye, and I would snicker if I wasn't currently afraid for my life.

"Stay down, boyo!" Da yells, but I'm already up and shooting.

Shooting, Finn comes in from the back where he was waiting for us.

A bullet whizzes by my ear as I keep shooting, and then I realize that the men are... retreating?

There's about four of them, so it's a fair fight, and they've already shot through half the windows in the warehouse. Dust is pouring out of a couple of crates where they've been shot.

Da takes a shot at the man who fired first and catches him right between the eyes.

The other men curse and scramble, into a minivan that takes off just as Jimmy and Finn run after them, shooting.

I stand up. "Jesus crow."

The world tilts around me for a second, probably from the adrenaline. I look at Da to see how he is and his face is pale as he looks at me.

"You're hit," he says quietly.

"What?" I look down at my chest is covered in blood. The world tilts around me again, and I brace myself up against the crate.

"Finn!" Da screams, and then I go down.

20

BREE

How could I be so dumb? So blind.

My dad will come any moment now. I just know it. I just hope Declan and Patrick aren't back by then.

And I'm not sure what I'll do when he comes. I don't want to live with a monster, but I don't want him to take his revenge on the Burkes. I can't be the reason they are hurt. Or worse.

God. It crushes me just thinking about something happening to anyone in this family, but especially Declan. Because I don't think I can deny for much longer that I love him.

Men yelling and a commotion make me run downstairs.

Is this my father coming now? Oh, lord, please no.

As my eyes land on the front door, I freeze in my steps, and my heart stops in my chest as soon as see him.

Declan.

He is being carried inside and he is leaving a trail of blood behind him.

No.

No, no, no, no, no.

This is all my fault.

He is not moving. Why is he not moving? He can't be dead, can he?

My feet start moving of their own accord and a keen sound surrounds me before I realize it's me. I'm screaming, my heart shattering as I go because I did this.

I killed Declan.

***

HE STILL HASN'T WOKEN UP.

The family doctor has come and gone after working hard to save his life.

He's in our bed, resting, and I refuse to leave his side, as do his father and brother.

His eyes flutter open and he croaks out, "What happened?"

Tears start running down my face. Thank god he is awake. But how can I look him in the eye, knowing I caused this to the man I love?

"You got shot, boyo." Patrick helps him sit up. "Doc was able to take the bullet out and fix you up. It was a close call for a second there."

Declan winces when he adjusts his position and I want to rush to him, but I'm the one who did this to him, so do I even deserve to be here?

"Sorry." He looks at his hand on his lap since the other is closely wrapped around his chest to prevent movement.

Patrick frowns. "Sorry for what, son? You were right in the line of fire."

"Who was it?" Declan looks up at his dad. He is ready to take on the world, even if he was just in death's door.

"Callum Murphy."

My breath leaves me. I knew I was responsible for this, but hearing the confirmation just about destroys me.

My father really is a monster. He could have chosen to save me, to come get me. Instead, he used my information to try and kill these people.

And I share his blood. I did this. I'm just as much of a monster as him.

"Niall's cousin," Declan's shocked voice pulls me out of my head. "How the hell would the Murphys know we were there?"

Patrick shrugs. "Probably came to steal another one of our shipments."

Declan frowns, and I want the earth to swallow me whole.

His eyes find me, and his face softens. "Hey, it's okay. I'm all right, princess."

I sniffle, rubbing at my eyes with the back of my hand.

"I'm sorry," I blurt out. Because I am. So sorry. I could die for him, and he almost died because of me.

He frowns. "What are you sorry for? You were the one shooting at me."

"I... I..." I can't tell them what I did. They'll kill me. And though I may deserve it, I need to make sure he recovers fully. "It's my family's fault. So, I feel the need to apologize for them." I hate myself.

He smiles. "You're a Burke now, so no apologizing needed."

Patrick kisses Declan on the forehead. "I'll leave you two alone. You need to rest, boyo. So, make sure you do."

He lays a hand on my shoulder and squeezes before he leaves.

Does he know?

Oh god. What will happen if they ever find out the truth?

I HAVEN'T LEFT DECLAN'S SIDE OVER THE PAST COUPLE of weeks. He is almost back to normal but still tender in places.

I'm kneeling by him as he looks down at me. God, I want him. I miss his body so much!

These weeks have been good for us to get to know each other a bit better, but we haven't had sex in weeks.

"Bree," he starts, and his voice comes out hoarse.

I look up at him with hungry eyes and put my hands on his thighs.

"Let me take care of you," I murmur, and raise my hands to his belt buckle.

He lets out a long, shaking breath. "Thought you'd never ask."

I smile, hungry as I look at Declan, as he strains against his slacks. I've removed his shirt in order to see if the wound still needs any dressing. It doesn't.

And now he's sitting there shirtless, his abdomen rock hard.

I touch him there, and he trembles, grinning down at me.

"Don't tease," he groans, and I grin back.

"Wouldn't dream of it."

I unbuckle his belt and unbutton his pants, reaching inside to free him from the fabric, and he bounces forth, long and thick. I think about how heavy he'd feel in my mouth.

My mouth starts to water.

I pump him slowly to be sure he's at full mast, and Declan lets out a low growl. He puts his hand on my head, gathering my hair into a ponytail and yanking it so I look at him.

"I said, don't tease," he warns.

I lick my lips, feeling the delicious sting as he tugs my hair. Pleasure shoots through me.

Finally, he releases me, and I slowly take him into my mouth, not teasing but wanting to do a good job.

He's big, after all, and I'm probably going to gag.

He chokes out a moan when I dip my head and take him in further, nearly choking but managing only to gag a little, tears streaming down my face.

He rolls his hips up, fucking my throat, and I let him, putting my hands on his thighs for purchase.

"Oh, fuck," he manages. "You look so pretty with your mouth full of my cock."

Pleasure settles in my lower abdomen, and I take him deeper, bobbing my head up and down, letting my saliva coat him and make the glide easier.

His breath starts to hitch after just a few strokes, and he yanks at my hair again, pulling me off him with a popping sound.

I pout. "You taste so good."

"Want to come inside you," he mutters, still holding my hair. "Hands and knees."

I can't comply fast enough.

He bunches my dress around my hips as I face away from him, lowering my panties to my ankles.

This is going to be rough and dirty, and I, for one, love it. I need something to take my mind off my guilt, my feelings for him, this mess with my father, and this is the perfect distraction.

I stop thinking when Declan rams inside me, no hesitation, and at first, it's a tight stretch but I'm already wet just from sucking him off.

He slides in and out of me, grunting, rough and with no rhythm, but I'm reaching an orgasm quickly.

"God," I cry. "I'm going to come, Declan, please, faster. Harder."

He does exactly what I say, fucking me hard and fast and when I drop my head to my folded hands, he grabs my hair again, yanking. The pinch mixed with the pleasure he's giving me makes my eyes roll back in my head.

"Want you loud for me. Let the world know who's fucking you this good."

"Oh, god," I gasp. "You are, Declan. Declan!" I yell his name when I start to come, and he groans, dropping my hair and taking hold of my hips to brutally thrust into me.

God, I *love* it when he's like this, when he's rough and fast and dirty, and I cry out when I start to come again.

He stills inside of me when he comes, and I don't want him to pull out.

I thrust back against him, and he chuckles.

"Not done yet, princess?"

"Want to come again," I whimper. "Just one more, Declan, please."

Declan huffs out a breath.

"Greedy, slutty baby," he croons, and his words make my stomach clench with need.

"Only for you," I tell him, rocking my hips back against him as he starts to move again.

Declan reaches around us to finger my clit, and I come again almost immediately, stars appearing behind my eyes.

He slowly pulls out of me, and I whine, collapsing on the floor.

He chuckles. "Look at you."

I roll over, hiding my face in my hands, but he takes them away.

"You look gorgeous all fucked out," he whispers, and I moan softly as the aftershocks of my orgasms rush through me.

"Let's go take a shower," he suggests, smiling softly and helping me up.

I stumble on shaky legs, but we manage to make our way to the bedroom and then the shower.

I pull the dress off, feeling sore in the most delicious way, but for some reason, I'm almost embarrassed.

I've had some hot sex with Declan, but I've never been that wanton about wanting it.

He doesn't seem ashamed or disgusted, though, smiling and helping me wash my hair as his half-erection bounces against my hip.

Soon, he's taking me again in the shower, bending me over in front of him and holding one leg up on his good side.

I come another time before he's finished, and he kisses along the back of my neck, showering me off again.

"I'd be able to hate you a lot more if the sex wasn't so good," I tell him after we're out of the shower and he's brushing my hair.

It's become sort of a tradition for us, the hair brushing. It makes me feel safe and loved in a way I've never felt, so I don't complain.

Declan snorts out a laugh. "Ain't that the truth."

It dawns on me when he sets the brush down and plops down in bed, his hair falling over his blue eyes as he watches me fondly.

I really am in love with him.

It's not just that I'm falling or that I'm developing feelings—I've actually fallen in love with him. And it's not Stockholm syndrome like I thought before, it can't be. It's more like... he saved me. He saved me from a monster I didn't even know was imprisoning me.

Declan is my knight in shining armor and for the longest time, I thought he was my warden.

I swallow hard.

I can't be in love with a man who would probably be disgusted I felt this way. He must hate me for who I am, for having my father's blood, even though he'd said that he didn't.

How could he be happy married to the daughter of his mother's killer? And worse. Now I've betrayed him. Sicced my father on him, even if that was never my intention.

What am I going to do? It's not like I can come clean, because God knows what Patrick would do to me. I've become the enemy just by virtue of wanting to get out.

I don't know what to do. I don't know how to handle this.

21

———

BREE

"Bree?" Declan calls, and I look at him, surprised. "What are you thinking about?"

"Nothing." I crawl into bed with him and put my head on his chest.

"You were thinking something." He cups my chin in his hand and tilts my head up. He's frowning, and I know I have to say something.

I swallow hard. "I'm just worried about you. You were shot not long ago and—"

"It's nothing." His face softens. "Almost healed."

"You almost died," I complain, my heart racing.

I almost lost him. It would have killed me.

"I'm fine, *a ghra mo chroi*," he murmurs, wrapping his good arm around me. "Almost fully healed."

He's right. But what won't heal is the fact that I was the one to get him shot by sending a message to my father. I had no idea that he would attack Declan and his men. His letter made me think he was coming to rescue me.

I'm still wrapping my head around what an awful

monster my father is, but I never thought he'd rather leave me here to go after them.

I'm being treated well, and most of me doesn't ever want to leave, but my father doesn't know that. For all he knows I'm being tortured, daily, and it hurts to think that he doesn't care beyond what it looks like for his image in the clan.

"Everything's going to be all right," Declan assures me, but he doesn't know what I've done.

I came from a monster, and maybe he's turned me into one, too.

My FATHER STANDS OVER ME, SHAKING MY SHOULDER.

"It's time to go, Bree," he says in a low tone, nearly whispering, and I look over to see Declan, sleeping soundly beside me.

I wrench away from my father. "No. I'm not going anywhere with you," I hiss. "And If you don't want a bullet in your throat, you should leave."

"What's wrong with you? You've become a Burke now?"

I tremble, sitting up quietly, trying my best not to wake Declan. I feel numb all over, cold as if I've been dipped in ice water.

"I'm not a Murphy anymore, that's for sure."

"You're my blood," my father says, slowly drawing his gun.

Panic rushes through me. "Stop. Don't. I'll... I'll go with you. I'll go, just... don't hurt him."

"I'll kill him just like I killed his mother," Niall says cruelly, and now I can't even think of him as my father. He's

just Niall Murphy, and he's the real Irish scourge, not Declan.

I start to scramble up, but then Niall squeezes the trigger, and the sound of the gun going off echoes through my head as I scream and scream.

Then I'm running, and I have no idea how I got out of the house. All I know is that I'm running from Niall, the monster I once had thought hung the moon.

Brambles scratch my skin, and I'm jumping over roots in the woods outside of Declan's mansion, and my heart feels like it's been torn from my chest.

I've done this. I've done all of this. I've gotten Declan and his family killed, and now I'm alone and scared.

He's coming after me because I'm a Burke now, after all, and even though I'm his blood, that won't save me.

I run and run, panting, my breathing ragged, and I slam into a hard wall of a man. When I wrench away, he's calling my name.

"Rory?" I gasp as I get a look at his face, but he's got this wicked, twisted grin on his face.

"Come home, Bree," he says, and then his mouth opens impossibly wide, his teeth razor sharp, and Niall comes up behind him, with those same sharp teeth, the same too-wide smile.

"Come home, Bree," Niall repeats, and there's a stench coming from both of them, a death-stench from all the people Niall has killed, all the lives he's ruined.

I can't move, my feet stuck like glue, and as they come toward me, I think of Declan. His wicked smile, the way his blue eyes light up when he laughs.

I close my eyes and wait for the end to come.

I'm startled out of the nightmare by Declan's hand on my shoulder.

"Bree?" His brows are furrowed, his blue eyes dark with worry. "You were screaming, are you all right?"

I throw my arms around him, trembling, and he holds me as best he can.

I bury my face into his chest and sob.

"Bad dream?" He rubs my back.

I nod, sniffling. "It was about my father."

Declan stiffens, but when I pull away to look at him, he doesn't look angry.

"I know it's hard for you."

"I didn't know," I whisper. "I didn't know what he'd done to you and your family, Declan, you have to believe me."

He searches my face. "I believe you, princess. I really do. You're a good person. Just because you have Murphy blood—"

"I don't want to talk about it," I blurt out, wiping at my face with the heels of my palms. "I don't ever want to talk about being a Murphy again."

Declan nods slowly. "All right, baby. Can I get you a glass of water?"

"Please." I snuggle back under the covers.

Declan goes into the bathroom and fills a glass up with water, bringing it back to me.

I gulp at it greedily. I've been neglecting to eat much or hydrate lately because I've been so upset, so guilty.

Declan deserves better. He deserves to know what I've done.

I open my mouth to tell him, to come clean, but I can't speak. Nothing comes out. Instead, I lean forward and put the glass on the nightstand before turning to Declan and pressing my mouth to his.

Declan makes a surprised sound in the back of his throat, but he kisses me back, softly, sweetly.

I deepen the kiss, hungry, and he smiles against my mouth.

"Eager, princess?"

"Yes," I breathe. "I want you to make love to me."

That's the first time I've said it like that, that I've used the word love when it comes to Declan, and his blue eyes widen slightly.

He's going to tell me he doesn't want me anymore. That how can he make love *with me if this was never about love for him.*

My heart clenches in my chest.

He's going to tell me that I'm a monster just like my father. He never wanted this anyway. he could never fall in love with a Murphy.

But Declan doesn't speak at all yet, just lying down next to me on the bed, facing the ceiling.

"I'm afraid you'll have to do most of the work, princess," he murmurs after a moment. "Shoulder's aching like a sonofabitch right now."

"We don't have to."

Declan frowns, his head jerking up for me to climb on top of him.

I do, straddling his hips, and he's half-hard against the fabric of his underwear.

I'm just wearing one of Declan's t-shirts that I threw on after the shower, so I'm bare from the waist down. I rub against his erection with my sex, and Declan bites his lip, watching me, his arm in the good side behind his head.

I don't want to think about anything anymore: not my father, not my estranged brother, not the Murphy blood flowing through my veins. I don't even want to think about how I've fallen in love with Declan and how I don't deserve him.

I just want to think about how he feels inside me, so I reach between us and free him.

Declan hisses as the air hits his erection, and I guide him inside of me, seating myself and rocking my hips slightly.

He throws his head back, nearly banging it on the headboard. He groans.

"Don't tease me, princess," he warns.

I giggle, feeling giddy with him inside me, letting go of everything that's been bothering me.

"I should," I say. "You always tease me."

Declan nearly pouts, and it makes me smile because it's so cute.

I roll my hips, starting to bounce on top of him, and his free hand clamps down on my hip.

"Christ, you keep moving like that and—," he curses.

I just smile and continue to move, letting him slide almost all the way out of me before he thrusts up and goes back inside.

"I'm not going to last," he tells me. "That little lap dance you're doing is something else."

I grin wider, proud, and I continue my slow and steady pace, rocking forward and backward again before bouncing on him.

He chokes out a moan when I start to move faster, bracing myself on the headboard and chasing my orgasm.

At first, I'd wanted to tease him, but now, all I want is to feel him spilling inside me.

I come after just a few moments, riding him hard, and when I start to pulse around him, Declan cries out my name, coming himself, too.

When it's over, I slump against him.

"I'm not hurting you, am I?" I mumble against his skin, and Declan chuckles, dragging his fingers through my hair.

"No, of course not."

I slowly roll off him, missing his warmth immediately, but then I snuggle up against him and put my head on the good side of his chest.

"Do you feel better now, baby?"

I've noticed that he's using pet names a lot more than usual. I wonder if that means that he feels more for me if he's accepting me as his wife.

I want that, so desperately, but I also know now that he deserves better. He deserves someone who wouldn't try to get out, who didn't almost get him killed. He deserves someone without the blood of a monster flowing through her veins.

I think about it, briefly, about what it'd be like if I saw him with someone else, and it makes me want to vomit. I can't imagine Declan with another woman. It would kill me.

I sniffle, tears coming to my eyes. "I do feel better," I say shakily, and Declan frowns.

"You don't seem like you feel better."

"I do," I insist, biting back the tears. "It's just... a lot. Everything that happened and finding out about my father..." *Falling in love with you...*

Declan pulls me closer with his good arm, kissing the crown of my head. "I can't imagine what you're going through. Just know that I'm here for you, okay?"

God, he's being so sweet. It's not even out of character, though. Declan is a good man, and that's becoming clearer and clearer to me.

Paige and Lara were right when they told me that

Declan is a good guy. I just hadn't believed them... not until it was too late.

I know that I need to tell him what I did. I know that he'll cast me out if I do, though, maybe even kill me, so I can't bring myself to do it. Even if maybe I deserve whatever the family decides to do to me.

I tell myself I can enjoy this for one more night, and squeeze my eyes shut, hoping that my slumber will be dreamless.

22

DECLAN

THANK GOD I'M BEING DISCHARGED BY DOC. I'M READY to get back out there.

We're finishing up when Gray walks into my office.

"I'm done here," Doc says, and I hand him a stack of cash before he leaves the room.

"How's everything healing?"

I roll my shoulder around, only a minor pull reminds me of the shot in the chest. "Good as new." I look at him. "I assume you have business to discuss with me."

"It's about Murphy."

I frown, putting my shirt back on and buttoning it before turning back to him. I'm sitting behind my desk.

Paige and Lara just got back from Paige's new home that dad bought for her, and they took Bree upstairs, giggling and talking like schoolgirls, so I'm not too worried about Bree listening in.

Gray looks at me with the most serious expression. "We can't figure out what happened that day you and dad were checking the shipment. There are no leaks in our organization."

"You can't know that for sure."

He sighs. "You don't think it's a little too coincidental?"

"What do you mean, *coincidental?*" I already feel defensive, and I can't even pinpoint why.

"You sent a letter from Bree to Murphy, and then suddenly, he knows when we're checking a shipment?"

"Doesn't he always know?" I clench my jaw. "He's always got his little spies around, listening to us. Besides, we never discussed anything while she was around, so how exactly would she know?"

"But the only people who knew about that shipment were Burkes and Jimmy."

"Exactly. So, what about Jimmy?"

Gray gives me a dark look. "Jimmy's been loyal to us for twenty years, Declan."

"I know what you're implying," I say, just as darkly.

Part of me wants to hit him, but I don't. I push down my anger at him because if I'm honest, I have my own suspicions. The timing does seem a bit convenient. "But I read the letters—both of them. There was nothing in them."

"Maybe they have some kind of code."

I sigh. "You're reaching, Gray. It's probably just that someone used an unsecured line. It doesn't always have to be something nefarious."

"You're blind." Gray rubs a hand across his face in frustration. "You're blinded by that girl, Declan, and this isn't going to end well."

"I don't know what you're talking about." I look up at him. "Besides, you and Da were the ones who pushed me into this marriage."

"It was Da's idea, not mine," Gray insists.

"Nevertheless, you went along with it. And she is never around when we discuss business, so again, Gray, how would she know?" I open the door to my office. "Now get out. I've got work to do."

"You and I may butt heads from time to time," Gray grumbles, "but I'm still your big brother, and I only want what's best for you. Bree may be pretty. She may act sweet. Hell, she even snowed me here for a while. But she's still a Murphy."

"She didn't know," I say fiercely. "She didn't know who her father was until Da explained everything."

Gray scoffs. "You really believe that?"

"I do." My fists clench. "Now, get out before I throw you out."

Gray finally leaves, slamming the door, and I sigh, looking down at my desk, which is scattered over with papers, mostly bookkeeping.

Usually, Lara deals with the books, but lately, I've been trying to do it myself. I need to learn how to run it. Da won't be around forever, and one day Lara will get married and move out.

But I'm not worried about money right now. All I want is to think this through.

I find myself wishing that my best friend, Kael, was in town. He's been away for a bit for business, and I usually hash this kind of thing out with him.

Perhaps it's for the best that I call Cillian instead of Kael, though. Cillian is only peripherally involved in the business, so maybe he'll have a clear head about this whole thing.

Besides, I need to let off some steam.

I pick up my phone and dial his number. He picks up and I don't even give him time to say hello.

"Meet me at the gym."

He groans. "Aren't you injured or something?"

"Almost healed and just cleared by the doc. So, I can do cardio."

"You're a madman," Cillian complains. "I'll see you there."

I head upstairs, changing into a pair of basketball shorts and a tight shirt. My biceps bulge in it, and I like seeing the difference in size after I'm able to lift. Unfortunately, I can't lift today or for a while, not wanting to ruin all that is healed already.

I head to the gym, and I don't see a glimpse of my sisters or Bree, which is also probably for the best. I don't know how I feel about her right now. Everything has gotten so confusing.

I'd thought, for a while, that I was swiftly falling in love with her. But it turns out that I don't even know what that means. I've never been in love before, after all. And can I fall in love with a woman who comes from our greatest enemy? The man who killed my mother?

She didn't know, I remind myself as I step onto the treadmill next to Cillian.

"What's on your mind?" Cillian asks quietly as I start up an incline.

"How do you know something's on my mind?"

"Well, you've practically ignored me ever since you got married to that Murphy chick, so I figure you showing up now means something."

"I didn't ask to get married," I say. "You know that was my father's doing."

"Yeah, but you've certainly been missing in action ever since."

"Sorry," I mumble, starting up a three miles per hour pace, just walking at first to warm up.

Cillian shrugs. "No reason for apologies. I'm just curious. What's it like being married to a Murphy?"

"It's something," I mutter.

Realizing that I don't want to talk about it, Cillian hums. "How's your chest and shoulder?"

"Getting better every day," I tell him.

"Have you figured out how Murphy knew when the shipment was being checked?" Cillian asks. Even though he's just a driver, he's friends with a lot of the Burke clan, so of course he's heard about it.

"He always knows," I repeat what I told Gray. "He's got people everywhere."

"Maybe," Cillian agrees.

I sigh. "I know what you're thinking."

"Do you, oh psychic?"

I snort out a laugh.

Cillian is usually pretty laid-back, which is one thing I do like about him. There's a reason he's my go-to when my best friend is out of town.

"You're thinking it has something to do with Bree Murphy."

"Your wife," Cillian points out.

"My wife." I start to move the incline up even further, and Cillian sighs, doing the same.

"You're going to try and kill me today, aren't you?"

I grin at him. "You're getting heavy. You can use the exercise."

Cillian slaps at his flat abdomen. "Heavy where? In my pants, maybe."

I bark out a surprised laugh. I've been so stressed I didn't even know I *could* laugh.

I sigh. "Gray thinks that my wife has something to do with it."

I need to talk about this. I can't work out as hard as I usually would because of my injury, and I need some kind of outlet.

"Gray thinks the worst of everyone."

I nod slowly. That much is true. Gray doesn't trust easily.

"I'm worried he may be right," I grumble.

"You really think she'd betray you? After all this time?"

"It's not like she chose this marriage, either. It was Da's crazy idea. And sure, it's worked. It's started a war between us and Murphy, but I'm not so sure that we're winning."

"Because she might have gotten ahold of him?"

"She sent a birthday card," I explain. "And he sent a letter back."

"You read them, of course."

"Of course." I nod. "And there was nothing in them. No weird phrasing or something that sounded like a code."

Cillian glances over at me. "But it's suspicious, the timing."

"It is. And what am I going to do if she's still loyal to her father?"

"It's hard to tell," Cillian says. "It's just a letter, after all, but if they have a code, it might be one you haven't cracked."

"Maybe." I turn up the speed on the treadmill.

"What are you going to do if she did?"

"I don't know."

Cillian whistles. "You must really like her."

"Why do you say that?"

"Because usually, you'd kill anyone who even smells like a rat."

He's right. I've always been brutal about people who became disloyal to the Burkes.

But it's different with Bree, and not just because of my feelings for her. As well as we've treated her, at the end of the day, she didn't choose this. How can I expect her to be loyal to the Burkes right away?

But of course, if she did do it, I'll have to deal with it. Gray will want blood, but there's no way I'll let him handle it. I'll handle it myself.

Bree has been so strange ever since the accident. It's like she's just going through the motions, and she's so pale and drawn all the time.

Is it guilt? Or is she just still traumatized by hearing about her father's many sins? It's hard to tell.

I haven't asked her, face to face, so maybe that's what I need to do. I'm afraid, though, that she'll come clean, and then I don't know what I'll do.

I take in a breath and pull out my phone, calling Lara.

She answers right away. "Declan? What's up?"

"Are you with Bree?" I ask in a quiet voice.

"Sure. She and Paige are in the pool. Do you need to talk to her?"

"No, no," I say quickly. "I don't want her to hear this conversation."

"What's going on?"

"I want you to keep an eye on her. Don't let her out of your sight unless she's in the bathroom or the bedroom."

Lara goes silent for a long moment. "I ask again, what's going on?"

"Nothing," I lie. "I just... want to keep a better eye on her after Murphy attacked us."

"All right," she says quietly. "I'll watch her."

"Thank you." I hang up the phone and turn up the speed again, needing to run, needing to get some of this worry and suspicion out.

I focus on the run, trying not to think, and it's thirty minutes before Cillian shuts his off and gets down.

"I need water."

I nod, continuing to run.

"You do, too." He turns my treadmill to a slow walk.

I sigh but I know he's right, so I turn it off and walk over to the duffel bag he's brought with water and protein bars.

I chew on a protein bar and suck down half a bottle of water.

"You know Kael is coming back to town tonight," Cillian points out. "Maybe we could all go out."

Cillian, Kael, and I had been thick as thieves in high school, and we haven't all gone out together in forever it seems. Cillian is by far the craziest out of all of us, with Kael being sort of a teetotaler, but somehow, it works.

"I know you've got work to do or whatever," Cillian says, apparently thinking I'm going to say no.

"Fuck work. Let's do it." I throw the gym towel into the laundry area and start toward the shower.

Lara continues to keep an eye on Bree, and I don't even know if I want to see Bree when I get home to change before heading out to the bar.

I shower and get dressed and it's already about eight in the evening when I'm seating in bed, putting on my shoes, about to head out.

Bree comes into the bedroom, wearing a towel and a bikini, soaking wet.

"I haven't seen you all day." She leans down to kiss my temple.

I force a smile at her. "Been busy."

"Anything I can do to help?"

She sounds so sweet, and part of me wants to pull her down into my lap and be late for my boys' night.

"It's all done, now. I'm going out with Kael and Cillian."

"Kael's your best friend?" she asks. "I think Paige mentioned him."

"He is," I nod. "Him and Cillian."

"You should have fun." She smiles. "Paige and Lara want a sleepover, anyway."

I chuckle. "I'll save you when I get home."

She smiles wider and heads off to the shower, and I watch her ass jiggle as she drops the towel to the floor at the doorway.

I bite my lip and walk toward her, undressing and getting into the shower with her.

She looks up at me. "Won't you be late?"

"They'll live."

I need to bury myself inside her, need to distract myself from all the thoughts I've been having about her possible betrayal.

Bree grins back at me before facing the wall, bracing her hands against the shower wall.

I slide my hand down between her lower lips, finding her slick enough for me to work myself into her.

I hold up one of her legs with my good arm, looping it around my elbow.

She gasps while I push myself into her, and I groan, biting down on her shoulder, reaching around her to cup her breasts and play with her peaked nipples.

"Declan," she breathes, and the sound of my name on her lips makes me thrust harder, the glide getting easier as she gets wetter, closer to her orgasm.

It's quick and hard and not intimate at all, but when we

both finish, almost in unison, I lean down to kiss the bites I've left on her shoulder and the side of her neck.

"Come and get me when you get home," she murmurs as I step out of the shower.

"Just try and stop me." I lean back into the shower to kiss her goodbye.

It does help, seeing Bree before I go out, because I'm reminded again that I do care for her. I don't know if it's love, exactly, because of the way it started, because I've never felt this way about any other woman.

When I arrive at Kelley's pub, Cillian is already there, but Kael is nowhere to be found.

I frown.

"You're late," Cillian says, sounding slightly drunk. "Kael and I started without you."

I blink. "Kael is taking shots with you?"

"I know, right? I guess he missed us." He laughs, and Kael comes out of the bathroom to stand at the bar. He orders us a round of vodka shots, top shelf, before he greets me. He grins and claps me on the shoulder. "I've heard that congratulations are in order."

"I don't know about that," I say, but his grin is contagious and soon I'm smiling back.

We take down our shots, and Cillian is already eyeing a redhead on the dance floor.

"No girls tonight," Kael warns. "Just us guys."

"No girls?" Cillian pouts.

"That's probably for the best," I say, sipping my beer. Beer and shots, maybe a few Irish car bombs, are our usual drinks of choice.

"Since you're a married man and all," Kael teases. "How did that happen, anyway?"

"Ask my da," I say flatly, but I feel a little bad that I'm not exactly telling Kael the truth.

I sigh. "She's a Murphy."

Kael's eyes widen. "I'd heard you got married, and that Niall was pissed, but I didn't put it together. How the hell did that happen?"

"It started out as a plan to piss Niall off," Cillian says helpfully, and I glare at him for running his mouth, but he's drunk and doesn't notice. "But I think our boy has feelings."

"Shut up," I growl, but Kael is looking at me, eyes squinted.

"I can't believe that out of the three of us, you're the one who got married first."

Cillian scoffs. "Wasn't going to be me."

"Do you have feelings for her?" Kael asks.

"Yes," I groan as Cillian orders another round of shots. "I don't know what to do about it."

"You don't have to do anything," Kael says. "You're married, aren't you?"

I end up explaining everything to Kael, swearing him to secrecy, and I know he'll keep to that. I trust him more than anyone in my life other than my family, after all.

Cillian has been known to run his mouth, but he doesn't know everyone in the clan the way that Kael does.

"Jesus," he mutters after I'm finished. "That's a lot, man, I'm sorry."

"Yeah."

"But even if she did have something to do with it, can you blame her?" Kael asks.

Cillian has broken our no girls rule and is tearing it up on the dance floor with the redhead from earlier.

No one is surprised.

"I mean, I guess I can't," I agree. "She's been forced into

this just the way that I was, but I just… I thought maybe she felt the same way that I do." I don't say that her life will be in abject danger if she did betray us, but Kael knows that.

"And how is that?"

"I think I might love her," I admit, and I don't think I would have said it if I wasn't tipsy nearing drunk, but there it is.

Kael's eyes widen. "Are you sure?"

"Hell no, I'm not sure," I huff. "I've never been in love before."

"First time for everything," Kael says.

It does feel better to get it all out, to tell them everything, and by the time I make it home, I'm feeling no pain. It's not just from the booze, but from getting everything off my chest.

Bree happens to be in bed when I get there, but she's snoring away.

I don't wake her, just climb into bed with her and kiss her sleeping mouth softly.

I pass out feeling better than I have in several days.

I know that won't last.

23

———

BREE

Declan's horribly hungover when I wake up, groaning and spitting into the wastebasket, and I can't help but laugh a little.

"Don't laugh at me; I'm dying."

I snort. "You're not dying. You just need to eat and hydrate. I guess you must've had fun?"

"I guess," he mutters.

It's easy to get lost in it, lost in the marriage, in our relationship.

I go downstairs and grab him a plate after dressing, bringing it back up to him.

"Marisol's steak and eggs will cure what ails you."

"All food sounds like death right now," he groans.

I smile, feeding him a couple of bites of eggs, and when he keeps them down, I feed him some toast and a few bites of steak.

After he downs a bottle of water, he seems to feel better.

Declan's sweet all morning, cuddling me in bed and kissing along the side of my face, but something seems to change when he gets a text message.

He sits up, before standing and quickly dressing.

I frown. "Is everything okay?"

"Another one of our shipments has been hit."

I swallow hard.

Does my father have anything to do with this? It makes everything crash down around me, and my good mood is spoiled.

"Be careful," I whisper, and Declan nods tersely, his mood changed, just like mine, as he walks out of the door and leaves.

I sigh, gathering up my book, a true crime novel, and heading to the sunroom.

It's peaceful here, with the open skylight and the big windows, the stained glass making different colors stream into the room.

I try to read my book but end up reading the same paragraph about twenty times before I give up, closing the book and putting it in my lap.

What am I going to do? Declan isn't going to take this kind of betrayal lightly. For all I know, he already knows and is plotting to kill me.

But would he act that way with me this morning? And even last night, he was all over me in the shower. Surely, he wouldn't be so close to me if he still hated me.

But at the end of the day, I have no idea how he feels about me.

It's only about half an hour before someone walks in, and I look up to see Lara.

I'm grateful that it isn't Paige. I love Paige to death, but her bubbly, outgoing personality can be a lot when I'm in such a weird mood.

Lara smiles and sits next to me. "What are you reading?"

"Truman Capote." I flash the book cover at her.

"*In Cold Blood*," she murmurs. "A classic."

"I've never read it. Paige recommended it."

Lara blinks. "I'm surprised she reads that kind of stuff."

I laugh. "She doesn't. But I told her I didn't want anything about love."

"Not much love in that novel, that's for sure." Lara gives me a small smile. She looks at me for a moment longer before speaking again. "So, what's going on with you?"

I stiffen. "I don't know what you mean."

"You've been in a weird mood ever since Declan got hurt."

"I'm just worried about him." Not exactly a lie.

I've been hoping ever since he left that he won't get hurt again, and who knows what my father is up to?

"It's more than that," she says. "You've seemed really... off the last couple weeks."

I bark out a laugh. "As if any of this is normal."

Lara smiles softly. "I guess you're right about that."

I'm quiet, hoping that she'll get the hint and leave, but it appears like she's settling in.

I could leave, I suppose, but that would seem rude.

Lara isn't a bad person. None of the Burkes are, and I think I'm falling in love with all of them, not just Declan. Of course, it's not the same kind of love, but I have always wanted a stable family.

"I know how you must feel sometimes," Lara murmurs. "Like no one is on your side."

I look at her, my eyes widening. "How could you possibly know how I feel?"

I don't say it to be harsh, but it comes out that way.

Lara hums, rocking the rocking chair she sits in backwards. "After Ma died, it was easy for everyone to forget about me. I was so young, but of course, not as young as Paige. I'm the middle child for all intents and purposes. Everyone was grieving, and everyone was trying to distract Paige from it because she was too young to understand. I just felt so confused.... and alone. It seemed like I was the only one that felt guilty that I was alive, and she wasn't."

I nod slowly, my heart aching. It was my father who'd killed her mother, and I don't even know how she can sit here and look at me.

"But after a while, everyone started noticing me again. We all moved on, as much as it hurt. And my family rallied around me when it took me a little longer than the others. They were patient, and kind, and soon enough, I realized that I was still loved and supported by them. It was hard, at first. And I remember how hard it was. I think about it a lot. So, I just wanted you to know that I do understand, and I'm here if you need to talk."

I shake my head. "It's different, though, Lara. You were already a part of the Burke family, already loved by them. You were never their enemy like me. You were never confused by feelings of guilt and loyalty and love."

The last part comes out before I know what I'm saying.

"Love?" Lara raises her well-groomed eyebrows. "You love Declan? That's amazing, that this marriage turned into a love match!"

She sounds excited, almost like Paige, and I can see their resemblance more than ever.

The chuckle I let out is bitter. "It's not like that," I say quickly. "Declan doesn't love me, and there are things..." I shake my head.

I sigh and shrug. "He never will. And I have to come to terms with that, with live with whatever this damn war brings. I just hope that everyone I care about survives. I don't care what happens to me."

"What do you mean, what happens with you?" Lara's brows draw together.

I stand up, shaking my head. "Nothing. I'm just thinking out loud. Sorry, I'm all over the place. Over-thinking things."

She leans forward, taking my wrist in her delicate grasp. "Bree, please. Stay and talk with me. It'll make you feel better if nothing else."

"I have to go." I pull gently away from her, heading back up to the bedroom and locking the door, panting and feeling anxious, my heart racing.

Like I don't already feel bad enough, now I'm lying to Lara. She and Paige have become my best friends, and I'm lying to both of them. I'm lying to everyone I've grown to care about.

The Burkes don't deserve this.

I plop down in bed, face down, groaning into the pillow.

What am I going to do now?

I don't realize I've fallen asleep until there's a banging on the door.

I go to it quickly, worried that something might be wrong with Declan, but instead of my husband, it's Paige and Lara standing there.

"You're coming with us," Paige says, grabbing my hand, and she drags me out into the hallway.

I blink.

Do they know? Did Declan send these two to kill me?

"Where are we going?"

"Shopping for ourselves and Paige's new house," Lara says with a small smile.

I pause, frowning. "We can't go out in public. At least, I can't."

"It's not public," Paige pipes up. "We rented out the local mall."

"You can... rent out a *mall*?"

"With enough money, you sure can." Lara grins. "It's only going to be us and the employees."

Thirty minutes later, we're pulling up at the mall, and I look around at the empty parking lot. The driver lets us out at the door, and Paige bustles inside.

"I don't even have my purse," I say, and Lara snorts.

"What would you need your purse for? We're treating you."

"You guys don't have to—" I start, but Paige cuts me off by dragging me into a photobooth.

She, Lara, and I make funny faces at the screen and the pictures that come out are dreadful, but funny.

Lara wrinkles her nose. "Let's take one classy one."

We try, but at the end, Paige sticks out her tongue.

"You're the worst," Lara complains, but she puts the second set into her purse with a smile on her face.

I'm smiling too by the time we go into the first store. I can't seem to help myself.

We go through decoration and fabric as if we are professional designers.

When Paige is happy with all we have for her house decor, it's time to have real fun. We head to the first clothing shop.

Lara instantly picks out a beautiful gold dress and heads into the dressing room. Paige picks a shirt and a hot-pink blouse, and she frowns when I just stand there, watching them.

"Pick out an outfit," she says. "You'll need it, for tonight."

"Tonight?"

"Declan got to have a boys' night out," she says. "So, Lara and I rented out that local club, Sphynx. We're going to tear it up!"

I blink at her. "I don't know if I'm in the right mood."

She frowns. "You've been in a bad mood for weeks, you and Declan both. I'm cheering you up if it kills me, dammit."

I laugh, unable to hold back. "All right, all right."

I look through the clothes, and I finally decide on a hunter-green dress with cut outs on each side, showing my pale skin. The color compliments my eyes, and it has a deep V-neck.

"That's *gorgeous*," Paige gushes, and we both head into individual dressing rooms, coming out about the same time as Lara in our new outfits.

"I love it." Lara swirls around and smiles. She looks statuesque and graceful, and it's really the perfect color to bring out the gold tints in her hair.

"I don't know how I feel about mine," Paige complains, plucking at the lace on the top.

"The blouse is very you," I say. "But I think a black or gray skirt would work better."

Paige beams at me. "Thanks!" She heads over to get a black, A-line skirt, and when she puts it on, she gasps at herself in the mirror. "This is perfect! Bree, you're a genius."

I laugh. "I'm only doing what Melissa taught me."

"God, it's been so long since I've actually been shopping," Lara says after we get undressed and buy the outfits. We're headed to a nearby shoe store.

"Why is that?" I ask.

"Da doesn't want us out and about unless we're with our brothers," Paige mutters. "I can't stand it."

"Between Declan, Gray, and Da, we're protected maybe too much." Lara chuckles.

"We're luckier than some," Paige points out. "I know that Felicity Sullivan never gets out of the house."

My eyes widen. I know that my father has done some business with the Sullivans, but I didn't even know a daughter was in the mix.

"Anyway, we're going to let loose tonight." Paige bounces into the shoe shop.

We browse among the shoes, and I think about Felicity Sullivan, how maybe things would have been easier if my father locked me away like a princess in a tower. Then I would have never been kidnapped, would have never learned what a monster he is. Never would have messed up the Burkes' lives.

Shaking my head to get those thoughts out of my head, I walk over to look at the heels, picking out a pair of white stilettos. Lara goes with a pair of gold, strappy heels, and Paige gets a pair of hot-pink pumps to match her outfit.

We trail over to the makeup store and pick out a few things, and then we're on our way home to get dressed.

Declan is locked in his office, and I swallow hard, wondering what's going on in there. Did something happen? Does he know what I did?

But Lara and Paige are determined to keep my mind off things, and Paige disappears into the kitchen while Lara and I head upstairs to relax.

Paige returns with a pitcher of frozen margaritas, and we all sip as we chat.

"Have you met anyone new lately?" I ask Paige, and she snorts.

"That's exactly why I wanted my own place. You've met my family. When would I meet someone?" she asks. "I never get out of the house unless Declan or Gray or one of my father's men are with us."

"We still get to go to dinner parties and events," Lara points out.

"Yeah, but those are all the same guys in different clans," Paige sulks. "I've met them all, and they're all terrible. I can't wait to move out. Almost." She is squealing and doing a little happy dance.

I laugh. "You have discerning tastes."

"Very," Lara agrees. "But I guess high standards are a good thing."

"It is." I sip more of my margarita. The alcohol is doing a good job at taking away my worries, or at least putting them away for a later date.

By the time we get ready, I've stuck to one margarita to Lara and Paige's two, and I'm feeling a little anxious. I haven't seen Declan since this morning, and I worry maybe he knows what happened and is just biding his time.

We head into the hallway, and Paige is giggly and tipsy, pulling my hand.

I freeze when I see Declan at the top of the stairs.

"Declan," I greet in a hushed voice.

"Bree." He looks me up and down with dark blue eyes.

I swallow hard, doing a little twirl and trying to keep my anxiety off my face.

"You like?"

"Love it," he says. "Where are you three going?"

"We're going out." Paige giggles, and Declan raises an eyebrow.

"Who's going with you?"

"We rented Sphynx out," Lara explains. "Jimmy is taking us."

Declan's face relaxes, if only slightly. "Have fun, ladies."

He puts his hand on my hip, leaning forward to kiss me deeply, making my knees weak. He smiles at me softly before walking up the rest of the stairs.

"That was kind of intense," Paige says, and Lara grabs her hand, leading her out to Jimmy's car.

It *was* intense, and I'm not sure what it means. Is it that Declan doesn't know? Or does he, and that was some kind of kiss of death?

I can't be sure. I know the way the Irish clans work. They'll smile in your face as they stab you in the back.

"Don't get all mopey again," Paige pleads as she pulls me into the club.

No one checks our IDs, presumably because Lara and Paige have rented the place out.

We walk into the bar and the music booms.

It's so strange to see a club with no people in it but the bartenders. It's a gorgeous club, with red and blue lights strobing overhead. A tiled, huge dance floor sits in the middle of the building, and the bar stretches around it in a square. The chandeliers look to be made of real crystal, and there's a disco ball in the corner.

We grab drinks at the bar and go right out to the dance floor, and by the time I'm halfway finished with the drink, I feel happy and free.

It's not just the booze, either. Paige and Lara have become like my own sisters. I'm closer to them than I have ever been to Rory. Even now that we are closer since he decided to leave the family.

Paige does a little twirl, giggling, and nearly falls.

I can't help but double over, laughing, as Lara tries to help her up.

Jimmy stands in the corner, watching us with a small smile, and other than him being there and the club being empty, it's like a normal night out with the girls.

We have the time of our lives, and I stop drinking around midnight so that I'm not unsteady on my feet, although I'm definitely tipsy.

Paige and Lara aren't too much the worse for wear either, and we all pile into Jimmy's car, in the backseat so that we can whisper and talk like young girls.

I guess we *are* young girls. It just seems like so much has happened that it's aged me.

When we arrive back at the mansion, Paige and Lara say their goodbyes, and I head up the stairs to the bedroom. I am a tiny bit unsteady, but I blame it on my new heels.

I expect Declan to be asleep, since it's nearly three in the morning, but when I open the bedroom door, he's sitting on the bed. A sheet only barely covers his abdomen, and I know he's naked beneath.

"Hey, princess," he calls in a low tone, and I stumble slightly as I take off my heels. He chuckles. "You good?"

"Fine," I mumble. "I'm not even that drunk."

"You're not, huh?" He stands up, nude, and walks over to unzip my dress, his hands lingering on my hips and ass.

He whispers into my ear, "You look absolutely stunning tonight."

I shiver, letting the dress fall to the floor. I turn, wearing just a white thong, and Declan looks me over.

"Are you drunk?"

"No." I pout.

He chuckles. "I think you're a little tipsy."

I shrug. "Not much," I say, but my head is starting to spin slightly now that I'm home.

"I think maybe we should just cuddle tonight." Declan smiles, and I whine but let him take me to the bed, let him draw me into his arms.

"Declan," I whisper, and Declan hums in response. "Are you mad at me?"

He's quiet for a long moment. "No, baby."

"Okay," I say in a small voice, and bury my face in his chest.

I sleep like this every night, listening to his heartbeat, and tonight, it's strong and steady, relaxing me to the core.

This is where I feel most at home, in my father's enemy's arms.

24

DECLAN

I want to eat breakfast earlier than Bree, trying to get some time to myself, but my father is there already, chatting with Marisol.

He looks a little red when I come down, and I wonder what they were talking about.

I smile. "Am I interrupting?"

"Of course not." Marisol bustles back into the kitchen.

My father gives me a look like I'm definitely interrupting, and I chuckle.

"Why don't you go ahead and ask her out?"

"I don't know what you're talking about, boyo," my father says, shoveling food into his mouth so he doesn't have to answer.

I shake my head, thinking about my own relationship, and I lose my smile.

He looks at me and frowns. "What's up with you?"

"What do you mean?"

I take a page from my father's playbook and start to eat my waffles, not being able to talk while the food is in my mouth.

"You've been acting strange for weeks."

"No, I haven't."

He snorts. "Oh yeah? Is that why you totally zoned out during our morning meeting yesterday?"

I wince. I had just been looking into space, not listening to anything that was said, and Gray had nudged me when my father asked me the question.

"I guess I've just been worried." I shrug. "Murphy hasn't retaliated, exactly, and I don't know where or who he's going to hit."

"He hit *you*," he points out. "In the chest, remember?"

"But he knows he didn't kill me," I argue. "And if it were Paige or Lara in Bree's position—"

"I'd kill the man on sight," my father says darkly.

"Exactly. So, what's the hold up?"

He shrugs. "He probably wants to steal us blind before he strikes like the snake he is."

"Maybe."

My mood is bad again at dinner, which Bree doesn't attend, having gone to bed early. She's been acting strangely, too, and I don't know how to deal with it. I don't know what it means.

Is it just finding out who her father really is, or is it something more? Did she betray me, or not?

I'm always thinking about it, in the back of my mind. It's like an obsession, and I can't get my mind off it.

"Why are you so quiet tonight?" Paige raises her eyebrows. "And where's Bree? Don't tell me you two are fighting again."

"We're not fighting."

Gray gives me a cool look, but I ignore him, remembering how he suggested she is a traitor just a few days ago. I will him not to say another word, and he doesn't.

"You're just being weirdly quiet." Paige chomps down on her lamb chop.

"It's okay to be quiet sometimes, Paige. I guess you wouldn't know that," I snap.

"Hey!" Da shouts. "You don't talk to your sister that way."

It's like I'm twelve years old and sullen all over again.

Paige is pouting at me, clearly hurt, and I sigh.

"I'm sorry, kiddo," I tell her softly. "I've just been so busy lately. It's been stressful."

"It's okay." Her face softens. "Just don't be a jerk."

"Noted."

I'm just in my office making some calls when Gray bursts into the office

"Have we made any progress?"

"What?"

"On finding out more about the attack," he huffs, a frustrated tone to his voice. "Remember, the one where you were almost killed?"

"You know if we had, you'd know already. Why?" My jaw tightens. I know where Gray is going with this.

"Your wife." Gray narrows his eyes at me. "And that suspicious letter she sent."

"She didn't know anything! You know what?" I sigh, standing and thrusting the letter at him. "You read it and tell me how she possibly could have given him any information."

Gray scans the letter and then frowns, looking back at me. "Where's the one he sent?"

I huff out an angry breath and take the first letter from him, handing him the one Niall sent in response. He scans it, too, and his shoulders slump.

"There's nothing here."

"I told you."

"That doesn't mean there's not a code we haven't cracked," he insists. "And if I find out that she had something to do with it—"

I take a couple of steps toward him. "Then what?" I growl. "What are you going to do?"

Gray clears his throat, throwing the letter down on my desk, staring at me.

"If that little bitch has anything to do with this, I'm going to—"

I don't let him get the next word out, tackling him around the waist.

We burst through the half-open door, rolling into the hallway.

I punch him in the kidneys, and he yelps, finally managing to get me on my back by sweeping his leg under mine.

He hits me in the face once, twice, before I punch him in the solar plexus, taking his breath.

"Fuck you," I hiss, and Gray gasps in a breath, hitting me in the stomach and trading spots with me as I gasp.

"*Póg mo mhóin.*"

"As if you could ever make me kiss a hairy ass like yours," I pant, still in a fighting stance, but Gray pulls away, slumping down the wall and holding his stomach.

"Fuck, that *hurts*," he groans. "I haven't been hit like that since high school."

"You deserved it then, too," I spit, panting and sitting up with a grimace, my chest and shoulder aching something fierce.

Gray chuckles. "Probably. But I don't know why you're going so hard for some girl you didn't even want to marry."

"She's not just some girl. She's my wife."

Gray raises an eyebrow, still panting. "So, you're actually accepting it?" He shifts, grimacing. "You sound like you like her."

All I can do is put my head in my hands.

Gray whistles. "Shit, Declan. You *do* like her. What the hell?"

"I know," I groan. "I don't know why it happened. I don't know how. She's a Murphy, for fuck's sake."

"Well, she's a Burke now," Gray says almost cheerfully, standing up unsteadily and coming over to help me up. He claps me on the back before pulling away.

"What am I going to do?" I ask, hoping for some brotherly advice, but instead Gray just shrugs.

"I don't know, brother. You'll figure it out."

And then he just walks off toward his room, rolling his shoulders.

Great. What a good chat.

I FIGURE THAT GRAY WILL GO TO DA RIGHT AWAY AND tell him about the fight, about his suspicions about Bree, but he doesn't. Da doesn't even approach me until after dinner the next night.

Bree has already gone up to bed, and I'm drinking Scotch with Da since Gray is out on a job.

"I need you to go and pick up this next shipment," Da says.

I raise an eyebrow. "Not Gray?"

"Gray's otherwise occupied," he says. "You can take Kael with you, he's back home now, aye?"

"Aye." I keep my eyebrow raised. "What's the trouble?"

"You were attacked when we went to check that shipment. I'm worried there's a rat in our midst."

Things have ramped up since that first attack.

I'm afraid Bree might be the rat, but how could she? She sent one letter weeks ago. Even if she said something then, nothing that has happened since can be her fault.

Murphy is retaliating with all he has, trying to get us out where he can slaughter us. That's the only explanation I can see.

But did Bree betray us? Betray me?

I'm still knocking it around my head, trying to figure out the potential code. I've read those letters dozens of times, and I've come up with nothing.

"Is this a test?"

"Not for you," Da says. "For Jimmy. I told him the wrong location."

"You suspect *Jimmy*?"

Da sighs. "I don't want to suspect anyone, son, but you know how this business works. He wouldn't be the first man to be swayed by Murphy's money."

I nod slowly. This will help me, too. If it turns out to be Jimmy, I can stop suspecting my wife.

If not... I'll cross that bridge when I get there, I guess.

"Call Kael and see if he's available," Da says. "Six in the morning, the westside warehouse."

After I finish my Scotch, I go up to my office, thinking I'll probably be sleeping there. I can't be around Bree without wanting her, without touching her and kissing her, and it's just making me more confused.

I call up Kael, and he answers on the third ring.

"What's up?"

"I've got a job for you," I tell him. "Easy. Just picking up a shipment."

"Hell, yeah," he says. "I've been missing working with you."

I snort. "There won't be any heads to bust, so don't get excited."

"Boo."

I can't help but laugh. I've missed him while he was away.

"See you at six in the morning, the westside warehouse."

"I'll be there."

I go to the linen closet down the hall and grab a blanket and a pillow, heading back to the office.

Bree has come out into the hallway, looking around, wearing her pink negligée and looking good enough to eat. She frowns in my direction.

"You're sleeping in your office?"

"Just for tonight. I've got a really early morning."

"I don't mind," she says, and I'm tempted to go into the bedroom and climb into bed with her, but I don't.

"I do," I say softly. "Don't want to wake you."

She pouts a little. "Just one night?"

God, she's so beautiful. So sweet when she wants to be. But could she secretly be a snake just like her father?

"Just one night. See you tomorrow."

I close the door to my office, sighing.

Staying away from Bree is harder than I thought.

KAEL IS ALREADY THERE WHEN I ROLL UP WITH THE rented truck, and it's only five-forty-five.

"You really did miss me." I chuckle as I get out and head into the warehouse.

"I checked the perimeter," Kael says. "No one around for miles."

"Good."

I look at my phone and nothing. No text with news of an attack anywhere.

Is this good news or bad news?

I can't say anymore. I'm so screwed up in the head right now.

"Why do you seem so depressed?" Kael asks.

"All is clear on all fronts."

"And that is a bad thing? You can't have hoped there was a rat."

"I kind of did," I admit. "Because if there isn't.... the attack on us that day could be my wife's doing."

Kael nods as he takes a crowbar to the first crate.

We start unloading the guns, putting them into the truck and replacing them with money, which the Russians would pick up later tonight. We changed all our routines and started doing these shipments like this to protect our men ever since Murphy attacked.

"And you've fallen in love with the enemy's daughter." Kael chuckles and shakes his head. "I can't leave town for a few weeks without you or Cillian doing something stupid."

I laugh. "Bet you didn't think it'd be me."

"I didn't."

We continue piling the guns into the truck. He bangs on the back of the truck once we get it all done.

"You want to go get some breakfast?"

I'm hoping for any reason not to go home yet, and Kael hops up in the truck's cab with me.

At the diner, I order a big breakfast with a short stack of pancakes, and Kael orders steak and eggs. My mind goes to

Bree feeding me Marisol's steak and eggs the other day, and my shoulders slump.

"What are you going to do?" Kael asks.

"What do you mean?"

"If it was her," he says. "Are you going to do it yourself?"

I shiver just thinking about it.

I know what Da would tell me. He'd say she's a Murphy, that she's just like her father. That she needs to be dealt with.

"I can't even think about it," I admit.

"Will you forgive her?"

"It's not up to me to forgive," I point out. "She's put the whole Burke clan in danger, if it's true."

"But you can't kill her."

"I don't know what I would do," I say honestly. "I guess I'd be angry, but I'd try to get around it, somehow."

I sigh. "I don't think Gray would forgive it."

He nods. "Gray can be kind of a hard ass."

"He's been pretty against it since the beginning."

He'd been shocked when Da suggested it. So had I, but so many things had changed since then. "But she's grown on even him, I think."

Kael raises an eyebrow. "Paige likes her?"

"Paige *especially* likes her," I say, and Kael snorts.

"Didn't know she liked anybody."

I blink at him.

Paige likes *everybody*, or at least everybody but Kael. But I don't say that, not wanting him to feel worse.

"She's a good person," I say. "Despite being born of a snake, she's got a really good heart."

"You do love her." Kael looks at me with wide eyes.

"Is that so hard to believe?"

"It is to me. Just never saw you as that kind of guy."

"I didn't either," I say honestly.

I'd never thought I would ever get married, never thought I would ever have a family outside of the rest of the Burkes. I didn't know that someone would fit so well into my life. Now, it feels strange to have even slept in my office last night, felt strange not having her in my arms as we slept.

"What's it like?"

"Hm? What?"

"Being in love."

"Jesus." I chuckle. "It's rough. Like there's always butterflies in your stomach. But when you're with them… it's like nothing else matters. Like no one else matters."

"I can't imagine that."

"Neither could I, until it started happening. I'm honestly as surprised as you are, Kael."

He laughs, finishing up his breakfast and sipping coffee. "Well, you should get back to your wife."

I frown. "I don't want to. Not until I really know what's going on."

"Have you asked her?"

"It's not like she's going to admit to it." I shake my head.

"She might. If she feels the same way—"

"She doesn't," I grumble.

Bree probably still hates me for what I've done, for kidnapping her, and I can't blame her. That may be why she did it in the first place. She wanted me gone.

The idea makes my heart drop into my stomach.

I hate the way it feels when I think about Bree betraying me. She acts so sweet, acts so loving, but I don't know how she really feels.

Kael doesn't argue, but we fight over the bill for a moment before I slip cash into the server's apron. Kael's still complaining about it when we get back into the truck.

I drop him off at his car a couple of blocks from the warehouse.

When I make it back home, Bree's in the living room, stretched across the couch and dead asleep. I smile a little, crouching next to her.

"Princess?" I call, and she snorts awake, yawning.

"Oh, you're home," she says. "I couldn't sleep last night without you."

She pouts again and this time, I do give in, scooping her off the couch and carrying her bridal style up the stairs.

She wraps her arms around my neck, nuzzling into my neck.

"You should get some more rest," I tell her, and she makes grabby hands at me when I put her in bed.

"I won't sleep unless you're here," she whines.

I chuckle. "All right, then."

I shed my shirt so the buttons won't be uncomfortable, and slide into bed next to her.

She cuddles up to me like she does every night, her head against my chest.

It's like she's meant to fit there, like we're two puzzle pieces.

Bree drifts off while I stroke her hair.

What the hell am I going to do?

I'm in love with my enemy's daughter, and there's nothing at all I can do about that.

What will I do if she has betrayed me?

25

BREE

When I wake up, Declan is gone, but he's left me a note.

Tonight, we're having a private dinner together. Wear something sexy.

I smile a little, looking down at the paper in my hand.

It seems such a sweet idea, but then, in the back of my mind, I'm questioning it.

What if he knows? What if today is my last day on earth because he's figured it out, and he's going to take me out?

I need a distraction, so I throw on my bikini and head out to the pool. It's quiet out there, no one at the patio or in the water, so I'll have some time alone.

I jump into the end of the pool, doing a few laps back and forth until my muscles are tired and trembling.

There's no way I can think when I exhaust myself, so I do it again, only stopping when my thighs are cramping. I don't want to drown. Or do I?

I get out of the pool and head to one of the patio chairs, sitting down and finishing reading my book.

It's an interesting plot, and it's even more interesting

when I relate it to my own life. Capote starts to believe and trust the man who killed all those people, and he doesn't know how to feel about it.

It reminds me of myself and Declan. At first, I'd thought he was going to kill me. I thought he was really the Irish scourge, really a brutal, hateful man who wanted me and my family dead.

And I guess he does want my father dead, but I cannot blame him. If he had done that to my mother, I don't know what I would do.

It reminds me, though, that I don't really know *what* happened to my mother. She was just gone. Can I trust my father to have told me the truth?

I used to believe him. Now? I just don't know.

There's so much that I don't know, but I do know that if I die tonight, I want to go out in style.

I make my way back to my bedroom and take a quick shower before rifling through my closet.

There's a knock on my open door, and I turn with a huff.

It's Paige. "Just wondered if you wanted anything for lunch," she says. "Da said we could order takeout."

"Sure," I mutter, still flipping through my clothes.

"What are you looking for?"

"Some outfit to wear tonight. Declan wants to have a private dinner."

"Ooh la la," Paige teases. "Why don't you come up with me and we'll look through my things? I know you have a little more junk in the trunk than I do, but we're pretty much the same size otherwise."

I laugh softly. "Thanks, Paige. I appreciate it, but I don't know..." I pause, trying to figure out how to say we have different styles without being offensive.

"I bet I have *something* you can wear." Paige takes my hand tugging me toward her suite.

I walk into her huge closet, and I almost lose myself in all the clothes.

She's right, she has to have something in here I can wear.

I pick out a few outfits, and Paige picks out some shoes, a pair of bright red heels and a pair of strappy black sandals.

I choose the sandals and pair it with a cream-colored dress that fits me a little snug around the backside.

Declan likes my curves, though, and the plunging neckline shows off what I have for cleavage.

"My brother's eyes will pop out of his head," Paige says happily as I tie the sandals on to be sure they fit.

"What are we getting for takeout?" I ask, but I'm so anxious I'm not sure I can eat.

We go down to the dining room after the food gets there, Thai food, and I pick at my glass noodles.

"You seem nervous about this dinner," Paige points out. "What's going on? Is Declan still being an ass?"

I blink. "Has he been?"

"To me, he has," Paige huffs. "He told me I talked too much the other day at dinner."

"I'm sorry, Paige," I grumble. "It's probably my fault he's been such a jerk."

"Why? What happened?"

"I can't really talk about it," I mutter, hoping she'll drop it, and wonder of wonders, she does.

She pushes her salad to me. "Take a few bites. You're wasting away, you know? I've barely seen you eat in the last couple weeks."

I take a couple bites just to placate her, smiling.

"You know, Paige, whatever happens…. I want you and Lara to know that you've been great sisters to me."

Paige frowns. "Why are you talking like that?"

I shake my head. "No reason. Just overthinking things, I guess."

"Well, stop it. We're going to be sisters forever."

I chuckle a little, and then head back up to the bedroom, taking a hot bath and shaving everything so that I'll be fresh and bare for Declan. I want him to know what he's missing if he decides to off me, and if he doesn't…. well, I'm hoping for some post-dinner sex.

It's the one thing we're good at, after all.

As I'm doing my hair, just curling it at the ends, someone knocks on the door. It's Marisol and another maid, one I haven't met, and they smile sheepishly.

There's a small table out in the hallway.

"We need to set up, ma'am," Marisol says.

"Please, call me Bree."

She smiles wider but just ushers me out.

I finish getting ready in the hallway bathroom, taking my makeup with me.

When I return, the small dining table is set up in the middle of the room with a candelabra in the middle. There's a white, lacy tablecloth covering it, and I find it quite adorable.

I smile, looking at it, and then Declan comes in behind me, putting a hand on my hip.

"You look amazing," he says, right in my ear, and I shudder at his low tone.

I turn to look at him, and he's wearing a black pair of tailored slacks and a silk shirt, halfway unbuttoned.

"You look great, too." I smile.

He smiles back and goes to pull one chair back, gesturing for me to sit. I do.

He sits across from me as I cross my legs, and then Marisol and the other maid bring in the food.

The plates are huge, covered in what appears to be shrimp and steak.

My mouth is watering.

"I know how much you like surf and turf," Declan says. "So, I asked for a special dinner."

"Is that a T-bone?" I ask, loving my steak large and rare.

"Rare, just like you like it." He grins at me.

He waits for me to take a bite, and I hesitate, wondering idly if it's poisoned. But then he cuts into his steak, and I do the same.

The first bite tastes like sawdust on the back of my tongue.

Is this it? Is this the last moment I'll have with Declan?

But Declan just frowns, pushing my plate toward me with his fork.

"Eat up, princess." He grins wickedly. "You're going to need your strength."

I nod and continue to eat, and eventually, it starts to taste amazing. "God, it's so good. Perfectly cooked."

"Marisol is a culinary genius." Declan nods, chewing.

Marisol has also poured us a glass of wine—white for me, and red for Declan.

I hate red wine, and I guess she's noticed that over the time I've been here. It strikes me as very sweet, and tears almost come to my eyes.

Declan seems to notice. "Baby, what's wrong?"

"This is just all so sweet," I sniffle. "What made you think of this?"

I freeze, waiting for him to reveal that he knows, that

he's cracked the code. But as I wait, looking at him, I realize that there is a bruise across his cheekbone, and his knuckles seem raw.

"Did someone hurt you?" I ask, worried that it was my father's men.

"Gray and I had a difference of opinion."

I can't help but roll my eyes. "Fighting with your brother? Isn't that a little immature?"

"I was defending you," Declan says fiercely. "He said some things that he couldn't take back. Made accusations..." he trails off.

I soften despite myself and put my hand on top of his for a second. "Well, thank you. But still, why are we here tonight?"

"You've just seemed so sad lately, princess. I wanted to cheer you up. See if there was anything I could do to help."

My heart clenches in my chest. I put my fork down, making a decision. Even if this is it, even if this is my last night on earth, I won't end things without telling him the truth.

It's now or never.

"You're right." I take a deep breath. "I haven't been okay lately, and it's all your fault."

Declan looks at me, raising an eyebrow.

"You kidnapped me. You brought me here to your family, forced me to marry you."

Declan's face falls, but I keep going.

"But I've come to realize something. It's not easy for me."

Declan reaches across the table to take my hand.

I squeeze it softly, trembling all over. "I don't even know how it happened. It probably *shouldn't* have happened, given everything. But I'm in love with you, Declan Burke."

The room falls silent, and I keep searching his face, but his expression is blank.

"You mean that?" His voice is raspy. "You really mean that, princess?"

"I really do," I shrug, looking down at my plate. "I know it's stupid, but—"

Declan stands up, pulling me to my feet and putting his arms around me. "You don't understand," he says in a low tone. "I'm in love with you, too, Bree."

All the air leaves my lungs. "Wh-What did you say?"

"I'm so fucking in love with you I can't see straight. God help us both."

We laugh almost in unison, and it's the only sound in the room before Declan leans down to kiss me, slowly, sweetly.

I deepen the kiss, sliding my tongue against his.

Declan kisses me over and over, pulling away briefly to look at me and then kissing me again as if he can't get enough.

He pushes me toward the bed, and my knees hit the back of it as I fall back down on it. Instead of covering me with his body, though, he bunches my dress over my hips, sliding down my body until he's crouching on the floor.

He loops my legs over his shoulders, looking down at my bare sex with hunger in his dark blue eyes.

He presses his face against me, and I moan as he laps at my clit, sliding two fingers inside me and angling them up to hit my g-spot.

I can't breathe for a brief moment while he works me over, and then I'm coming, so quickly I can't believe it.

"God, you taste so good," he murmurs against my inner thigh, kissing me there, leaving his mark on me.

I want him to leave it everywhere.

I feel giddy, drunk even though I've only had half a glass of wine.

Declan loves me. He really loves me, feels the same way that I do.

Declan doesn't let up, pressing his face against me again, locking his lips around my clit and pumping his fingers in and out of me.

Eventually, he adds a third finger, and I feel so full that I come again, crying out his name.

"That's right, baby. Come all over my tongue," he moans, and then I put my hands in his hair, pulling him up.

"I want you," I pant. "Want you inside me."

"You don't have to ask me twice." He wipes his hand across his mouth.

He takes off his shirt, discarding it, and unbuttons his slacks, stepping out of them and his underwear at once. His dick stands thick and heavy in front of him, and my mouth is watering all over again.

I wish I could have him in my mouth again, but I'm too worked up after two orgasms, want him inside me, looking into my eyes as he makes love to me.

And this time, it will be making love for both of us. Because we love each other.

I'm in awe of it, can't believe that he feels the same way, but I'm grateful nonetheless. I can't believe I thought I might die tonight but in reality, I'm getting everything I want.

Guilt rockets through me, but when Declan guides himself inside me, I moan out his name, unable to think any further.

He looks into my eyes, cupping my face as he moves inside me, and tears start to fill my eyes almost immediately.

"Are you all right?" Declan whispers and stops his movements.

I whine, rocking my hips forward. "I'm fine. I just... I feel a lot."

"I feel a lot too." He groans as he thrusts in and out. "God, I'm so close already. I love the way you taste."

"Don't worry." I giggle. "This can last all night."

"We've got all the time in the world." And he thrusts into me harder, more sloppily.

I know that he's close, and I dig my nails into his shoulders.

He hisses at the sting before spilling inside of me, and when he's done, he collapses on top of me, holding himself up with just his forearms.

I smile, kissing along the side of his face, and Declan chuckles.

"We didn't finish dinner."

"Let's have naked dinner," I say wickedly, wiggling out from under him and standing to take off my dress, unzipping it and letting it fall to the floor.

Declan grins and, already naked, takes the table and pulls it closer to the bed, taking our plates off it and handing me mine.

I take off my strappy shoes while Declan discards his socks and shoes.

"Naked dinner. Can't believe I didn't think of this before." He cuts into his steak and eats a big piece. "It's even good lukewarm," he groans.

I pop a shrimp into my mouth, grinning at him.

"When did you know?" I ask him, and he stops chewing, thinking.

"I honestly don't know," he says quietly. "It happened

so gradually that all of a sudden, it just hit me. I think I was watching you sleep, actually."

I've never seen Declan flush, but his cheeks are a little pink as he looks away.

"That's so sweet." I feel like a girl who's just gotten her first boyfriend, but I can't help it. I'm in love, and we're married, and he feels the same way. It's like everything else doesn't matter anymore.

"What about you?" he asks.

"Same as you," I answer honestly. "I don't know how it happened, it just... one day, I was in love."

"It's so weird," he comments, finishing his food. "I think there's dessert downstairs."

"I'll put on a robe and get it."

He grabs my wrist as I get out of bed. "Hurry back."

Smiling, I throw on a robe and go downstairs for dessert.

Marisol and Patrick are in the dining room, and they're awfully close to each other.

They break apart as I grab dessert, two individual lava cakes.

"Bree," Patrick says, his cheeks flushed.

"Patrick." I grin. "And Marisol."

She heads into the kitchen, not looking at me, and I wonder what's going on with them.

I head up the stairs, eager to tell Declan what I've just seen.

"Declan, does your da have something going on with Marisol?"

"God, I hope so." Declan takes the cake from me.

I giggle. "I just caught them downstairs standing really close to each other."

"I hope it happens."

"Really?"

Declan nods, eating his cake. "Da's been in love with the memory of my mother since... He deserves some love and happiness."

"You told me she wasn't here before your Ma passed." I still feel a large amount of guilt that it was my father who did it.

"She wasn't. She came shortly after because Da couldn't do it all himself. He soon realized someone had to cook for us."

"Ah," I say quietly. "I understand how that could be hard."

"But he deserves to move on. To love again. To be loved."

"You all do." I think of what Lara told me the other day. They'd all been so affected by their mother's death. I wish there was something I could do.

Declan puts our desserts, mine uneaten, on the nightstand, and pulls me into his lap.

"I hope you didn't think we were done yet, wife." He gives me a wicked grin.

"I was hoping we weren't." I grin back, feeling him hard against my ass as I straddle his lap.

I hope this night lasts forever.

26

DECLAN

BREE ROCKS HER HIPS AGAINST MINE, HER AMPLE ASS sliding against my erection, and I groan, lifting her up by her hips.

I slide into her, thrusting up, and she cries out, bracing herself on my shoulders.

I'm almost all the way healed, so it doesn't hurt when she drags her nails through my chest.

In fact, I love the sting of it, want it to burn later while I'm in the shower, so that I'm always thinking of her.

"I love you," I tell her, panting against her ear, taking her earlobe into my mouth.

"I love you too," she says, her voice pitching up into a moan when I slide my hands up her back and let her bounce on top of me, rocking her hips desperately for friction.

"Make yourself come, princess."

She mewls out a moan, rolling her hips faster and faster.

I grit my teeth, my balls aching, to keep from spilling into her.

I want this to last all night, want to be inside of her as

much as I possibly can be, but when she starts to pulse around me, breathing out my name over and over in a chant, I can't hold back.

I flip her onto her back, making love to her slowly and steadily, kissing along her neck, her chin, her mouth.

I capture her tongue with my mouth, sucking on it, and she moans against my lips.

"I'm going to come again," she gasps, and I grin, fucking her in longer strokes as she starts to clench around me.

"I wish I could do this forever," I groan, knowing that my orgasm is approaching, and when I come, I stiffen, leaning down to kiss her deeply.

I nip at her lip as I pull away, plopping down next to her, and she puts her head on my chest, just like always.

I smile, playing idly with her auburn curls.

"I can barely believe it," she says after a long moment when we've both come down.

"Believe what?"

"That you love me back." She lifts her head to smile at me. "I was going crazy. I thought I was alone in all of this."

"I thought the same thing," I admit. "I thought I was the crazy one, and you still hated me."

"I only hated you when I didn't know you." Bree nuzzles against my neck. "I fell in love with you as I got to know you."

"Same here." I hum, smiling, closing my eyes, the sheets tangled all around us.

I don't want to leave here. I don't want to separate from her after this night, especially when I know it can come crashing down on top of me.

I think I know, deep down, that she sent a message to her father. I'm pretty sure that it's the only way they could have known what day we'd be out and about. Now that Jimmy has been cleared...

I was hoping that tonight, she would come clean. I thought maybe she'd tell me, and that would go a long way to me forgiving her.

But instead, she told me that she loves me. That's so much better.

Bree drifts off with me playing with her hair, her breathing low and even.

I want to stay here, wish I could drift off with her, but I'm not sure I can sleep tonight at all.

I slowly extricate myself from Bree's arms and legs, and she whimpers but doesn't wake, cuddling my pillow instead.

My heart clenches in my chest.

She's so sweet and beautiful. How could she have betrayed me? I don't even want to think about it.

Instead, I decide to clean up the mess in the room, taking the dishes downstairs.

Marisol and my father aren't in the dining room or the kitchen, so I guess Bree scared them off. I really do hope they're able to start something. They both deserve happiness, and my mother would have wanted my da to have it.

It's not Bree's fault that her father killed my mother, but it's hard to understand how I fell in love with her.

I guess I can understand Gray's anger.

After cleaning up, there's nothing more I can do so I put on a pair of shorts and a tight t-shirt and head to the gym. It's nearly two in the morning, but it's an all-night gym, and no one will be there.

I'm shocked when I see Cillian on the treadmill. "What the hell are you doing here?"

"I could ask you the same thing," he pants, slowing

down the treadmill. "Just couldn't sleep. Thought I'd tire myself out."

"Same here." I step onto the machine and put it on a high incline so we can talk.

"What's wrong with you?" Cillian asks.

"I'm in love with my wife, who happens to also be a Murphy," I tell him.

Cillian whistles. "I hate to say I told you so, but I thought this might happen. You're sure you're in love?"

"Pretty fucking sure," I mutter, walking at a slow pace to warm up. "We had dinner tonight, alone, and she told me she loves me, too."

Cillian raises an eyebrow. "Isn't that good news?"

"It should be. But I'm still not sure if she got a message out to her father. If she did, she set me up to be killed."

Cillian shakes his head. "That's a hell of a thing to think about your wife."

"I'm just going to have to crack that code. That's the only way."

"Look for inconsistencies." Cillian shrugs. "Things that don't seem quite right."

"Thank you." I nod. "That actually helps."

I need to reread the letters. There's something just at the back of my mind that I can't quite put my finger on. But for now, I need to work out, let off some steam. If I don't, I feel like my head will blow off.

I turn the machine up and break into a run, and thirty minutes later, I've sweated through my shirt.

Cillian and I hit the showers, and after, we part ways with a fist bump.

Cillian's a good guy, but he's not exactly the kind of guy you have deep conversations with.

Somehow, though, he's given me an idea.

I rush home and head into my office, taking the letters and reading them side by side.

But it doesn't help. There still doesn't seem to be any inconsistencies. The mention of the dog is kind of weird, but Bree mentioned the cocker spaniel once at dinner. I guess she really doesn't talk about her much, though.

Is it something to do with the dog?

It's nearing daylight when someone knocks on my open door.

I look up to see my father standing in the doorway.

"Can I come in?"

"Of course." I gesture to the chair in front of my desk.

He sits down, looking at me intently. "So, you know that Jimmy is cleared."

"I know, Da. I know what you're going to say. I've been looking over the letters, trying to figure out the code—"

"You *don't* know what I'm going to say," Da says. "I want you to drop it."

"What?"

"It doesn't matter. Murphy is going to come for us no matter what we do. So, just let it go."

"I can't let it go!" I exclaim. "If someone's lying to us—"

"The truth always comes out, boyo." It's something he's always said.

Then he simply stands up and walks out into the hallway.

What the hell? Was he telling me that he believes it's Bree, too, but to let it go? He can't be saying that.

And even if Da did forgive it, that doesn't mean that I will. She's been lying to me all this time. For weeks.

I won't forgive that. I can't.

I look down at the paper and still, I can't find anything. My eyes are crossing, and I'm feeling tired and irritated, so I walk across the hall to my bedroom, slowly opening the door.

Bree is sitting up in bed, her auburn hair mussed from our sex last night. She frowns at me.

"Where have you been?"

"Working," I mutter.

She raises an eyebrow. "You're in a mood."

"I'm not." I walk over to the bed and sit down on the edge, taking hold of her ankle in one hand.

"Declan," she mutters, looking up at me from under her long eyelashes. "About last night... if you didn't mean it—"

"I meant it." And it's true. I do love her, but I don't know what that means for us—especially if she's betrayed me.

Can I forgive something like that, especially when I still have an ache in my chest from the bullet? How do I know she doesn't want me dead, just like her father?

Bree smiles, relief clear on her face. "Me, too."

I try to smile back at her, but it feels forced, and she must notice, too.

"Something's going on. What's wrong, Declan?"

I shake my head. "It's just boring work stuff, princess. Nothing to worry your pretty little head about."

Bree rolls her eyes but she's still smiling, and I think I've thrown her off the subject.

"I'm not some wilting violet, you know? I can handle some work stuff." She pauses. "After all, I used to do my dad's books."

Did you? Did you see where he stole half of our shipments? Did you know about it?

I can't stop thinking about it. I can't stop wondering if she isn't nearly as innocent as I thought she was.

I don't blame her for what Murphy did, at least not to a

point. But regardless of what she said before, I need to know if she knew. If she knew the kind of man he was and still sent him after me. Because if she did, I don't know if I can forgive her. I don't know if I even want to.

I clear my throat, needing a distraction.

I climb up onto the bed on my knees, grabbing Bree's ankles in each hand and spreading her thighs. She's only wearing the sheet, and it rides up around her waist as I position her.

I spread her thighs with my hands, watching her face.

Bree grins up at me. "Didn't get enough last night?"

"Don't think it'll ever be enough," I murmur, and yank her closer to me.

She squeals and then moans as I roll my hips against her sex.

"I know the feeling," she murmurs, blinking those big hazel eyes up at me. The green in them seems more pronounced in the sunlight streaming through the window.

She's beautiful, and my heart aches, wondering if she's not nearly as innocent as she seems. Murphy blood runs through her veins, but has he gotten to her heart, too?

I can't imagine I'd feel the same way about her if I knew she'd really betrayed me.

Not wanting to think anymore, I push down my sweats, freeing my bobbing erection, and she looks at it hungrily.

"Sit up," I order in a low tone. "Want to fill that pretty mouth of yours."

She scrambles into a sitting position, eagerly leaning forward and wrapping her small hand around my base. As she takes me into her mouth, I hiss in a sharp breath as pleasure rockets through me.

"Good girl," I murmur, gathering her thick, auburn hair

in a ponytail and moving her head up and down in the rhythm that I want. "Good fucking girl."

She moans around me, and the vibration sends an ache through my cock.

I start to move her head faster, and she relaxes her throat, letting me fuck her mouth.

I roll my hips, and she gags, tears streaming down her face. The sight only makes me hotter, and I look down at her.

I pause but she drags her nails along my thighs to encourage me, making eye contract.

She can take it. She wants to.

Thrusting harder, chasing my orgasm, my balls start to ache as I get close.

When I tug her hair sharply, she cries out at the sting, popping off me.

I pull her head up so that she's looking at me and attack her mouth, kissing her deeply, tasting the salt of me on her tongue.

I push her down on the bed after I pull away, pulling her legs over my biceps.

She feels hot against me and when I slide my fingers through her lower lips, she's slick and ready.

Grabbing myself by the base, I guide myself into her, pushing into her, thrusting forward instinctively.

Bree moans, throwing her head back and fisting her hands in the sheets. "F-fuck."

"So fucking hot," I mumble, not even sure what I'm saying.

All I know is that I don't want to think anymore, don't want to worry that she's broken my trust and my heart and I just can't accept it.

I want to empty all these bad feelings into her body,

leave my mark on her so that if she has betrayed me, she'll remember me forever.

I thrust into her roughly, riding her hard, and Bree goes limp beneath me like a rag doll, like a sex doll for me to use. It's so hot that I'm close to the edge already.

When she starts to mewl like a kitten and pulse around me, I can't take it anymore.

I rock my hips into her in a decidedly unsteady motion, and finally spill inside her, gasping out her name.

"Declan," she answers, and the sound of my name on her mouth makes me grab her by the hair again, kiss her dirty and deep.

"God, I love you," I mumble against her lips, knowing that it's true, knowing that it might be my ruin.

"I love you, too." She smiles at me, her hazel eyes as innocent as the rest of her body is wanton.

I roll to the side, panting, and just like always, Bree puts her head on my chest.

My heart thuds too hard against my chest plate, but she doesn't seem to notice.

She's dozing in minutes, and while she's napping, I extract myself from her arms, padding into the hallway, planning to go downstairs for a snack.

All that activity last night and this morning has really taken it out of me, and there's no way I can sleep with all the thoughts swirling in my mind.

I walk down the hallway, and the sound of sniffling makes me lift my head from where I've been looking down at my feet, dejected.

I look up to see my baby sister's room with the door slightly ajar, and her sitting on the bed, tears streaming down her face.

"Paige? *A'stor*, what's wrong?" I ask, instantly going to her.

She throws herself into my arms, pressing her face against my chest and sobbing as if her heart is breaking.

"Are you all right?" I stroke her hair, and she starts to calm down.

"I'm fine." She pulls away and wipes tears from her face with the back of her hand. "It's just…"

"You can talk to me." I hate it when my sisters are upset.

Her eyes well with tears again as she looks up at me. "I'm just… alone. I'm so alone, Declan."

"You're not alone, *a'stor*," I promise her. "You've got us—"

"It's not the same!" she bursts out. "You have Bree, and you're so happy…"

Happy isn't exactly the term I'd use, giving what's going on lately, but Paige wouldn't know much about that. We try to keep her out of the loop when it comes to business, because Paige is sensitive, probably the most innocent of all of us.

"Oh, honey," I say, smiling a little. "You're so young. You'll find someone."

"You think?" she sniffles.

"I know. Especially now that you are moving out like you wanted." I smirk. "No more need to sneak out like you did back in high school."

Her eyes widen, but she barks out a laugh in spite of her sadness, and I smile widely, giving her a quick hug.

"You'll find the one, Paige. It just takes time."

"What's it like?" she almost whispers. "Being in love?"

"God," I answer, laughing softly. "It's crazy. It's like being on a roller coaster—one minute you're having a blast and the next you're scared out of your mind."

"That sounds scary."

"It is a little scary." I pat her shoulder. "But it's worth it."

"It is?"

"It is. Because when it's good, Paige... it's the best feeling in the world."

She sniffles once more and then rubs her eyes. "I'm sorry. I really am happy for you, Declan. It's just... it's hard to watch someone get everything I want."

"You'll get there, *a'stor*."

"You promise?"

"I promise. Your new life will have it all."

"I guess you're right. I'm just nervous because it's time for me to move out, and I'll be really alone. I've never been by myself before, so..." She shrugs, looking at her hands.

"We are just a phone call away, and the doors here are always open for you."

"Thank you." She smiles, leaning up to kiss me on the cheek, and lies down on the bed.

I leave her room, shaking my head as I head down the stairs. I don't know what precipitated that breakdown, but I'm grateful for the distraction.

Gray is downstairs, eating from a bowl of fruit, and I sit next to him, grabbing a couple of grapes and slices of apples. He grunts and pushes the bowl toward me.

It's all the apology two brothers need, and we eat in silence for a few minutes.

"Marisol says I'll spoil my lunch." Gray chuckles.

"With fruit?" I scoff. "No way."

The Burke boys eat like horses, and a little bowl of fruit between the two of us is barely a drop in the bucket.

"Did you talk to Da?" Gray looks at me sideways.

"I did." I nod, hoping he's not going to bring up Bree again.

He just nods, and my shoulders slump in relief.

Gray has a point—it's strange that Murphy targeted the warehouse that day, since we weren't even getting a shipment—and he's probably right. Bree probably did send her father a message. What I need to know is *why*.

"I'm glad Jimmy's not the rat," Gray comments. "I'd hate to kill him."

I snort out a laugh. "Jimmy's as loyal as the day is long."

Gray looks at me for a long moment, as if he wants to ask me something, but then he looks away, sipping his tea. "There's more in the pot if you want some," he grumbles, and then gets up, leaving me alone with my thoughts.

At least Gray isn't on my ass about Bree anymore.

That's something.

Now, if I can just convince myself that she's innocent, I'll be on easy street.

But can I do that? Can I put my family at risk just because I'm in love with my wife?

27

———

BREE

As happy as I've been the past few days, I'm still losing my mind. Guilt is eating me up, knowing that Declan was hurt by what I did. In my defense, I hadn't expected my father to go after him. I'd expected him to come rescue me, but knowing now who my father is, I should have expected things to go sideways.

And now, I don't know what to do. It felt so good after Declan confessed that he loved me, but how can he love me if he doesn't know what I've done?

I'm going crazy, like I don't know which end is up.

I need to clear my head. It's been a few days since Declan confessed, but he's still acting strangely. He doesn't talk to me unless we're making love, and Gray and Patrick seem to be avoiding me. The only Burkes who aren't acting weird are Paige and Lara.

I put on my swimsuit, just a one-piece this time, and go down to the pool house, wearing a pair of flip-flops that clack against my feet as I walk.

I'm hoping to get in a few laps by myself, hoping that

it'll help me decide what to do, but when I arrive, Lara is sunbathing out at the pool.

She's so pale I assume she needs a high SPF, but she seems to be enjoying the sun. She looks at me over her sunglasses as I pad up to her.

"Bree," she greets. "Where have you been lately?"

I wince. I guess I've been avoiding Paige and Lara just a little bit. Their exuberance would just make me feel more guilty.

It's easier now that Paige is moving out today, but I'm sure she'll still be here all the time. At least Lara is more low key.

"Just... existing," I say awkwardly. "Declan has been keeping me busy."

Lara smirks and winks at me. "I can believe that."

I snort out a laugh, surprised at her suggestion of vulgarity. Lara always seems so classy.

"What have you been up to?"

She shrugs. "You know, just living the life. Shopping, going out with my friends..." She trails off, probably remembering my circumstances here.

"Must be nice."

"You know, after some time, Declan will let up on the whole..." she trails off again.

"Keeping me prisoner?" I ask dryly.

She laughs. "Something like that."

"Honestly, lately I haven't minded it," I admit, sitting next to her on one of the lounge chairs. "I haven't felt much like going out or socializing."

"Because of Declan getting hurt? Honey, that wasn't your fault."

I bite the inside of my cheek so hard I taste iron on my tongue.

It *is* my fault. If I hadn't sent that coded message to my father...

"I guess," I mutter, not sure how else to respond.

"Things seem... different between you two," Lara comments. "Not as contentious."

I smile slightly. "He told me that he loved me."

Lara sits bolt upright. "He did?"

I nod, my smile widening.

"Do you love him back?"

"You know I do."

Lara grins, bouncing on the lounge chair. She looks almost like Paige when she does that.

"I'm so excited for you, Bree, you have no idea."

"Excited?"

"I always hoped this would happen," she explains. "I hoped that you would sway Declan. He's always been so serious, so focused on work. He needs someone like you in his life."

He deserves better than me.

"I don't know about that," I mutter.

Lara frowns, opening her mouth like she's going to say something, but then Paige squeals and runs toward us, wearing her bikini.

"Bree!" she exclaims, leaning over to draw me into a hug.

I pat her back, smiling. "Hey, Paige. Excited about moving out?"

I'd hoped that I would miss her and she'd be gone already. She is too cheery for my current mood.

But now that she's here, I'm grateful for the distraction.

"Oh, my god. I can't believe that is today! My things are being taken to the house as we speak. Da only wants me to

go when all is in its place. But I have to make us some cele-
bratory mimosas."

Lara mock-gags. "I'm still hungover from last night."

Paige huffs. "I'm still mad you went out to that new club
without me."

"It's not *that* new."

"I haven't been." Paige plops down on the lounge chair
next to me. "I never get to go out without a chaperone. I
don't see why you do."

"Please," Lara snorts. "Da always sends someone out
with me. I just learned how to have fun in spite of it."

"Oh, great one, teach me your ways," Paige says dramatically, and Lara laughs.

I smile at the two of them, glad that they're here. If I'd
been out here by myself, I probably would be going down
some kind of spiral.

"Did you meet anyone interesting?" I ask Lara.

"No. Just the regular joes."

"Regular joes can be fun," Paige points out.

Lara scoffs. "Not to me. I need something different than
the Irishmen who do business with Da."

"I think it's kind of exciting." Paige shrugs. "Guys in the
life, I mean."

"How is it exciting?" Lara's chin almost hits the floor.
"We deal with that kind of stuff all the time. I'd rather have
a guy who probably isn't going to get shot, personally."

"You're a stick in the mud," Paige accuses, and Lara
frowns at her.

"And you're a—"

"Guys, guys," I say, trying to keep the two of them from
fighting. "How about *one* mimosa?"

Paige stands up, smiling at me before glowering at her
sister, and heading inside the pool house to the bar.

Lara sighs. "I try not to let her get to me, but sometimes..."

"Sometimes sisters butt heads. I get it."

"Are you like that with your brother?"

"Rory?" I think about it. "I was before he left home. Weirdly enough we became closer since he turned his back on the family business. We're still not close close, but we talk here and there."

"And why's that?"

I shrug. "I don't know. Maybe we just don't have the same interests."

"What is Rory interested in?"

I laugh. "Who knows?"

Lara laughs with me, and by the time Paige gets back, it seems like their little tiff is over with.

I sip my mimosa slowly, not wanting the depressant part of alcohol to bring my mood down again.

Lara takes one sip and then winces and puts it down. Paige drinks hers like a fish, as usual.

I'm the first one to jump into the pool, and Paige follows suit while Lara continues to sunbathe.

Paige splashes water at her until she finally gets in, sighing as if she's terribly put upon. I can't help but laugh when Paige dunks her and Lara comes up fighting and sputtering.

I swim a few laps and then start to wonder about Declan—where is he? I know he does work during the day, but I've seen both Patrick and Gray around the house this morning. Usually, one or the both of them go with him, especially ever since he got hurt.

I pull myself out of the pool and Paige boos after me.

"First one out is a rotten egg!" she yells, and I turn to smile at her.

"I'll be back," I promise. "I want to go and check on Declan."

"Because you loooove him," Lara shouts, and Paige blinks, bobbing in the water.

"She admitted it?"

"He did, too," Lara says excitedly and Paige dances in the water.

"Yes, I knew it!"

"You did not," Lara groans.

"I did! I told you weeks ago that Declan was crazy about her."

I laugh. "Well, thank you both for the vote of confidence."

As I walk away, Paige is talking excitedly. "It's like she's really our sister now!"

My heart feels somehow full and empty at the same time. If they knew what I've done...

I dry off at the door and walk into the house, padding up the stairs in my bare feet since I've left my flipflops behind.

The door to Declan's office is closed, so I knock lightly.

"Come in," he calls in a grunt, and I slowly open the door.

He looks up at me, and there's something I can't quite name in his expression. Is it hurt? Anger?

Does he know?

He's holding up two sheets of paper, staring at them.

"Wh-what are you doing?" I stutter in an almost whisper.

"Close the door," he barks, and fear rushes through me. *He knows.*

I almost feel relieved. If he knows, then it can just be over. I can just be done.

"I need you to be honest with me, Bree."

I nod slowly, standing in front of his desk.

What happens when he finds out? Does he come after me right away? Shoot me between the eyes? Will he make me suffer first?

"Did you send your father a coded message? I need to know. I need to know if you betrayed me and my family. If you almost got me killed." His face is blank, his blue eyes hard as he stares into my soul.

Tears fill my eyes, and I can't stop them from falling. "That was before," I whisper.

Declan's hands fist, crumpling the papers, and he stands up, nearly knocking the chair over.

"So, you did it. You're the reason we were ambushed, the reason I got shot. You nearly got me killed." His voice is flat and steady, but it cracks at the end. "How could you? How could you tell me that you love me when you betrayed me? Damn you." He throws the papers at me.

They hit me in the chest, and I let them fall to the ground. Tears keep streaming down my face but something like anger is rising up within me.

"That was before, Declan. Before I knew that you loved me. I know it's not much of an excuse, but this is not all on me. You kidnapped me, made me marry you. You made me fall in love with you. Made me torn between my family and yours. Damn you for that!"

"I thought my family was your family." His jaw is tight, and I know he's gritting his teeth so hard his jaw will ache later.

I take a step toward him. "You ripped me from my family. I haven't seen my father in weeks!"

"Your father is a monster!" he roars, slamming his hands down on the desk. "I saved you, can't you see that?"

"I'm not some fucking princess in the tower waiting for

my white knight, Declan," I shoot back. "Nobody asked you to save me. And fuck you for even saying that. You didn't do this out of some need to *save* me. You did it to start a war, and you know that."

"That was before," Declan says softly, his shoulders slumping. "That was before I fell in love with you."

"Then why can't you understand why I did what I did?"

"Because you betrayed me!" he shouts. "Because you lied. Do you even have a dog?"

"I did," I admit, crossing my arms over my chest. "She died years ago."

"So, that was it," he seethes. "It was the fucking dog, all along."

"Does it really matter, Declan? What matters is that this is done. This is over. Kill me if you want to. I'm tired of worrying about it."

He freezes, staring at me, his gaze boring through me. "You really think I could do that? You think I'm just going to jump across this desk and strangle you with my bare hands?"

"I don't know." I tilt my chin up. "How am I supposed to know what you do to someone like me? To a dirty Murphy who got you shot?"

Declan stalks toward me, putting his hands on my shoulders, his fingers digging into my flesh, but I don't wrench away. I look right at him, wanting him to see me before he kills me.

I'm not afraid.

I'm *angry*. How dare he kidnap me, force me into this life, and then get mad at me when I try to escape it?

"What would you have done?" I demand to know. "What would you have done if someone uprooted you from your life, showed you a whole new way? Would you just take it? Or would you try to escape any way you could?"

Declan loosens his grip, and I wrench away from him.

"You act like you and your family are perfect, like you've done nothing wrong," I accuse. "But who was it that started all of this? Because it damn sure wasn't me."

"You can't argue that your father isn't a monster."

I scoff. "And you can't argue that yours isn't one either!" My voice raises. My skin feels hot all over, and looking at Declan, I can't believe this is the same man who had his arms wrapped around me all night.

"It's different," he insists, and I bark out a bitter laugh.

"Of course, it is. It's always different when it's you, isn't it? If I'm so beneath you, then why did you ever make love to me? Why did you tell me that you loved me? Why did you *marry* me? And why won't you let me go?"

He's trembling enough that I notice it. "The Burkes don't sexualize children. The Burkes respect women, not send them to prostitute themselves. There's a difference between Niall Murphy and my da."

"No, you just sell drugs and guns to adults," I grit out. "That's *so* much better. Do you know how many people the Burkes have gotten hooked on dust? How many sisters, daughters? Do you know how many of them turned to prostitution to support their habit? How many people have your guns killed, Declan? You have no room to be on the moral high horse, here."

Declan doesn't answer, just staring at me. He knows I'm right.

"Your family isn't better than mine. You're just kidding yourself. And you've been in the game longer. So *yes*, I sent a message to my father. I didn't know he was a monster then. I didn't know he would have you shot. I thought he'd come and save me. Because you *kidnapped* me. I didn't choose this. I didn't choose *you*."

Pain flashes across Declan's face. "Is that what this is all about? You lied when you said you loved me?"

I pinch the bridge of my nose between my thumb and forefinger. "No, Declan. I told the truth. I wanted out. I wanted to go home. But that's before I realized that *you* were my home. I've been sorry, sick to my stomach ever since you were injured. I didn't want that. I didn't ask for that."

"That doesn't matter," he growls. "You still betrayed me."

"I *know* that it doesn't matter. I know there's no forgiveness, but the least you can do is be completely honest with yourself. You may say you love me, Declan, but you'll never truly see me as anything but a weapon against my family."

I stare at him for a moment longer before yanking the door open and stalking into the hallway. Paige is at the top of the stairs, her eyes wide.

"Not now," I grind out, and storm into the bedroom, slamming the door.

I plop down on the bed, the tears coming now, faster than I could have expected.

Someone knocks on the door.

"Go away!" I scream, but a small voice comes through the door.

"It's Paige. Please let me in."

"I can't right now, Paige," I sob, but she comes in anyway, quickly shutting the door behind her.

"I'm not going to ask what happened." She sits on the edge of the bed. "All I know is that you seem sad and angry, and I know that feeling. I just want to be here for you."

She draws me into her arms, and I fight her at first but

eventually, I bury my head in her lap, sobbing like a child as she strokes my hair.

It feels comforting. My mother used to do this for me when I was young and full of big emotions. Right now, I feel like my heart is tearing in two.

Who am I? Am I Bree Murphy or Bree Burke? Am I some combination of the two? How dare Declan accuse me of being a monster like my father is when he's the spitting image of his?

After some time, I manage to calm down, and Paige smiles at me.

"God, I left a snotty wet spot on your cover-up," I sniffle, and Bree laughs.

"That's okay. I've got a million more." She pauses. "If you ever *do* want to talk about it..."

"I don't." I shake my head, but then give her a weak smile. "But thank you. Thank you for being here."

"I just wanted to help."

I take her hands in mine, squeezing them. "It really did help."

I'm telling the truth. Paige and Lara are like the sisters I never had.

Paige stands up, leaving me be and turning off the light as she leaves.

I bury myself in the sheets that smell like Declan and look up at the ceiling, replaying our argument over and over in my mind.

I don't regret a single thing I said because I said the truth.

Declan may hate me for what I've done, and that's fine. I deserve it.

But I refuse to let him lie to himself.

He's as much at fault as I am.

28

DECLAN

I CURSE, SLAMMING MY FIST INTO THE WALL, RIGHT BY where Bree was standing. My fist goes through the sheetrock. I remove it with a wince and my knuckles are bleeding.

Usually, when I'm in the midst of an argument, I know that I'm right. Right now, I'm not sure.

Bree said some things that make sense—I *had* taken her from her home, her family. I imprisoned her here, and now I'm punishing her for trying to get out?

But on the other hand, she told me that she loved me. She'd said that she feels the same way about me as I do about her, and that implies trust. She could have come to me. She could have asked me if she could go.

Would I have taken that well, though?

I sigh, knowing that I wouldn't have. We would have had this same fight, and maybe I'd feel just as betrayed.

I head into the bathroom in the hallway, bandaging my knuckles, because I'm going to need to go to the gym. I can't stay here, god knows, and I can't keep pretending like everything's okay when everything's falling apart around me.

I don't bother calling Cillian, knowing that I'll be terrible company. I just drive there like a maniac, trying not to think.

What if Bree's right? What if we're just like Murphy?

She's definitely right about the dust, and she's right that it's hooked a lot of people. How many bullets from my guns have gone into women? Children?

I've wanted this fight to be over for so long, but I'd never quite understood that we're also in the wrong.

When I arrive at the gym, I run on the treadmill until I want to throw up, and then go over to the punching bag, beating the hell out of it.

Each sting in my knuckles reminds me of the bruises I've probably left on Bree's shoulders. Each sting reminds me of the ache in my heart.

She betrayed me.

But why am I so shocked? I knew it all along. I knew she was a Murphy at heart.

Bree made some good points in that argument, though, I have to admit. She's right. We do bad things. We tell ourselves it's for the greater good, but is it?

Da always says that if we didn't run drugs and guns, someone less responsible would. And maybe he's right, but that doesn't make it moral. Bree said that our family was just a different kind of monster, and that makes more sense to me than I like to admit.

Cillian walks in just as I'm punching the bag so hard that it shakes on the hook.

"Declan? What are you doing here?"

I grunt, punching the bag again.

"Declan," he says again softly, catching my arm. "Your hand... it's bleeding."

When I pull away, blood is running down my arm. I curse and walk toward the locker room. Cillian follows me.

"Why are you following me around instead of working out?" I snap.

He holds up his hands. "Because you're my friend and you're clearly upset. What's going on?"

I slam the locker door shut after grabbing my towel to wrap around my bleeding knuckles. They were already injured. It's no wonder I'm bleeding.

"She did it. She betrayed us."

Cillian doesn't look shocked. "Is it really that much of a betrayal?"

"I could have *died*, Cillian."

"But you didn't. And even if you had, she didn't pull the trigger. Her father did. But can you blame her? She wanted to be rescued."

"That's not what happened," I say stiffly.

"No, but Murphy's to blame for that, not Bree. She just wanted to go home."

Cillian's words repeating what Bree said are driving me up the wall.

"And why would she want to go home?" I burst out. "I've given her everything."

"Not everything," Cillian murmurs.

"Money, clothes, a roof over her head, protection—"

"Freedom." Cillian raises his eyebrow. "You took away her freedom, Declan. You gave her no choice."

I frown, glaring at him, but in the end, I know that he's right. She didn't have a choice in this marriage. She didn't have a choice in any of this.

So, how can she love me?

My shoulders slump.

Of course, she doesn't love me, after what I've done.

How could she? When she asked me to put myself in her shoes, it had shaken me a little.

She is right. About all of it.

And what am I supposed to do now? Now that I love her. Now that I've lost her.

"You wanna come to my place and get fucked up?"

I let out a breath. "Fuck it. Let's go."

Two hours later, we're singing Irish ditties and drinking Jameson. I keep getting these waves of despair, a depression that makes my shoulders slump.

"You're thinking about her again," Cillian warns.

"I can't stop thinking about her."

He shoves a glass at me, but the amber liquid doesn't seem appealing to me anymore.

"Maybe I should go home."

"You should stay here. Don't want to say anything to her that you might regret."

"Too late."

I let my head fall forward, banging it on the kitchen table, and Cillian snorts out a laugh.

"Man, this is why I don't get close to women. One-night stands are all I need."

"Not like I planned this," I mutter, taking the drink glass and rolling it around in my hand before taking a sip with a grimace.

It still burns, so I'm not drunk enough yet, I suppose.

"Has there ever been a woman for you?" I'm curious, and since we're both close to shitfaced, he might actually tell me the truth.

"Not since high school." Cillian's voice sounds hoarse and far away.

"That young?"

"Everything feels so *big* when you're young, you know?"

I nod, but I'm not altogether sure I know what he means. Seems like things have always been big for me, but my mother used to always say that I was a sensitive one.

I fly off the handle when I'm angry, drown in despair when I'm sad. Which is why being in love has been such a roller coaster for me.

"Everything feels big now."

"You love her?" Cillian leans back in his seat, looking at me.

"Fuck. Yeah." I chug down the rest of my glass of whiskey, and the world tilts on its axis.

Finally.

Maybe I'm on the verge of a blackout so I can forget this whole, awful day.

The next thing I know, I'm in a car on the way home, trying to look out of the window so I don't throw up.

"You all right, boss?" somebody, maybe Sean, asks.

"Fine," I slur, but when I try to get out of the car, I nearly fall flat on my face.

Sean—it is Sean, I can tell even through my swimming vision—all but carries me into the house, making it as far as the couch before he drops me.

I bounce on the couch, and I'm out before my head even hits the cushion.

I wake up to someone standing over me, thrusting a glass of water into my hand.

When I look up, I realize that it's Lara. She's frowning down at me.

"I see you tied one on last night."

"What's it to you?" I mutter, sitting up and putting a hand to my aching head.

"Drink the water." She pushes the glass of water into my hands, and I drain it.

It does help my head a little.

"What happened with you and Bree? She wouldn't come out of the bedroom all day."

"None of your business."

Lara huffs out a breath, crossing her thin arms over her chest. "This family is my business, Declan, and Bree is a part of that."

"Is she?" I stumble to my feet, walking into the bathroom, but Lara just follows me, and once I'm done, she's leaning against the wall outside the bathroom.

"What is that supposed to mean?"

"This marriage was forced on us. Forced on her."

"Maybe, but things have changed since then."

"No, they haven't. She's still a Murphy, and I'm still a Burke."

"No." Lara's voice is raising. She's clearly mad at me, but my head and my heart hurt too much to care. "She's a Burke now. She chose to stay."

I snort. "No, she didn't."

"You're still drunk. Talking nonsense! Sober the fuck up and be real with me for one fucking second."

"She wanted out," I roar. "She sent her dad a message, wanted him to rescue her. She doesn't want to be here. What else can I tell you?"

Lara blinks at me, her face going suddenly pale. "Wh-what?"

"She betrayed us, Lara. She's a Murphy, just like her father. Snake blood runs through her veins," I sneer, and Lara promptly slaps me across the face.

"Don't talk about her like that. She's your wife."

I chuckle bitterly, wondering if I'm still a bit drunk and deciding I don't care.

"She's nothing to me," I mutter, and head up the stairs.

I pass Bree as she is almost at the bottom of the stairs, but I don't even look at her. I can't. Because I know I said that out of hurt. Out of spite. And if I look at her, I'll cave. I'll beg her for forgiveness.

And right now, I think I want her to hurt just as bad as I am.

I make my way up the stairs, my head spinning, my stomach nauseous, and I barely make it to the bathroom before throwing up whiskey and bile. I've barely eaten today.

I breathe hard through my nose, trying not to throw up again, and finally, I stand and splash water on my face, looking at myself in the mirror.

"Get it together," I tell myself. "She's nothing to you."

Maybe if I say it often enough, one day I might believe it.

My reflection looks tired and drawn, looking back at me like I'm the fucking idiot, talking to myself in my own bathroom.

"Fuck her," I whisper. "I don't need her."

The way my heart aches tells me I do, but I ignore it.

I stumble to the bed, lying down fully clothed, and I pray that my sleep is dreamless.

29

———

BREE

"She's nothing to me." Declan's words are running inside my head on an endless, hurtful loop from hell.

I've never been so devastated in my life. I've never been in love before, and I didn't know it could hurt this much.

"He doesn't mean it." Lara reaches for me, but I'm already running back up the stairs to the guest room I've been sleeping in.

I slam into a wall of man, though, and arms go around me.

I try to fight, thinking it might be Declan, but I look up into faded gray eyes.

Patrick.

My lip starts to tremble, and he gathers me into his arms, and I can't help starting to sob, burying my face in his broad chest.

He rubs my back, singing something in a different language—Gaelic, I suppose. It's comforting, and I lean against him, sniffling.

Finally, I pull away, and he smiles down at me.

"Why don't you come into my office?" he asks softly, and I worry for a slight second that he may be angry with me.

It's not like mobsters tell you outright that they're going to kill you.

But at this point, does it even matter?

I follow him into the office, and he gestures to the couch.

I sit down, pulling my legs up beneath me.

"You know what I've done. Who I am."

"Yes." Patrick nods. "I do."

"Are you... are you going to kill me?"

Patrick snorts. "No, no, *a'stor*. Nothing like that. Not over this."

"I know how this kind of stuff works."

"Do you, now?" Patrick gives me a slight smile and raising a silver eyebrow. "Please, enlighten me."

I sigh. "Someone betrays you; you get rid of them."

"Maybe that's the way Niall Murphy does things, but you get more than one chance in the Burke clan."

"Really?" It seems crazy to me that he wouldn't be brutal and swift with his punishment.

"Speaking of Murphy..." He takes his phone to slide across the desk toward me. "You can call him, if you want."

I stare at him, starting to tremble. "You don't mean that."

"I do. All I ask is that you stay in this room while you talk to him."

I just keep looking at the phone, and finally, I pick it up and dial my father's number.

"Hello?"

There's a lot of background sound, like he's throwing a dinner party or something.

My blood starts boiling.

"*Daidí?*"

"Bree," he breathes. "Where are you? Have the Burkes let you go?"

"No," I state. "And I don't want to go."

My father pauses for a long moment. "What was that?"

"I said I don't want to go. I know what you did. They told me what you did to their family, and I don't want anything to do with it or you."

He snorts. "Oh, so they've filled your pretty head with lies, have they? I didn't know you'd turn traitor so easily, Bree." He pauses and then mutters something I can barely understand under his breath, but I know it's about my mother.

"What did you say?"

"I said you are just like your mother."

"What are you talking about?" I stand up. "Did... did you do something to her?"

I don't want to believe he could stoop so low, he could be this much of a monster. But he killed Declan's mom knowing who she was. Could he have done the same with mine?

He wouldn't, right?

He loved her.

My head spins.

"Did. You. Do. Something. To. Her?" Ice and fire run through my veins. I need this answer, but I'm not sure I'm ready for it.

He's silent on the other line for a long moment.

"Same thing I do to all traitors."

My world crumbles as my heart shatters. I can hardly breathe, but he will not get the satisfaction of witnessing me break. "Is that supposed to be an answer or a threat?"

"It's a warning, *wean*. I love you, but I won't hesitate to kill you before you become a Burke, a dog traitor."

"Too late," I hiss. "You should have rescued me like you were supposed to. Back then, my eyes were still blinded to who you are. Now, it's too late. I'm not a Murphy anymore. I disown you. I'm a Burke now, and I'll be the first in line to make sure you get everything coming to you, Niall Murphy."

I hang up the phone, sliding it back across the desk and putting my face in my hands, sobbing. My mother didn't abandon me at all. She was hurt, maybe killed, by Niall Murphy.

He really is the monster Declan claims he is. He is the snake.

And all this time, I've been a pawn in his fucking chess game.

Patrick comes around the desk to crouch and comfort me, drawing me into his arms.

"I've ruined everything!" I sob into his chest, and Patrick chuckles, stroking my hair.

"Declan will calm down, *a'stor*. The truth of the matter is… I don't really blame you, and once he stops being a hothead, he won't, either. You were taken from your family, from everything you ever knew."

"Y-You mean it?" I stutter. "You're not like, lulling me into a false sense of security so you can stab me in the back?"

He laughs out loud. "By god, you're a suspicious soul. I like that about you. It'll keep Declan on his toes. No harm will come to you over this." He pauses, looking at me with a small smile on his face. "You're perfect for Declan, you know?"

I shrink back, withdrawing into myself.

"He hates me."

"There's a very thin line between love and hate, Bree. He's upset with you right now, upset with himself, but he doesn't hate you. If he did, he wouldn't be losing his mind right now. He loves you. Just like you love him."

"I do love him," I whisper, and Patrick smiles wider.

"I know you do, sweetheart. And he knows it, too. He'll come around. It'll all work out."

I stand up, my legs a bit shaky, and Patrick gives me one last hug before I walk out of the office, still sniffling.

Lara meets me in the hallway, holding a champagne glass that appears to be full of orange juice.

"How about mimosas and a horror movie on the big screen?" she suggests.

I blink at her. "You don't... hate me? Don't you know what I did?"

She scoffs. "You did the same thing any of us would have done in your position. Declan's being a dick about it, but he'll get over it. You're our sister, Bree. Of course, we don't hate you."

She takes my arm. "Now. Paige is waiting for us. She says she needs this one last night here with the three of us together, and she'll start her new life tomorrow."

Tears spring to my eyes all over again, but this time, I manage to fight them back and let Lara lead me into the entertainment den.

Paige already has a slasher queued up, and she grins at me.

"You're here!" she exclaims. "I thought she'd never talk you out of bed."

"She didn't. Your father did."

"Knew the old man was good for something."

I sip my mimosa, and she's already pouring more in my glass. I pull my glass back a little, but Paige frowns.

"If anyone needs this, you do," she says, and I nod after a moment.

"I guess you're right."

Champagne doesn't tend to give me the headache that wine or liquor does, so I suck down my mimosa and let her refill it.

Two hours later, the movie is over and I'm laughing, doubled over, at Paige's impression of one of the dead teenagers.

"Thought I'd never hear that laugh again," Lara comments, and I smile at her, sobering somewhat. My vision is doubling but I feel lighter and freer than I have in a long time.

Everyone knows what I did, and the world didn't end.

I know Declan hates me, and I know I deserve it. He'll probably hate me forever.

The only thing keeping me going now is the hope that Patrick might be right.

He might never love me again, and I don't know if he'll ever forgive me, but I'll do everything I can to show him that I'm sorry. I'll do everything in my power to make it up to the Burkes.

I'll show Declan, show all of them, that I belong with them. That this is where I want to be. That I am worthy of being a Burke. If they'll have me.

"I'm glad you became a Burke, Bree," Paige squeezes my hand, a little tipsy, and I smile at her.

"I'm happy that I did, too." And I mean it.

My life was a lot emptier before the Burkes took me from my father, and I was living a lie. I didn't know the kind of monster my father truly was, and now that I know, I know that I don't want anything to do with him.

Talking to him on the phone had only exacerbated that truth.

He is a snake, just like Declan always said. The problem is, Declan thinks that I'm one, too.

"Don't start getting glum," Lara warns.

"I can't help it," I mutter. "Declan's so mad at me."

"He gets mad at the drop of a hat," Paige scoffs. "He'll be over it in a couple of days."

I hum, not so sure about that. "I don't even know why I did it."

"Because you were scared," Lara suggests. "I'd be scared if I was alone in enemy territory. You didn't know that we were good people."

"*I* don't even know if we're good people," Paige jokes, and I can't help but bark out a surprised laugh.

"Morality is pretty gray around these parts," Lara agrees, and she flips through the streaming service to find the sequel to the slasher. "Now, drink up. Every time you hear a scream."

I chuckle and we go back to watching and drinking.

By the time the movie is over, Paige is passed out on the chair, and Lara and I are fading fast.

"Why don't you stay in my room?" Lara suggests. "You shouldn't be by yourself right now."

"You wouldn't mind?"

"Of course not." She pauses. "Besides, I have to get you to help me carry Paige to bed."

I laugh, and we help Paige up, getting her to her room. Paige snorts, but she's snoring as her head hits the pillow.

Lara leads me into her bedroom, and it's just as neat as I

had imagined. We've been in Paige's fairly messy room a lot, but I don't know if I've ever seen Lara's.

She has portraits up of the Burke family on the wall, and there's a huge bookcase in the corner.

"You read all these?"

"Not yet." She smiles. "But some of them I've read a dozen times."

"I know how that goes. I have my favorites, too."

Lara hums, tossing me a shorts set to wear to bed. It's a little long on me because she's taller, but it fits well. I slide into the bed and moan at the feel of the silk sheets.

"Nice, right?"

"It's wonderful," I mumble, the alcohol finally getting to me and making my head spin. "Lara?"

"Yeah?"

She flips off the light and gets into bed.

"You really think Declan will forgive me?"

"I think he already has. I just don't think he knows it yet."

I murmur something under my breath and I'm not even sure what it is, and then I'm drifting off into sleep.

It's not dreamless, though.

I stand on a beach, my toes in the sand, my butt on a beach towel.

"Baby?" someone calls, and when I turn my head, it's Declan, his blue eyes fond and soft as he looks at me.

"How'd we get here?" I look around. I have no idea where this is.

The ocean air feels good on my face, the sun beating down on my shoulders. I can feel everything so vividly I wonder if I'm awake or asleep.

"I'm not sure." He is smiling. "But aren't you glad we're here?"

I look down, and I'm wearing a wedding dress, not the pretty dress that Paige loaned me on my wedding, but a real wedding dress, with a train and embroidered shapes on the skirt.

I look over at Declan, and he's wearing a tuxedo.

"I thought we already did this."

"Not for real."

And then instead of sitting, we're standing under an arch, and he cups my face in his hand and kisses me. "Mrs. Burke,"

"Declan?"

His voice sounds farther and farther away, and his hands are slipping from mine.

Panic rolls through me.

"You'll never be a Burke," he snarls, and now he's ten feet away from me.

Now twenty.

Now thirty and I can barely see his face, but I can hear his voice loud and clear. "You'll always be a Murphy snake."

"Wait!" I cry out as he starts to disappear, but then he's gone, and all I can feel is the tears on my face.

I wake up with a start, and Lara rolls over, still sleeping.

My heart beats out of my chest.

Are Lara and Patrick right?

Or is my dream a prophecy of sorts?

DECLAN

I wake up hungover and more pissed off than ever, and I head out of the house immediately, not waiting for Gray. He catches up to me in the driveway, though, looking exasperated.

"You can't just go off by yourself," he says. "Not after what happened."

"Doesn't matter," I mutter.

I don't much care if I live or die at this point. Maybe that's dramatic, but Cillian was right—I have big feelings.

It's annoying, especially for a guy who tries to fight those feelings. I've been fighting my feelings for Bree for weeks now, and I'm tired. Tired of being angry at her. Tired of feeling hurt. And all the whiskey I poured down my throat last night didn't help matters.

I grunt to Gray, and he rolls his eyes and gets into the passenger side of my car. We take off, and I can't even appreciate opening the car up on the highway, driving it as James Dean must have.

I used to love this car, used to love the adrenaline of

going a hundred miles an hour, but now, I can't muster up any feeling but irritation and, deep down, hurt.

It's not so much that Bree sent her father a message. It's that she did so without me knowing. Sneaky, behind my back.

"Are you going to talk or just grunt at me this whole time?"

I grunt at him.

Gray raises an eyebrow. "What was that?"

"I said I don't want to talk."

"That much is clear."

"Well, then shut up."

We have a full day today, including visiting Paige at her new home to see how she is adjusting after moving out a couple of days ago. Dad gave both me and Gray keys to her place. It was either that and a man stationed outside her house twenty-four-seven or she would not be allowed to move out.

She was not happy.

I'm glad we are keeping busy today. I need to have my mind away from Bree and all this fucking hurt I can't seem to shake off. This need to still be with her all the time, even after she confessed she betrayed me.

I hate being this weak.

We arrive at the first warehouse to drop off money and grab our guns.

Gray huffs out a breath and gets out of the car, taking a crowbar to the first of the crates while I back the car up to put the guns in the trunk. It's not many this time, just some handguns and a few kilos of dust. Usually, we bring a truck to big shipments, but right now, we're running small.

Mostly because of Murphy.

She'd told him what day we'd be out of the house, and

though she had no idea where we would be, that nugget of information had still nearly gotten me killed. It pisses me off all over again just to think about it.

Gray and I hit up the second warehouse, this time just picking up money from the Bratva. It's about two hundred thousand dollars short, and Gray curses.

"Fucking Russians."

"Da isn't going to care about a couple hundred thousand. A couple million, maybe."

There's a rustle in the back of the warehouse, and I freeze as Gray draws his gun. I draw mine from the small of my back, walking toward the back, and as I do, something darts out over my feet.

"Fuck!" I yell, but I don't pull the trigger. "It's a fucking cat."

"Kittens, too," Gray points out, gesturing toward the litter.

I curse in Gaelic and jerk my head toward the door. "Let's go. We'll call animal control on the way out."

Once the cats are handled, we head to the next warehouse, where we meet with Jimmy.

"Anything else stolen?" I bark, and Jimmy shakes his head.

"No sign of Murphy. I think it was a fluke."

I scoff but don't explain that it was my wife who ratted us out. I don't want to say anything like that in front of Jimmy. It's embarrassing to have your wife betray you, after all.

The worst part of all of this is that I'm not just mad. If I was just mad, if I just hated her, this would be so much easier. But I'm hurt, and I feel betrayed, and I don't know if I can forgive her.

Even though in her situation, I might have done worse.

Can I really blame her for sending a simple message to her father? Wouldn't I have done the same? I probably would have already tried to escape, would have fought tooth and nail for my family. Can I blame her for doing the same?

We're about to leave the third warehouse when I catch sight of a familiar car—Paige's little red Corvette, parked down the street. I can tell it is hers because of her license plate—PBURKE.

We are meeting her later at her place, so I ignore it, but Gray has other ideas.

"There's Paige," Gray points out. "Should we call her? Go to lunch together? Maybe we can head to her place after that?"

I'm not really in the mood to go to lunch, not feeling like this, and I open my mouth to tell him so but then Jimmy stiffens.

"Who's that?"

I look toward where his gaze is and three big men are walking toward Paige.

One of them has a red beard, and I recognize him as one of Murphy's men—Conan O'Leary. He's called Redbeard because of not only his beard, but because he only has one eye. He's pretty hard to miss with an eyepatch like a pirate.

I curse, taking off running toward her on the street. It seems to take me an hour to get there, and I draw my gun, right there in the street.

Jimmy and Gray flank me, and Paige turns around when I shout her name, looking at me with wide eyes.

"Get down! Get the fuck out of the way!" I yell at her, and it takes her a moment to process but she hits the deck, covering her face with her hands.

Gunshots ring out, one, two, three.

Paige tries crawling toward me, but Conan grabs her

around the ankles, dragging her to him before grabbing her by the hair.

Fuck, no!

She screams, and I know her knees must be bloody because she is being dragged instead of walking toward a van.

She thrashes and fights, and the sonofabitch punches her on the face.

I grit my teeth, advancing toward Conan, but he's fast as well as big, dragging her to the door of the van before I reach them.

Three gunshots ring out, and Jimmy cries out. I turn to him, and he's been hit high up in the upper thigh and blood is flowing down his pants.

"Fuck!" If we don't do something fast, Paige will be taken, and Jimmy will die of blood loss. "Are you good, Gray? Are you hit?"

"Good." He advances toward the men, shooting one in the throat and the other in the kneecap. The third man gets away, sprinting toward the van where Paige is still fighting hard not to be hauled into.

I chase him down, tackling him around the waist and his chin hits the ground, making him spit blood.

I kick him in the ribs before shooting him in the upper thigh.

He screams, and I contemplate shooting him again. "That's where you got my friend, you sonofabitch." I kick him in the ribs. "If you survive, tell Niall Murphy he just signed his death warrant."

I run toward Paige. I need to save her. Now. She is already half inside the van.

Gray shoots Conan in the head.

I get to my sister and haul her up.

She wilts against me. "Is it safe?"

I look around. Gray is already getting Jimmy back to the car, trusting me to take care of Paige.

"Let's not wait to find out."

We jog to where Gray and Jimmy are and get inside the car, Paige in the back with Jimmy before we rush him to Doc.

Doc lives downtown, and it'll be quicker to get Jimmy there instead of waiting for Doc to show up at home. Jimmy's hit close to his femoral artery, and I'm terrified that he's going to bleed out before we get there.

Paige has her small hand clamped around Jimmy's thigh, and he seems in and out of consciousness.

I double park on the street, and we file out of the car, with me and Gray carrying Jimmy inside and Paige trembling, still holding his thigh to try and slow down his bleeding.

I bang on Doc's door, and he opens it with his dark, curly hair all mussed, his brown eyes wide.

"Oh, fuck me sideways," he mutters and helps us get Jimmy to the couch. He cuts off Jimmy's jeans leg with a pocketknife, cursing under his breath.

"How bad is it, Doc?" Gray asks.

"Shut up and let me work. Hand me my bag," Doc barks to Paige, and she picks it up, but it falls to the floor because she's trembling so much.

I pick it up, handing it to Doc, and turn to comfort Paige, pulling her into my arms. She sobs against my chest, and I stroke her hair.

"Come on, let's sit down for a second, okay?"

I lead her to the couch and sit beside her before releasing her and taking a couple of alcohol swabs from

Liam's bag to start cleaning up her bloody knees. She winces, still crying.

Her eye is turning purple, so I stop for a second, get her some ice for it before I continue taking care of her knees.

Doc is still working on Jimmy, and I watch with a grimace as he dives a pair of small tweezers into Jimmy's flesh.

"The bullet's still in there," Doc mutters. "Hold him down, Gray."

"Sorry about this, Jim." Gray's face almost a testament to his name as he holds Jimmy down.

Jimmy starts jerking around and I reach out to do my part to help hold Jimmy's leg as still as I can as Doc does his thing.

"Got it."

The bullet clinks on the glass coffee table as Doc discards it, and then he starts to stitch Jimmy up.

Jimmy's sobbing at this point, no longer screaming, and I'm proud of Paige when she crouches next to him and takes his hand.

"You're okay," she croaks. "We're both okay."

Doc wipes his brow when he's finished, leaving a trail of blood across his forehead.

"He should be all right, but he's lost a lot of blood. Might be touch-and-go for a bit. I'm going to give him some saline, but I don't have any O neg blood lying around."

Gray sets his jaw. "I'm O negative. Can I help?"

Soon enough, Doc sets Gray up in some kind of ex-army medic contraption with a needle in his vein and his blood going into a bag.

When the bag is over half full, Doc disconnects Gray, shakes the bag a couple of times before hooking it to Jimmy, and brings Gray a cookie afterward, like it's a real blood donation.

Gray still looks pale, but otherwise none the worse for wear.

"Leave him here for tonight. Call his family," Doc says. "Just in case."

Fuck.

It must be worse than he let on.

I nod. "I'll call his sister."

She answers on the first ring because I call from my personal phone.

"Jesus, what happened?"

I close my eyes, hating this part of the job.

"Jimmy's been shot. Upper thigh. He's lost a lot of blood."

She's quiet for a moment before she sobs. "Where is he?"

"Doc's. He says he'll probably pull through but... just in case."

Doc takes the phone from me. "I'm giving him a transfusion now, but he's out. He'll want a familiar face when he wakes up, yeah?"

Elena responds, her voice sounding tinny to me, and Doc hangs up, handing me the phone back.

Gray looks at me and then at Paige, and then back at me. "We should go home."

I hate leaving Jimmy like this. He's been a loyal member of the Burke clan for all his life, but Paige needs to come home with us tonight and be surrounded by the whole family.

I take Paige's arm and look at Doc. "Call me if anything changes. Anything."

He nods solemnly, and I lead Paige back out to the car.

She climbs in the backseat while Gray gets in the passenger seat and the ride home is silent and uncomfortable.

When we arrive back at the mansion, I help Paige out of the car, and she's still trembling.

"I'm okay," she mumbles. "I'm okay."

"You're okay, *a'stor*," I promise her. "And I'll make sure you stay that way."

Lara meets us at the door, her brow furrowed, and I know the second she notices Paige's black eye.

"What the hell happened?"

Paige throws herself into our older sister's arms, sobbing.

I sigh. "Fucking *Murphy* happened."

Bree comes down the stairs, her hazel eyes wide and worried.

"Paige? Are you okay?"

I grit my teeth, wanting to say something, wanting to be angry, but all I can feel is this stupid ache in my heart.

Paige moves from Lara's arms to Bree's, hugging her tightly.

"There was so much shooting, and Jimmy... Jimmy got hurt."

Lara takes my arm. "Is he going to be okay?"

I pull away gently. "Doc says probably. Gray gave some blood."

Lara hugs Gray quickly. "I'm sure he'll appreciate it."

Gray just nods, and my father comes down from his office, thunderous rage on his face.

"Niall Murphy better count his days."

Bree looks up at him when he says it, and I think that she might protest, but her face is blank and serious.

"Anyone have a problem with that?"

I am looking right at her, challenging her to say something, but she just looks right at me, her face expressionless.

She doesn't say a word.

Paige is safe, but Jimmy is touch and go.

And Niall Murphy's days are numbered. The only question now is on whose side his daughter will stand. Ours or his.

31

———

BREE

I FUSS OVER PAIGE FOR A BIT, OFFERING HER FOOD AND water, but she shakes her head.

"I just want to go back to bed." Her voice wobbles.

"Do you want to be alone?" Lara asks.

"God, no."

I follow them up the stairs and help Lara tuck her in, but I don't stay. I'm not sure Paige wants me there, given that it was my father who nearly had her kidnapped.

She is hurt. Her eye is swollen and dark purple and I could just throw up thinking this is all my fault somehow.

I go into the guest bedroom, which is fairly empty but has become my home over the last couple of days, and I sit down hard on the bed.

My head is spinning.

My father has just shot Jimmy, nearly kidnapped Paige, and now the Burkes want his head on a pike. I can't blame them. I can't even be upset about it. It's what he deserves.

There is nothing left inside me when I think about him, no warm feeling, no tenderness, no love. Nothing but this disgust of sharing blood with a monster.

I wish I could get ahold of Rory. Maybe he'd know what to do.

Right now, I don't know if I should stay or go. Declan doesn't want me here. The rest of the Burkes are shaken up by my father's actions.

Maybe I should just cut my losses and go. I'm a daily reminder of all that is wrong and all the bad things that happen to them.

I should ask Patrick. I'm sure by now he'd just let me go.

Yes, that's exactly what I do.

I stand up and head for the door.

When I'm halfway there, someone opens the door.

Declan is standing there, his face blank.

We stare at each other for a few beats. We haven't talked since that last fight, and he's the last person I expected to come and see me.

"I'm so glad Paige is okay," I whisper.

"Jimmy's not," he barks.

"Declan, I had no idea that he'd go after Paige, I swear to you—"

Declan holds up a hand to stop me. "I know that. This isn't on you, but I have other things to say to you."

I swallow hard, wondering if he's here to tell me to get out. I stiffen, ready to go if he wants me to. I don't want to stay where I'm not wanted. I don't deserve to be here, anyway, with my filthy Murphy blood.

Declan said himself I mean nothing to him.

"I can understand why you did what you did," he says quietly, looking down at me.

I keep eye contact even though tears well in my eyes.

"And I was wrong for some of the things I said. Hell, for a *lot* of the things I said."

What is going on right now?

I just nod. I don't know what to do. What to say.

I'll make his life easier. If he wants me out, this is his cue. "You said I mean nothing to you."

Declan sighs heavily, running a hand through his already messy hair. His shirt is covered in blood. Is any of it his? Is he hurt again?

I clench my fists, forcing myself to stay still, no not touch him and reassure myself he is okay, he is not hurt.

"That was maybe the biggest lie I ever told."

What?

"Declan," I start, but he lets out a long breath.

"Let me finish. I'm sorry for the things I said. I'm sorry for attacking you the way I did."

Is he.... apologizing? To *me*?

I never thought this would happen. I thought he'd hate me forever, and part of me wants to go to him, throw myself into his arms. Part of me wants to tell him I love him, and I always will, but another part of me is still angry. Prideful. Hurt.

"And I understand if you want to leave, to go back to your father. I won't stop you."

My breath is stuck in my chest.

"Is... Is that what you want?" I whisper.

Declan scoffs. "Of course not. It'll break my heart to do it, Bree. But I will if that's what you want. I want you to be happy. Even if it's without me."

I can't stop myself, flinging myself at him, and he catches me, chuckling slightly as he stumbles backward.

"I thought you'd hate me forever," I breathe. "I thought I ruined everything."

"I could never hate you," he murmurs, brushing his nose against mine. "I love you, Bree Murphy."

"Bree Burke," I correct, and kiss him.

Declan's the first to pull away, looking down at me. "You didn't say it back." His breath is labored. "Does that mean you don't—"

"No!" I exclaim.

His face falls.

I wrap my arms around his neck. "I'm so madly in love with you I can't see straight, Declan Burke."

"Yeah?"

"Yeah!"

A grin spreads across his handsome face, and he kisses me again, this time more insistently.

He pushes me down on the bed, covering me with his body, and I can't seem to stop talking.

"I promise I'll never betray you again, Declan. Never."

He murmurs a response against my neck, kissing me there, but I keep going. Babbling, at this point, but I can't help it.

"I'll be a Burke as long as you'll have me."

"Forever," he growls, and kisses my throat, leaving marks there that will sting later.

I don't care. I want him to mark me everywhere, mark me his.

I'm still wearing the shorts set that Lara gave me, and he pushes it to the side, shoving down his slacks over his ass to free his erection.

Declan presses into me, and I cry out against his mouth as he kisses me again.

When he's inside me to the hilt, he kisses the tip of my nose.

"I love you, Bree Burke," he says in a low tone, and I can't help but grin.

"I love you, Declan Burke."

I can't believe we've come this far.

Declan starts to move his hips, and I moan, arching my back, locking my ankles around the small of his back to bring him deeper.

I roll my hips, meeting him with every thrust, and he kisses me over and over until I'm breathless.

It's only a few thrusts before I'm coming around him, chanting his name.

Declan curses when he spills inside me, pulling back to look at me.

"I'm still kind of mad at you," he admits, but he kisses my nose, my chin.

I laugh. "That's okay, baby. Lara and Paige say you're a hothead, but you don't hold grudges."

"Oh, I hold grudges. But not against you. I don't think I could ever hold a grudge against you."

"Why not?"

"Because I love you." He shrugs, and my heart feels so full it could burst.

I grin, the smile hurting my cheeks. "I love you, too, Declan."

"You're a Burke now, right?"

"Right."

"Forever?"

"Forever," I promise, and he kisses me, leaving me no doubt about his feelings, and starts to rock inside me again.

He bites down on my neck when he comes this time, and I love the sting, the pain and pleasure that rushes through my body.

I giggle, and nothing can break this moment, nothing can take us away from this love bubble where it is just the two of us—until Declan's phone rings.

He answers, barking into the phone, and listens. His face is expressionless, blank.

"All right." He hangs up the phone.

His brow furrows when he looks at me.

"What is it? Is it Jimmy?"

He nods and then a grin breaks out across his face. "He's going to be okay. He woke up asking for food."

He chuckles, and I smile, sitting up on my knees to hug him from behind.

We don't leave the bedroom for nearly two days.

When I finally emerge from the room, it's to run downstairs and get something to eat. We're both starving, and Declan says he can't go again until he gets sustenance, so I must grab some food.

Lara is downstairs, eating by herself. It's nearly lunch time, so Marisol has prepared some soup and sandwiches.

I grin at her, and she grins back.

"I guess you and Declan made up?"

I grin. "You could say that."

"It was either that or you killed each other," she chuckles, and I can't help but laugh.

"Nothing like that, I promise. Everything's okay. We're going to be okay."

"All of us will be," she says quietly and stands up to hug me. She sniffs me, grimacing. "You and Declan need to shower. You smell like sex."

"Gross," Paige pipes up, walking into the room.

The marks of the attack are still there but she is better.

I smile sheepishly, saluting them.

"Noted."

I take the soup and sandwiches up to Declan on a tray, and he gulps down one of the water bottles before eating and pulling me back into bed.

"We're eventually going to have to leave this room, you know?"

He frowns. "No. I don't want to."

I laugh. "You sound like a little kid."

"I feel like a teenager. It's like... being sixteen all over again."

"I was never in love at sixteen." I shrug.

"Me, either. I guess this is just what I imagine it feels like."

He kisses my temple.

"We should shower and go down to dinner later. I think your family misses you."

"Miss you, more likely," he snorts. "They like you better than me, you know?"

I laugh. "Who wouldn't?"

He bites down on my shoulder playfully, and I start to undress, just wearing one of his button-up shirts. Declan looks at me, his blue eyes dark with lust.

He grabs at me, but I dart away.

"I need to eat," I state. "And then we need to shower."

He grins. "We're just going to get dirty again anyway."

I snort out a laugh and sit down, cross-legged and nude, shoving bites of sandwich and soup into my mouth.

He looks at me as if I am one of the most enthralling shows ever until I'm finished, and then I tug him up, leading him to the shower.

Before I even get the water heated up, he has his fingers inside me where I've bent over to turn on the faucet, and I cry out, arching my back.

"Get in the shower," I breathe, and Declan pops his fingers out of me, putting them in his mouth and sucking slowly.

"Yes, ma'am," he drawls, and I glare at him but there's no heat behind it.

"You're a menace."

"The Irish scourge," he jokes, and I laugh out loud, feeling lighter and freer than I ever have.

I sober, thinking about my father. "You know that this isn't over."

"What isn't over?"

"The war between the Murphys and the Burkes."

He sighs. "I know."

"For a while there, part of me hoped that this marriage would ease things between you," I admit, tears springing to my eyes. "Part of me hoped my father would come around."

His face serious now instead of lustful, he draws me into his arms. "Everything's going to be okay, *a ghra mo chroi*. I promise you."

"How can you know that?" I look up into his blue eyes.

"I just do," he says softly, and he kisses me so gently I feel my heart swelling with love for him.

"You called me that before. What does it mean?"

"Love of my heart."

He washes my hair and I finger over the scar from his bullet wound.

"Hey," he whispers against my neck after rinsing my hair.

"Yeah?"

"Do you want to get married again? Do this for real?"

I twist my head to look at him, surprised. "What? You'd do that?"

He shrugs. "You can't exactly invite your father, but..."

"I don't need another wedding," I blurt out, thinking about my dream. The dream where I lost him. "I don't need anything but you."

Declan still pouts, but I kiss him, pushing the thoughts of a real wedding out of my head.

I don't need it. I don't want a repeat of my dream, after all, don't want Declan slipping away from me.

By the time dinner rolls around, we're more than clean. In fact my fingertips look like prunes. We walk down to dinner, and Patrick grins at us.

"Didn't think you two would ever come out of the bedroom."

Gray snorts out a laugh, smiling at Declan, and Paige gestures me over to sit between her and Lara.

I go, lingering on holding Declan's hand as long as I can. His fingers slip from mine, and I feel a bit of panic, remembering that dream.

Was it a prophetic one?

I hope that I only dreamed it because I was worried about Declan hating me, but I can't be sure.

"Are we having another wedding?" Paige asks, and I shake my head fiercely.

Declan sighs. "She says no."

"But another wedding would be fun!" Paige insists, pouting at me just like her brother did. They look oddly alike in that moment, and I blink at her, really looking at her. She has dark circles under her eyes and looks drained.

Has she been sleeping? Eating?

"Maybe someday," I mumble. "But not now."

"You're no fun." Declan says the words, but he's smiling at me. He glances over at Patrick. "Jimmy's going to be okay."

"I know." Patrick nods. "Doc called me a couple of days ago."

Declan looks surprised. "Have we really been holed up that long?"

Gray laughs. "You sure have. What were you doing in there?"

"Playing checkers," I answer matter-of-factly, and the table bursts out into laughter.

There's always laughter at the Burke dining room table. There's always fun and crazy stories, and it's like what I always imagined a real family to be like.

As much as I'd told myself it was okay, I never felt that way with my father. And now that I know who he is, I want to find out more.

Like what really happened to my mother. What had she done to deserve such a fate?

I go silent as I think about it, and it's Lara who puts her hand on my knee to get my attention.

"Penny for your thoughts?"

I sigh, looking over at Patrick. "When I talked to my father last—"

Declan stares at me, shocked, and I reach out and take his hand.

"I let her call him," Patrick says.

Declan visibly relaxes, but my heart aches. It may take some time for him to trust me again, and I can't blame him.

"I have reason to believe he did something to my mother," I whisper. "I don't know what it was. I don't know if he hurt her or—" My voice cracks, and Declan squeezes my hand.

"We'll find out," he promises. "We'll do some research."

I know that "research" probably means interrogating a few of my father's men, but so be it.

Patrick speaks up. "We'll do whatever we can for you, *a'stor*. You just say the word."

I smile at him. "Thank you. Thank all of you, for accepting me as a Burke. For showing me the way."

"Thank you for proving not all the Murphys are snakes. Gray chuckles.

"I may have a little snake in me," I joke. "But it's like a garden snake. Not a cottonmouth."

Declan laughs at that, and we continue dinner.

It's not silent, or awkward. It's wonderful, like every dinner with the Burkes.

After it's over, Declan leads me upstairs as I'm saying goodbye to everyone.

Lara frowns at him. "You'll have to eventually give her up for a girls' night, you know?"

"I'm not giving her up for anything," he growls, and I nudge him with my shoulder.

"One night a month for a girls' night," I insist. "We can't be around each other every moment. You'll have to work."

"I guess," he grumbles and all but drags me up the stairs.

I undress, letting my clothes fall to the floor, and climb into bed, exhausted and sore all over, bruises on my thighs and my hip bones.

"I hope you don't think I'm going to let you sleep."

I groan. "You have to. We've barely slept in days."

Declan looks serious, but then his jaw cracks in a yawn. "Maybe you're right."

"I'm always right," I say, and he snorts, climbing into bed with me after undressing.

Declan draws me into his arms, pulling me close and kissing the side of my face.

"You're mine now," he mumbles. "Body and soul."

"And heart, too," I point out, and he smiles against my lips as I turn my head to kiss him.

I'm happier than I ever have been,

I've come a long way from where I started, and I'm so glad this is where the journey brought me.

Home, lying in the arms of the man I love. My father's enemy.

32

———

DECLAN

A week passes and Bree and I are happier than ever. There's only one problem—I want more.

I want all of her, all the time. I can't get enough, and I need us to have a do-over. I don't want our wedding memories to be of her being forced. I want a wedding story we can tell our grandchildren.

But Bree seems to not want to get married again. I ask her every day, and every single day she tells me she doesn't need it, that all she needs is me.

"Are you sure you want to do this?" Gray asks as I stand next to him at the courthouse.

I take a deep breath in. "Yeah, I think I do." I walk up to the clerk. "I'd like to file for divorce."

"Sorry to hear that, that'll be three-hundred dollars."

I slide her the money.

"This seems extreme," Gray complains.

"Maybe it is, but it's the only way I can get her to marry me again."

"Are you sure she's not going to be mad?"

"She's going to be *livid*." I chuckle.

But instead of livid, when I throw the papers down on the bed, Bree looks up at me with her hazel eyes swimming with tears.

"Declan..." Her voice breaks. "Why are you doing this? What have I done?"

"No, no, *mo chroí*." I hurry to the bed and draw her into my arms. My heart. My one true love. "You didn't do a thing. I just... I want to do this for real, Bree. I want you to choose me, and for you to know that I choose you back. I'll always choose you."

"I did choose you," she sobs. "It took me a little while, but I did."

When she calms down, she huffs, crossing her arms over her chest. "I'm not signing these."

"Listen." I take her hands in mine. "I want us to do this right. I want your friends there. Whatever family you have that won't try to kill me."

She barks out a laugh at that, and I smile.

"Besides, we can have a longer engagement," I offer. "Get to know each other."

She scoffs. "We already know each other inside and out."

"There's always more to learn."

It takes over an hour of talking and insisting that there's nothing she's done wrong before Bree signs the papers with a shaking hand.

We file for an uncontested divorce, and it goes through in a week.

Bree's moping around the house, though, looking down at her ring, and I grimace.

I hate that ring. It doesn't fit her at all. She likes

sapphires and rubies, not diamonds. I know her better now. And this time I actually care if she likes the ring.

I wake up early one day and grab Lara. We drive to Paige's, who has gone back to her place this past week, and get her to come with us. She is grumpy because she doesn't like to be up early, but Lara is excited.

We drive to the jeweler.

"I cannot *wait* for the wedding," Lara gushes, and Paige glares at me.

"Why do we have to do this so *early*?"

"Because Bree wakes up early." I drag her out to the car.

The jewelry shop has just opened when we walk in. By the wide eyes and almost salivating mouths, I can tell they took one look at my expensive clothes and know they're going to get a huge commission.

They start out by showing me the biggest diamonds, but I wait, letting Paige and Lara browse around.

Lara's the one that finds it—a diamond inlaid with sapphires *and* rubies, and it's dainty and beautiful with a white-gold band.

"It's perfect," Paige breathes.

"I know," Lara says, and I snort, walking over to the cashier.

"I'll take it."

"Very well, sir. That will be twenty thousand dollars."

"Do you accept Visa or Mastercard?"

"Either is fine." She swipes the card and gets the ring in a beautiful box that I put in my pocket before we leave.

As soon as we get home, I go up to my father's office.

"I want us to go out to Natalia's for dinner tomorrow," I tell him. "All of us."

"You might have trouble pinning down Gray."

"I won't." I shrug. "I've already told him."

My father looks up at me, eyes sparkling. "First the divorce, and now this? What's your plan, boyo?"

"I'm going to do this the right way. The way she's always deserved."

He smiles. "Then I'll be there with bells on."

Bree isn't dressed by six o'clock, and I'm in an Armani suit, standing over her as she lounges on the bed.

"I don't think I feel up to going," she grumbles, and I grab her by the ankle, yanking her to the end of the bed.

She squeals and giggles, her hazel eyes brighter as she looks up at me.

"You're going," I order, and she sits up before going to the bathroom.

When she comes out, she is wearing a blue dress and has her hair curled, makeup on.

I smile. "That's more like it."

"What, you don't like me barefaced and messy-haired?"

"I like you every way. But tonight, I'm glad you look so beautiful."

She looks at me. "Declan, what are you up to?"

I shrug. "I can't take my beautiful girlfriend out on the town?"

"Girlfriend," she mutters, and she's a little dimmed as we go out to the car. Gray, Lara, and Da have already left, and Paige will be meeting us there.

We arrive for our reservation right on time, and I'm antsy as they seat us.

Paige's a little late, and I glare at her, but she just shrugs, giving me a sheepish smile.

"Now," Da says. "What's everyone ordering?"

I can't wait.

"Champagne for the table," I say, and I discreetly hand the server the ring to put in her champagne glass.

When everyone has a glass poured, I smile and clink my fork on my glass.

"A toast," I suggest, and Bree looks up at me, surprised. "To Bree becoming a Burke, once and for all."

We all clink our glasses, and I watch her face as she starts to drink, her eyes widening when she realizes what's going on.

"Declan," she breathes. "You bastard."

My father and Gray both crack up, and I get down on one knee.

"Bree Murphy," I say quietly. "Will you marry me? Will you make me the happiest man on Earth?"

She huffs out a breath. "I already married you. And you divorced me."

"Will you marry me *again*? Forever this time?" I ask patiently, knowing that she's prideful but that her attitude is just a front.

"Of course I will," she mutters, throwing her arms around me, and Paige is recording and Lara's crying and it's a beautiful moment.

I'm glad I got to share it with my family.

THE MORNING AFTER OUR ENGAGEMENT, WE'RE IN A Catholic church and going through the religious motions of getting married.

Kael is finally back from out of town, and he and Cillian stand next to me as my best men.

Kael whistles as we wait for Bree to come down the aisle. "I can't believe you're doing this *twice*."

"I keep telling you, it'll happen to you."

Kael snorts. "Fat chance.

"I didn't think it would happen to me, either, but here we are."

"We're not the same, my friend." Kael smiles as he shakes his head.

It seems to take forever for the ceremony to finish, and I'm impatient for her to be declared my wife again. To be able to kiss my bride.

When the priest finally does proclaim us husband and wife and gives me permission, I grab her around the waist, kissing her so deeply that Gray whoops and hollers from the crowd.

She grins against my mouth.

"Where are we going for the honeymoon?"

"You won't know until we get there."

Bree pouts. "I don't like surprises."

"You do now," I tell her with a chuckle, and we head to the reception, accepting money and gifts from everyone.

Bree chose not to invite anyone from the Murphy side of the family. She did try reaching out to her brother, but never heard back from him.

Her father, of course, was never even a possibility. She told me more than once that she wouldn't want him here even if things were on better terms with our families.

Some of her aunts and cousins from her mother's side are here, though, and they are as nice as supportive as can be.

Bree seems anxious as we get into the limo to go to the airport, and I frown, cupping her face in my hands.

She sighs. "I know it seems stupid," she starts. "But I

had this dream, back when we were fighting. We were on a beach and... You slipped away from me. Told me I'd never be a Burke. And now I..."

I smile. "Well, too late now, since you just married me and I'm never letting you go ever again. Besides, don't worry. We're not going to a beach."

Her eyes widen. "We're not?"

I shake my head. "The opposite, actually. I'm taking you to the mountains."

"Oh, thank god," she blurts out, and I laugh.

"Do you really think that if we went to the beach, I'd leave you?"

"I don't know!" she exclaims. "It just scared me, that's all."

I kiss her, smiling against her lips. "It'll take more than a little sand to make me stop loving you, Bree Burke."

THE MOUNTAINS ARE SNOW-TOPPED AND BEAUTIFUL, and Bree's all bundled up in a parka and long johns, looking cute as a button.

"Maybe we should have chosen the beach," I comment. "You're wearing too many clothes."

She grins, darting inside toward the bedroom. "Guess you'll have to get me out of them."

I laugh as I peel layer upon layer of clothes off her.

"Jesus, you're wearing the whole closet."

She snorts out a laugh. "Consider me a very well-wrapped present."

"Best present ever."

The heat is on full blast when I finally get both of us out

of our clothes, and I move down her body, pressing my face into her sex and inhaling with a moan.

"Don't tease," she whines, and I latch around her clit immediately, pumping two fingers in and out of her until her thighs are trembling.

I take my time after her first orgasm, making her come twice more before I cover her with my body.

My erection presses against her thigh, and she reaches down, taking me in hand.

She pumps her fist slowly, and I grit my teeth.

"This is going to be over too soon if you keep doing that," I breathe.

She grins, spreading her thighs, and I spear into her, fucking her rough and fast.

We have all the time in the world to make love, but it's been a day since I've been inside her, and I missed being surrounded by her heat.

She arches her back, crying out my name against my mouth, and I roll my hips into hers, looking into her hazel eyes. There's such love and lust in them I could get lost.

When it's over and she's panting against me, wrapped around me with her head on my chest like a little puzzle piece, I kiss her forehead.

"Declan?"

I hum, still breathing hard.

"Have you ever thought about having kids?"

My eyes widen. "Why?"

"I'm not pregnant or anything," she blurts out, and I relax. "But we haven't been using protection, and... it could happen."

"If it happens, it happens."

She frowns. "That's a pretty breezy way to handle it."

"So?" I shrug. "I'd love to have a little you running around."

"What if it's a little *you?*"

"Oh, god," I groan, and she smacks my chest.

I laugh and catch her hand in mine, kissing her knuckles "I'm just kidding, *a ghra mo chroi.* Whatever happens with us and our future kids, I'll be happy."

"That's all I want," she murmurs. "For us to be happy."

"And we will be. With one kid or five."

"Five?" She blanches.

"The Irish have big families."

"Five," she mutters, and puts her head back on my chest.

I smile, wondering what she'd look like all full and swollen with my baby. The thought makes me happy and also, a little aroused.

What better way to show she's mine than to get her pregnant?

"I've decided we should try for number one." I slip my hand down her body to trail my fingers through her wetness.

She gasps. "What, we're going to name them all numbers?"

I laugh against her mouth before pressing back into her.

———

A MONTH HAS GONE BY SINCE WE CAME BACK FROM our honeymoon and life is perfect. Or so I thought.

Bree walks up to me, her hazel eyes worried and wet.

"Declan?"

"What's wrong, baby?" My voice comes out all gruff from sleep.

I've just started to get dressed.

"Number one is coming."

"Number what now?"

"Number one," she whispers, and she holds up a stick with two pink lines on it.

I'm frozen, just staring at it for a long moment, and her brows draw together as she looks up at me.

When my body finally catches up to my brain, I whoop, grabbing her around the waist and twirling her around.

She yelps, giggling, and I finally sit her down on her feet.

"I guess we have an announcement for dinner," I say, and she takes my hand.

"Can you wait until dinner?"

"Probably not." I want to scream it from the rooftops now.

She bounces away from me. "I'm happy it's family dinner day. Paige is here, so I'm going to tell her and Lara. You tell Patrick and Gray."

Her smile is huge as she blows me a kiss before running out of the door.

I look after her, thinking about how this all started, about how much I'd hated the idea of being married. Especially to a Murphy.

I'd thought she was like her father. Monstrous. Evil.

But Bree Murphy, now Burke, changed my life. Every day she makes me believe I'm a man who deserves love, makes me understand that I can have people that love me in my life other than my family.

My whole life, I thought I'd never be more than a gangster. I thought I'd die hard, just like my father probably will, his father before us did.

She taught me that I can be happy. *Really* happy, not just content, inside and outside of a war.

There's only one woman who has captured my heart, who owns me, body and soul.

And now she is making my life even richer by giving me a piece of us together. Our baby.

And I'll never forget that. I'll never let her go.